THE RULE OF WISDOM

BOOK ONE

THE FALL OF VARLANA

BY JOY SIMONS

Published by Warner House Press of Albertville, Alabama, USA
Copyright © 2022 Joy Simons
Cover Illustration © 2022 Debrey Taylor
Interior Design © 2022 Warner House Press

Warner House Press
1325 Lane Switch Road
Albertville, AL 35951
USA

Published 2022
Printed in the United States of America

Scripture quotations from The Authorized (King James) Version. Rights in the Authorized Version in the United Kingdom are vested in the Crown. Reproduced by permission of the Crown's patentee, Cambridge University Press

26 25 24 23 22 1 2 3 4 5

ISBN: 978-1-951890-34-6

This book is dedicated to Allie Weathersby: a faithful friend who is always honest about my successes and failings, a loving sister who is willing to listen for hours while I process, and a ballerina who can choreograph fight scenes. This book came alive in large part because of her.

Thank-you, Allie. I love you to death.

TABLE OF CONTENTS

CHAPTER 1
PROMOTION AND DEATH

A young man sat by the bed in the dark, musky room. Sunlight tried to sneak past the drapes, but only created shadows against the lines of tension across his brow.

"Father," he whispered.

A heavy sigh filled the lungs of the man who lay on the bed. His bagged eyes fluttered open and he turned his head to see his son. He weakly lifted his hand toward the young man.

"Ja'el, are you ready?"

Ja'el grasped the offered hand. "Yes, Father. I think so."

"Your mind must be settled in this."

"I am nervous, but I hope to make you proud."

"Do not concern yourself with pleasing me. You must grow *yourself* into this."

"But I am representing you, father."

"You are representing Varlana. It is to her you must pledge your allegiance. I will pass away, you will pass away, but Varlana must remain."

Morcon's voice weakened, but he pressed on. "Today, you are the Damon of Varlana, not the son of Morcon. Walk straight and tall. You are a good, strong man. Varlana will be proud of you and so I shall be proud of you."

Morcon struggled to raise up on his elbows. "The Great Telling is our most important day. Stand with confidence and ..." He broke into coughs. Ja'el quickly poured him a cup of water as the healer entered full of concern.

"Ja'el, leave him. He needs his rest." He moved between Ja'el and his father to administer a vapor for Morcon's breath. Ja'el walked to the front of the house and sat alone.

Only three months earlier he and his father had attended a ball at the king's palace. The great ballroom was ablaze with candles that flickered off the gold trim and glass chandeliers. The musicians played lively airs and the women, in layers of silk and lace, danced around the room with men in bright colored coats and sashes.

"Father, why are we here? I feel out of place." Ja'el wore the brown robe of a sage, as his father did, a sharp contrast to the festive atmosphere.

"Watch, son. There is work to do."

Ja'el watched the happy couples. His eye stopped on Jakfa, the king's nephew and heir to the throne. A strikingly handsome man, Jakfa turned the eye of almost every female in the hall. At the moment, he danced with Marguerite, the daughter of General Janell. She didn't look too happy and Jakfa began to turn her roughly around the floor.

Ja'el moved across the floor to interrupt the dance. "May I have a turn, Marguerite?"

Jakfa frowned, his eyebrows lowered, but Marguerite smiled and moved into Ja'el's arms.

"Thank-you, Ja'el."

"My pleasure." He whirled her gently through the next dance and deposited her next to her father. The General smiled. "You are as good a dancer as your father. How is he feeling today?"

"He is a little weak, but he sits over there." Ja'el pointed to his father's chair. The General turned to his assistant. "Captain Dugan, look after Marguerite while I talk to Morcon." He rose and walked across the floor. Captain Dugan looked very happy to look after Marguerite, so Ja'el left the couple to wander.

He slipped out into the hallway for some fresh air and there, tucked in an alcove, he saw Jakfa kissing a young woman. *He wastes no time. That poor girl.*

Ja'el had known Jakfa most of his life. They attended school together here in the palace. However, they hardly ever agreed and fought most of the time. Jakfa bullied the other children and Ja'el often rose to their defense.

I hope King Salak lives forever. I would hate to see Jakfa on the throne.

The hallway led to the royal gardens and Ja'el moved through the door into the familiar pathways. Juniper and rosemary covered the ground. Hanging pots of every variety of flower hung in arbors of fragrant honeysuckle nestled in beds of colorful petunias. A riot of fragrance filled Ja'el's nostrils as he slowly walked around. In the back were beds of herbs and medicinal plants. Ja'el loved the back garden. Morcon had taught him the healing arts and other family secrets here. The familiar leaves seemed to reach for him, but he had been too long away and turned to go back.

Jakfa stood in his way. "You never stop, do you?"

"What do you mean?"

"Marguerite. I meant to have her tonight, and you butted in."

Ja'el snorted a chuckle. "She does not want you. You see her with Captain Dugan. Why are you wasting your time?"

"I can have any woman I want."

"You are a child pretending to be a man." Ja'el tried to move past him, but Jakfa gripped his arm and punched him in the stomach. Ja'el doubled over as he gasped for air.

"That feel like a child? Leave me alone or I'll give you more of that." He turned and strode into the palace.

Ja'el slowly stood, took a deep breath, and…

The clock struck three and Ja'el's thoughts snapped back to the present. *How fast father has declined. He should stand at the Telling, not me.*

It was time to go. He stood, straightened his robe and walked into the prosperous streets of Varlana. The warm sun relaxed his tense muscles, but anxiety filled his mind. Today he graduated, whether he wanted to or not.

King Salak opened the treasury to decorate the capital for the Great Telling. Every Damon across Umberlan came to report the successes (or failures) of their regions, and people from all over Umberlan came to Varlana to witness the event.

He played with the sleeve of his robe as he walked. *Come on, Ja'el. You have worked for this for years. You should know what you are doing by now.*

He smiled to himself and looked around. Yards of colored silk draped every balcony. He watched the Damons dressed in their fine robes ride in open carriages for all to see; their horses crowned with tall, colorful plumes. Reins braided with gold and silver rope gleamed in the sunlight. Crowds thickened on the walkways as Ja'el approached the palace. People lined the streets to see the spectacle.

The richer merchants, dressed in all their finery, hoped for royal recognition as they strolled up and down the street. A smile from an influential Damon could boost sales. A visit to their store could put a rival out of business.

This whole town goes crazy for the Great Telling. His smile grew as he watched the wide-eyed children. *This day I like.*

What Ja'el didn't like happened the day before. Every big city hid its dark underbelly and Varlana wanted to hide hers completely for the next few days. Palace guards patrolled throughout the capital to keep the peace. Soldiers rounded up suspected criminals, even children, and jailed them until the end of the Telling and the departure of the Damons. Street urchins as young as six found themselves alone in cells with hardened criminals. The scarcity of food in the jails caused frequent fights over scraps. The guards seldom intervened. Ja'el heard them say, "One less to worry about," when a fight ended in murder.

Today, he pushed those concerns aside and when he approached the palace gate, he searched his pockets for his invitation. *Did I leave it at home? No. Here it is.* He brushed off the lint, his thin smile did nothing to hide his shaky hands. He knew exactly what to say, but he had never officially visited without his father and insecurity moved him to doubt himself. He opened his mouth to speak.

"Ja'el, son of Morcon, to report to the king." He handed the guard the official invitation. The guard looked at the wrinkled envelope and stared at Ja'el for a long moment. Ja'el met his gaze with false bravado, but the guard scanned his list, found Ja'el's name and moved aside to let him pass.

Why did I doubt? My father arranged it. Of course, it worked perfectly. He wondered if he'd ever be as efficient and thorough as Morcon. *He must recover. I'm not ready.*

But Morcon's illness had increased and with it Ja'el's responsibilities. Not much more than twenty, he didn't command the respect his father did. He needed to deliver his report well.

A soldier escorted Ja'el into the Grand Hall. It never failed to impress first-time visitors to the palace. Ja'el had entered this hall many times, but he still felt intimidated. The cathedral ceiling was painted sky-blue with puffy clouds. It seemed like the sky outside came in. He almost felt the sun on his face.

The tiles on the floor made complicated patterns in shades of red and gold, the colors of Varlana and King Salak. Red and pink flowers bloomed on golden fields painted on the walls. Warriors in golden armor roared in victory as their enemies bled red under their heel. Every step found a new picture of wonder and history.

The red and gold banner of King Salak blazed in the sunlight beside a huge staircase. It wound in a lazy circle up to a mezzanine that circled the room. Every piece of furniture and all the railings glowed with the luster of ivory. Its beauty and decadence always amazed Ja'el.

"Do not be fooled by beauty. It may hide a deeper ugliness." His father's wisdom echoed in his head. "Wisdom is a prize found only in the truth. Never close your eyes to it." He smiled at the sound of his father's voice in his mind, like a close friend's guidance.

He turned his head to the right. The music room, science room, library, and gardens dominated his life until now. His father's influence opened a desk for him to be educated here and games in the palace gardens became some of his fondest memories.

To the left, the halls led to official government rooms and the royal family's personal quarters. Ja'el remembered the last, and only, time he traversed these hallowed halls. Several weeks before his father escorted him to the empty throne room. "Moving into such an important day without preparation is foolish. You must understand this environment as much as you can."

As they entered, their steps echoed off the marble walls. The huge throne perched in the center on a raised pedestal commanded the room's entire focus. Wide steps led to the foot of the pedestal, designed to intimidate and never used. Another staircase hid behind, the last five steps secreted behind a great oak door. The king, alone, used these steps to ascend to the throne itself. From this lofty perch he ruled his subjects.

Balconies lined the upper tiers. Windows of glass let sunbeams caress the throne from all sides. Brightly colored banners hung from the railings. They represented all the Damons in Umberlan, but behind the throne, bigger and brighter than them all, hung King Salak's royal crest.

His father directed him to the floor and explained the tiles. Subtle color changes showed traffic patterns, where one waited and how one approached the king. Proprieties must be kept. A slight misstep and an official's life could be ruined.

"The colors are the key. Watch how the Damons move and you will learn more completely."

Ja'el tried to change his thoughts to the events of this day. The *empty* room intimidated, but now it would be full of dignitaries; the balconies packed with onlookers, influential citizens with no royal blood or decree. They would all stare at him as he delivered his report. His knees started to shake as they walked down the hall. *Breathe. Relax. Breathe.*

Too soon the guard opened the Throne Room door and Ja'el stepped in. The door clicked shut behind him and he tried to lose himself among the Damons who stood along the walls. They all waited, stiff with anticipation. The king would arrive soon.

"Clank." The great lock turned and the door behind the throne slowly began to open. The crowd fell silent as they stared at the throne.

Trumpets from somewhere heralded the king's arrival and he arose from under the royal crest. He wore ceremonial battle dress. Strong and virile, his ornate sword hung ready at his side. His leather armor creaked with every step saying, "Hero" and "Champion." His cape, lush with furs and velvet, draped over his shoulder and arm. A mass of jewels sparkled in the golden crown on his head. His presence dwarfed everything else in the room.

He began to speak. As his voice boomed out into the room, he strode back and forth in front of the throne. His cape trailed down the stairs in all its glory. His crown sparkled in the sunlight. The most important and powerful man in the room stopped in a bright sunbeam. The crown reflected a rainbow on the wall and the light made a halo around his face. The Damons and nobles stood silent before him.

"We have gathered here to witness the strength of Umberlan. Your Damons, rulers of regions, are my arms into our great country. They are a reflection of the light of knowledge and wisdom emanating over the land from our glorious capital, Varlana. This throne is the source of our life, the representation of all good things. Umberlan has known peace since my grandfather conquered the last of the rebels. Our lands prosper because of two generations of peace and strength.

"Now we bear witness to the truth of this camaraderie. When we are strong, Umberlan is a force for good. It has been for generations before me and it will be so for generations to come. Let your ears hear the truth of this. Damons come forth and report."

King Salak approached the throne, draped his cape over the arm with a flourish, and sat down as the light beamed on him from every direction. His father warned him there would be pageantry, but this… .

The Damons began to approach and give their reports. No money. No gifts. King Salak hated flatterers and his spies kept him abreast of the goings-on in his kingdom. As they approached him, they bowed deeply, cowed into reports of truth, good or bad. His kind face contrasted his sharp and terse words. The clear message, "Don't waste my time."

Ja'el felt underdressed. His father taught him, "The man in the clothes must have a bigger presence than the clothes on the man." He wore his best robe, but it looked paltry compared to the Damons' finery. One more thing to worry about. His knees still shook. He forced himself to breathe slower. His report came last. *Will I make it to the end?*

Then Ja'el heard his name. He slowly approached the king and opened his mouth to speak.

"I…uh…"

A giggle from the balcony cut him deeply, but also served to strengthen his resolve. He straightened his back and took a deep breath.

"My king," His voice echoed off the walls and surprised him. *I sound pretty good.* This little boost of confidence launched him into his report. "The report from Varlana is good." He would be damned if a giggling girl got satisfaction. His anger strengthened his voice and he continued the report with no more problems.

When he finished, the king smiled. "Your father will be pleased. The man has become bigger than his clothes."

Ja'el's feet hardly touched the floor. All the way home he relived the moment the king smiled at him. He burst through the door and raced to his father to tell him everything.

He stopped suddenly when he saw the healer. He turned with a somber look to greet Ja'el as he packed his bag.

"Is he sleeping?"

"No, but he's very weak. Don't talk too long."

Ja'el quietly approached the bed. "Father, it went well. I think I pleased the king."

"Good. Excellent. Tell me everything." Morcon's voice whispered, but his eyes smiled. "Everything."

Ja'el took his father's hand and began to relate his story. When he reached the king's speech, he stood and began to strut around the room while he swirled an imaginary cape back and forth. He turned back to his father to continue and heard the rattle of life's last breath.

"Healer!"

As soon as the healer entered his shoulders slumped. The pallor of death covered Morcon's face.

"I'm sorry, Ja'el. He's gone."

Ja'el stumbled out of the room and fell into a chair. *My best day and my worst day.*

* * * * *

In a daze, he moved through the next few weeks. Umberlan celebrated his father's life and honored him in death. All the Damons stayed a few extra days to pay their respects, which forced Ja'el to receive them graciously day after day. When Morcon's body finally joined his wife's in the family tomb, Ja'el felt the weight of his father's legacy laid on his young shoulders.

The day after the death service, the king called for him. The guard turned right from the Grand Hall and led him to the library. This surprised him, but the familiar books and tables gave him comfort. King Salak waited behind the teacher's desk.

"My king." Ja'el went to one knee and bowed his head.

"Ja'el, rise. I want to tell you myself how much I am grieved over your father's death. I valued his friendship above all others."

"Thank you, King Salak."

"But affairs of state do not grieve as we do and I need his wisdom by my side. You are now my chief advisor and the Damon of Varlana."

Ja'el knew this might be coming, but he didn't expect it so soon. "I am honored, sir, but am I ready?"

"No one is ready. I trust you and believe you will be a help to me. That is why I want you. Your father's loss is a hard one, but we must bear up and make the decisions of the day. He groomed you for this. I expect you to attend me in the morning."

When Ja'el left the library, he turned right toward the gardens. As he wandered among the topiary and flora, he heard the faint laughter of childhood memories. *This is the start of a new life. Father, help me to live it well.* He walked through the outer gate and left his youth behind him.

* * * * *

The next morning Ja'el overslept. He jumped out of bed, threw on his robes, and combed his hand through his hair as he ran to the palace. A few seconds to catch his breath and he entered the King's council. King Salak looked away from his argument. A smile curved up at the corner of his mouth as he waved Ja'el to the table.

"Ah, Ja'el you know everyone" He pointed to each man. "General Janell, Minister Talaene, Tobin – my Captain of the guard, and Kalaren of the Merchant Guild."

Ja'el knew them all and nodded to each of them. A wayward strand of hair flopped over his eye, but he ignored it as he sat down in the empty chair in the middle of the table.

"Now, General, you should start at the beginning for Ja'el's sake."

Ja'el saw the frustration quickly pass over Janell's face. Already embarrassed by his late arrival, he tried to make amends. "My king, I'm sure I can catch up quickly. Please, General, do not be inconvenienced for my sake."

King Salak laughed heartily. "You are your father's son. I knew you would not disappoint me. General, if you please."

"My king, your brother's army continues to grow. I don't believe he has your good interest in mind. We should be concerned."

"Nonsense, Janell. Gailen is my brother. He may not like me, but we are family and family does not turn on family. He raises an army to defend Umberlan. He has given me his word."

Silence around the table made Ja'el feel compelled to ask the question, "Who do we need to defend against? Is someone preparing to attack Umberlan?"

Tobin spoke quietly. "There are rumors of an Oberlan invasion."

Salak's hands hit the table. "No. Our treaty stands. King Ardenna will not move against us. I demand to know where this report came from."

The General tried again. "If not Oberlan, then where? Why does your brother feel the need to raise so many troops?"

"Am I the only one here who remembers my father's work to unify these lands? Gailen and I will not abandon his vision of Umberlan. If Gailen raises men to support me, then it proves he is for me. There's an end to it. What other business?"

They turned to matters in the city and spoke no more about war. As the capital of Umberlan, Varlana dwarfed the hamlets and towns that dotted the rest of Umberlan's map. King Salak left the governance of them to each region's Damon.

Varlana held the seat of national power. He believed his palace and the grandeur of Varlana directly impacted the country's prosperity. If Varlana succeeded, Umberlan succeeded. The king ruled the country, a much bigger concern than the squabbles of a small town.

This view left the Damons off the king's council. He trusted his Damons to rule and be loyal to the crown, but his blind trust weakened the government. He united Varlana, but neglected the rest of Umberlan. The resentment of the Damons turned into the sparks of revolution.

As the council left the room, Janell fell in beside Ja'el.

"What say you, Ja'el? What do you think of the king's council?"

His familiarity startled Ja'el. Janell never approached him like this. He knew of some Damons who switched their loyalty to Gailen, but he didn't know where the General stood. He measured his thoughts and chose to be cautious.

"Varlana prospers. And the regions seem to be doing well. Are you concerned?"

10

"Varlana prospers, but not all its citizens are happy. Have you heard of the rebel's scroll?"

Ja'el knew of the list of grievances against King Salak by some Damons, but he didn't trust Janell yet. "Yes, but I understand it represents only a very small faction. Should Varlana be worried?"

Janell pulled Ja'el aside to sit on a bench and leaned into his ear. "Are you for the king?"

"Of-course. What have I done to make you doubt my loyalty?"

"Nothing. But you remain neutral. I need to know if you're your father's son."

"I am loyal to the king. I do not know who to fully trust, so I remain uncommitted."

"Your father joined with us. You must see the sense of this."

"I see the sense of working for the good of Varlana. I have yet to know who these rebels are or where they come from. Do you know who's backing them? I will not move on rumor and speculation and, right now, it is all you have."

Janell rubbed his forehead. He took a deep breath and held Ja'el's eye. "I will speak plainly, but I will kill you if you betray me."

Now I will finally know the truth of this, thought Ja'el.

"The king is blind when it comes to his brother. Morcon worked with us to help him see the danger. Now you must join us against Gailen."

Ja'el knew about the division at court, but this news surprised him. "King Salak does not doubt Gailen's loyalty. Who are you to question it?"

"Gailen gathers forces to fight against whose army? Oberlan and Symbia don't prepare for war. I have spies in every kingdom and they tell me the king's treaties are holding. You know the history between Salak and Gailen. Who do you think Gailen prepares to fight?"

"I must know more before I decide." He needed to buy time to scour his father's notes. A wrong step like this could end the influence he built with the king.

They agreed to meet the next day and Ja'el continued home. He pulled his father's journals off the shelf and started to read.

It will not be obvious. He would not risk it.. What is implied? What is between the lines, Father?

He studied the notes all afternoon. Rebellion and treachery underscored the pages. His father worried about King Salak's safety even in his own palace. By sunset, Ja'el became convinced the General told the truth.

When Ja'el met the General the next day, he shared what he learned.

"It seems my father did leave evidence of his agreement with you. But I must make my own decisions. What more can you tell me?"

"You serve on the Council. What is your desire?"

Ja'el knew Janell tested him. "I desire peace in Umberlan and prosperity in Varlana. Like my father, I wish to see King Salak's reign be long and happy."

"Your sweet talk means nothing."

Janell's stern face made Ja'el sit up straighter. "Janell, my family has served the king for generations. I will not betray my father's trust or his father's before him. I tell you here and now, if you are not for the king, you are my enemy."

"You have your father's passion." He smiled and motioned Ja'el closer. "Come here. I have some hard things to say to you."

They settled on a shaded bench where trees sheltered them from the sun and the public. Janell carefully scanned the area and bent toward Ja'el.

"King Salak's greatest weakness is his desire to reconcile with his brother. Gailen plays him like a lamar. *His* desire is the throne, has been since their father chose Salak over him. We are afraid of insurrection."

"Surely Gailen would not be so brazen?"

"Gailen is a fighter. He will take with violence what he wants if it's not given to him outright. His influence grows stronger at court and we believe several Damons have sworn allegiance to him against the king."

"And the king still does not believe it."

"Yes. Now you begin to see the danger around him. We must work together to change his mind; help him see reason about his brother. We have tarried too long. Keep your eyes and ears sharp, Ja'el. Gailen has spies everywhere."

* * * * *

Janell returned to his rooms. Captain Dugan, his attendant, waited with Marguerite, his daughter. They dropped hands as he entered.

"General, is he with us?"

"I believe he is. He is young, but he will be a good ally."

Marguerite's face lit up with hope. "Will he be able to stop Gailen?"

"I don't think anyone can stop Gailen at this point, but I vow you two will be married as soon as the King puts him down."

They said their good-nights and Dugan kissed Marguerite gently on the cheek before she left the room. General Janell and Dugan sat together for a few more moments to discuss their plans against Gailen.

"Have you heard from Damon Noran?"

"He doesn't travel since he injured his leg. I've sent a messenger, but he hasn't returned."

"Aside from Varlana, the biggest regions are with Gailen."

A cloud of worry passed over Dugan's face. "And the king's regions isolated. Devonshire could be the difference between victory and defeat."

"We can't let it come to war. Morcon wouldn't have let it come this far."

"Is Ja'el as strong as his father?"

"He is passionate and smart, but he's young. I don't know."

"We can't go forward without him."

"I know. Tomorrow we bring Ja'el in."

"Can you trust him?"

"I trusted his father completely. Let's hope the son is the same."

CHAPTER 2
IN WHICH WE MEET AN INGRID

Chimaya Castle nestled in a box canyon to the west of Varlana. The colossus loomed high above, carved out of the rock wall behind it. Visitors approached through the open fields of the foothills along a winding road that climbed around the base and up the mountain. It ended at a massive gate which opened only by invitation and revealed a draw bridge to the castle door. A moat fed by ice-cold water from the snow-capped peaks surrounded three sides. The rockface behind it rose seventy-five feet above the tallest spire.

The harsh and imposing exterior didn't reflect its interior. Gailen lived in luxury. Tapestries lined the halls and thick rugs covered the floors. Dark wood paneled the rooms, polished to a rich glow. Elegant furniture testified of good taste and expense. Gailen wanted everyone who entered to understand his power.

Large windows remained open to let in light, but great, heavy shutters hung outside to protect against an attack. Designed for defense, Chimaya remained undefeated, even in the great wars fought many generations ago.

Gailen sat enthroned in the Library surrounded by loyal followers. A huge desk curved around him. Great numbers of impressive books lined the walls from floor to ceiling. Books were rare in Umberlan. The knowledge of binding scrolls emerged generations ago when dragons flew. The dragons gave many of their secrets to humans and books were plentiful. However, after the dragon wars, the knowledge disappeared. Books became rare. Gailen's collection had been in his family for many years; one of his most valued possessions.

His most cherished – the wisdom and ancestry of his family – he kept close at hand. The yellowed pages complained of age and wear. It had guided his family for many years. At this moment he held it closed. His thumb rubbed the spine as he thought about his immediate future.

He had fought his way into power, sometimes even armed in back alleys with knives. Rarely did he lose. He enjoyed the violence and he wore his injuries with pride. His twisted nose and pitted face chilled the bravest spine. Gailen had lost his left ear lobe, torn off in a fight. The ragged tear remained evident under his short-cropped hair. His smile revealed broken and stained teeth. The effect of his countenance brought fear into an opponent's eyes, a sight Gailen enjoyed.

When his brother closed the royal council to the Damons, it opened a golden opportunity for him. He invited all Umberlan's Damons to meet with him to find answers to their mutual problems. The meetings started cordially, but over time Gailen planted the seeds of discontent. Now his work bore fruit. They divided and those frustrated with King Salak's narrow vision of Umberlan aligned themselves with Gailen.

Three Damons, Arbak, Endar and Matoki pledged their allegiance to him already. Their lands, together with his, made almost half of the country. Gailen also employed loyal spies and guards at Salak's palace. Always hamstrung by the wily Morcon, the vacancy created by his death fell to his son, a young and weak replacement. *Now is the time.* His thoughts returned to the men before him.

"My army grows too big to hide. Salak has been informed, but still believes I am loyal to him. I need more soldiers to ensure victory, so I need to move forces into your regions."

Gailen moved pieces around on a map spread across his desk. "200 men here, Matoki, along your border with Varlana's region; and 250 men here just across the regional line, Endar. Our numbers will swell without arousing suspicion."

"And supplies to feed them?" Damons loyal to King Salak surrounded Endar's region. "I'm already feeding 150 soldiers. How will I hide wagons to feed 400?"

"I will send what you need." Gailen patience wore thin. *How did this whining pig become a Damon?* "If you're not strong enough to wage your small part in this campaign, I will be happy to relieve you of your responsibility. You may retire in the west wing of my castle. Shall I help you pack your things?" He smiled.

Endar blanched and took a small step back. The west wing held the dungeons. "No, Gailen. My only concern is to keep the troops in top physical condition."

"Go. All of you. We will meet again, soon." The Damons scurried out and prepared to leave the castle. Gailen's mind turned to domestic duties as he pulled a bell rope. He stared at a woman's portrait on the wall opposite his desk as the servant entered.

"Do you remember my wife?"

The man never knew her, but he knew the risk of a negative answer. "Yes sir. She's very beautiful."

"But weak. Just one son and she died. Such a waste. I would have been happy with her."

The servant's eyebrows lifted at his candor, but he remained silent. He didn't want to pay the penalty for offense.

"Bring me an Ingrid and a rider. I have work to do."

"Yes sir." The servant immediately left the room unnoticed by Gailen, who continued to stare at Ingrid's portrait. *Ah, Ingrid. Such beauty and grace. It is inconvenient you died, but your son is growing up well.*

He had loved her, but the need to be a strong king overpowered his need of her. He spent his energy in the study of how to rule instead of how to love. When his father gave the throne to Salak instead, Gailen was consumed with jealousy and resentment. His anger drove a wedge between he and Ingrid. Now his memories of her confused him; anger at her abandonment, love when he remembered her kindness, and bitterness because he believed her death cost him the crown.

Since her death, he always picked the most beautiful girl in Tenebray to be his consort. When she reached the age where her youth began to wane, he moved her to the east wing and found another. He didn't know their names. He didn't care. When one moved into the castle her name changed to Ingrid. While they lived here, they obeyed or died. After they left, if they left, they could call themselves whatever they wanted.

* * * * *

"Ingrid" stood outside the library door and straightened her dress. She wore her favorite, made especially to compliment her complexion and her best features. She hoped Gailen would be pleased.

"I hope he's in a good mood," she muttered to herself. The servant reached for the door handle. "No. Not yet."

She took a deep breath and steadied herself. The first time she had joined him for an afternoon in his study he was gentle and kind. Since then, these hours turned into nightmares. *Please let this day be like the first.*

As she hoped for the best, she nodded at the servant. He opened the door and she entered. Gailen sat at his desk and folded a letter. He didn't even look up as he dripped wax on the paper and said, "Ingrid, I wish to have you. Take off your clothes."

The dress was a failure. He didn't even see it. Her hands shook as she struggled with buttons and laces. Soon the dress dropped into a nondescript pile on the floor and she shivered in the cold air that meandered in from the open window. She slowly walked to take her place beside and slightly behind his chair.

Tears welled up in her eyes as she struggled to keep her composure. This afternoon would be a nightmare.

Gailen stood and turned to her as he began to unlace his pants, but the rider's entrance interrupted him. Ingrid stood rigid, naked in front of this stranger. *A boy. He's only a boy.* If she moved to hide her shame behind Gailen he would knock her to the floor. She bore her humiliation in silence.

The young man tripped over his feet when he spied her. She looked down as her face flushed and Gailen chuckled.

The rider approached the desk and tried to keep his eyes trained on Gailen. "You sent for me?"

"Yes. Here is a letter to deliver to my son at the Palace in Varlana. Give it to him personally."

The rider reached for the letter, but Gailen snatched it back and watched his discomfort. Ingrid stood rigid, but her muscles shivered in the cold. Gailen's fingers caressed her cheek and shoulder.

"Isn't she pretty?"

She cringed at his touch and he pinched her breast until it left a bruise. As the sharp pain jolted her body, a quiet yelp escaped her throat and Gailen kissed her roughly as he groped her. It was all show to upset the rider. It made her feel disgusting, but a broken arm would feel worse.

The rider's jaw dropped slightly as he gazed at the scene. He tried to control himself, but he began to desire her. His palms started to sweat as he realized he would be discovered. Gailen saw his eyes move over Ingrid's body.

"Do you want her?"

Ingrid stood still, but fear rose in her throat. Gailen often gave her to other men, but this was a boy. *This is too much. I can't do this, but if I refuse, he'll kill me, beat me until I'm dead. I'm only a toy for him. Do I want to die to preserve this boy's virginity for a few more days?* She waited silent, filled with dread.

The rider looked at the floor. "I would never take what is yours, Damon."

"But do you want her?"

"Y…Yes, but I would never…"

"Take her. I give her to you." He grabbed Ingrid by the arm and tossed her roughly on the floor in front of him. "Take her now before me."

The rider stared down at the beautiful woman in disbelief and shook with fear and desire. She cried in shame and sweat began to run down his face.

A laugh roared through the room and Gailen slapped the rider hard on the back. "You are ridiculous, letting a slip of a girl best you." He handed the young man the letter. "Get out. Deliver the letter and never come back, weakling." The young man received a kick in the backside for his hesitation.

As he left the room, Gailen motioned for Ingrid to stand. She rose on shaky legs and trembled in front of him. Suddenly, he slapped her back to the floor. "Why are you so weak? You are always so weak." He kicked her and she scrambled across the floor to get away, but Gailen was spry and quickly grabbed her by the hair. For a long while he had his way with her. When he finished, he laced his pants and left her to cry on the floor. "Be quiet, girl, I have work to do."

She hurt everywhere, but eventually summoned the strength to rise and return to her post at his desk. All afternoon she stood in humiliation while Gailen met with servants and city officials. In between, he toyed with her or beat her.

When he left to eat evening meal, she fell to the floor and crawled to her beautiful dress that lay forgotten in a pile on the floor. The soft silks soothed her body as she hugged it to herself and wept. *When will this hell end?*

CHAPTER 3
ADVERSARIES AND ALLIANCES

Once again Ja'el found himself in the council chamber at odds with Jakfa, the king's nephew.

"We cannot keep taxing the people. Your excesses will break the back of Umberlan."

"Excesses. We have to eat!"

"We do not have to eat like pigs, Jakfa. Show some restraint and think of the people."

"One of your father's old sayings again? Can't you think of anything yourself?"

"I choose to live in my father's wisdom rather than your self-indulgence. If we starve the people by taking all they have, we will eventually starve ourselves."

"The people serve *us*. A fact you seem to forget."

The king's staff hit the floor with a thud. "Enough. Jakfa you would do well to learn from Ja'el. His father was the wisest man I ever knew. Do not come before this council again unless you have something useful to present. This meeting is done."

The king strode from the chamber and motioned for Ja'el to follow. Over the past six months Ja'el and Salak worked closely together. Ja'el learned how to present the king's arguments in council and take the criticism with dignity. This allowed the king to be the wise judge. Salak now considered Ja'el a close friend. They walked in silence until the king led them into the privacy of his rooms.

Salak threw his staff on a table. "How could my brother raise such a loathsome, self-indulgent boy?"

"They both have always resented your crown. Remember, Gailen is older than you. Your father's decision to give you the throne turned the kingdom upside down for a while. I do not think Gailen has ever forgiven you."

"It wasn't my fault. Ja'el, how many times have I told you my father forced me into the crown."

"Still, you make a much better king than Gailen could ever be."

"Jakfa struts around like *he* wears the crown."

"He is next in line."

"I cannot bear the thought of Jakfa as king after me, Ja'el. We must do something. He has no heart for the people."

"My king, the only solution is to marry and have a son of your own."

"How many times must we talk of this? I do not trust my judgment in matters of the heart. I make bad decisions there.

"There are many women at court who could be queen. They are raised to live in the palace. Any one of them would be fine."

"I can't trust them, Ja'el. They're all vying for power, not Varlana. I have considered every one and none of them suit me."

"Why couldn't you love one of them? What kind of woman are you looking for?"

"It's not about love. It's the character of the woman you should think about. Is she strong enough to rule, especially a young son? Is her heart tender toward others? Will she stand with me or shrink from the battle-field? A woman like Adonna."

"Adonna is a legend."

"Yes. But if she lived, I would choose Adonna as my warrior queen."

"My king, you are being unfair. I am sure you can find a woman with a good heart here at the palace."

"No. I'm done with looking. It takes too much energy away from being king. I have given this matter much thought. *You* must find me a wife."

"My king…

"Don't 'my king' me. I know you're about to refuse. I won't have it. I won't waste my time with this anymore. You're a good judge of people. You must go out to the Damons and find me a wife."

"But I know nothing of such matters. I have never loved another."

"I will not hear it. You must go. I cannot wait any longer. You have watched Jakfa for a year now and see how his power grows at court. I think maybe Janell is right and he *is* planning a coup. If Gailen can't control him, I must."

Ja'el sat silent and stared at the king as he paced the room. He knew without a doubt now King Salak would never face the truth of his brother's betrayal. He ignored the obvious and believed Jakfa rebellious rather than obedient. *He will go to his grave thinking the best of Gailen.*

"You must hurry. I must be married by mid-summer. The announcement will be made immediately. That should keep Jakfa in his place. You have six months to find me a wife and get me married."

Ja'el slumped in his chair. He couldn't argue with the king when he made up his mind like this. But he didn't know where to start.

With a sigh he resigned himself to his fate. "I will prepare tonight and leave tomorrow."

"Good. I will begin arrangements. Six months, Ja'el. Six months and I will have a bride. Another nine and I will have an heir."

* * * * *

Ja'el left the castle and met Janell in a tavern. They pretended to drink and carouse until the early hours when, arm in arm they began to stumble home. Janell pretended to trip and leaned into Ja'el.

"What news?"

"The king is determined to marry and produce an heir. He believes *Jakfa* plans a coup and this action will be enough to compel Gailen to stop him."

"He will not see reason when it comes to his brother. This latest nonsense will just fuel the fire."

"I am to leave tonight. I will be back in four or five months with his new bride, whoever she is. The wedding is in mid-summer."

"Ja'el, your voice will be missed at council. Return as soon as you can."

"What of the Damons?"

"Five are loyal to the king. Four have sworn for Gailen. It will be soon, Ja'el. Hurry back."

No one walked the empty streets by the time he arrived home and began to plan. He covered the windows, retrieved a wide, shallow wooden bowl and began to carefully fill it with water. The practice of magic was a family secret. His family carried the gift since the age of the dragons and Morcon had taught him like his father before him. The old wooden scrying bowl had been treasured by every wizard in his family. He traced the patterns along the edge and thought about Morcon.

You are missed, father, by more people than me. The world spins out of control and I have no answers. You left too soon and now I go on a fool's errand because I have no answers for the king.

He sighed and began to slowly stir and chant. He looked for his trip's destination, a woman of character. *How do you scry character?* He imagined a woman he could love, since he and the king shared the same desires. She must be beautiful, but strong and brave. Slowly, a picture emerged.

A tall slender woman walked the streets of Varlana and stopped to admire the wares of several vendors. Although Ja'el could not hear sounds, she seemed to talk with them kindly. Her hair set off her face perfectly and her delicate fingers gently picked up a peach and deposited it in her pocket. As she left the booth, Ja'el realized she didn't pay the vendor. *Hmmm.* He disturbed the water and started again.

A sweet girl (*maybe too young?*) walked down a lane shaded by old-growth trees. She met a man and smiled. He returned her smile. It all looked congenial and happy. Then money exchanged hands. *Oh well, try again.*

Ja'el scryed for hours and almost gave up, until he saw…

A beautiful young woman walked in a garden. Her long raven hair cradled the fine features of her face. Gently she tended the flowers and thoughtfully pruned away unwanted limbs and dead blooms. Her warm smile complimented the joy and peace on her face. Suddenly she frowned in anger, stuck her nose into a thorny plant, and reached in to grab a locust who dared to dine on its leaves. She threw the interloper violently to the ground and stomped on it with all her weight. She took no notice of the scrape on her hand as she danced in victory. With a satisfactory smile she composed herself and continued through the garden as before.

"Perfect! She is perfect. Now, where *is* she?"

It took Ja'el until dawn to discover where she lived. Evan Castle near Devonshire. The farthest reaches of the kingdom. *Well, I should not be surprised. Any closer and she would have come to court.*

Weary, but hopeful, he saddled his horse in the morning mist and set off to find the king's new wife.

* * * * *

Jakfa received his father's letter and opened it as soon as he entered his rooms.

Jakfa,

The business of Chimaya continues. All is under control and the land prospers.

The road project is underway. The repairs will be started soon after you receive this letter.

I know your heart is loyal to Umberlan. Make sure the palace guards surround the king against our enemies.

Your father,
Gailen

The coded letter clearly spelled out the message. The business of the rebellion moved ahead successfully. The army grew and the Damons loyal to his father remained so. The first part of their plan would weaken the king's forces with attacks on his supply wagons. They would also infiltrate the palace guards with men loyal to Gailen. His heart remained loyal to his father's vision of an Umberlan free of King Salak. At least one of Gailen's men in the guards would be near the king at all times.

So, it begins. Jakfa sat down at his desk to plan.

* * * * *

The trip evolved uneventful and wonderful. Every few days the scenery changed and Ja'el stopped to examine new forms of plant-life. His father had taught him herb science and his favorite times were spent amidst a small library of illustrated books of far-flung plants not native to the lands around Varlana. He had packed his favorite and now the pictures seemed to come alive. He investigated every new plant.

At night he scryed the girl. He saw her read – good. He saw her play the lamar – good. He saw her bite her nails – not so good, but she's not perfect which means people will relate to her. So, another point in her favor. He saw her peacefully sleep – good, no snores. Night after night he watched her until he knew her before he met her. *King Salak will be pleased.*

When he finally arrived in Devonshire, he rented a room in town for one day and night. He wanted to give the castle a little warning. In the morning he went to market, asked several merchants about Evan, and casually dropped the tidbit he traveled from Varlana. In the afternoon he stopped a few walkers and asked directions to the castle. At the tavern's evening meal, he allowed the barkeep to draw out his connection with King Salak. Now he finally climbed into bed; his work finished. If Evan Castle didn't know he would arrive tomorrow on the king's business then he'd give up and go home.

At mid-morning he presented himself to Damon Noran of Evan Castle. The color drained from the Damon's face and he began to apologize for any unintended offense he might have done to the king.

"Fine sir, I sent a message with my thorough report for the Great Calling. I am so sorry, but travel is impossible with my leg, and my daughter and I are alone. I cannot leave her and I cannot travel. Please show mercy for an old sick fool." He struggled to deeply bow before Ja'el.

"No. Please get up. There is no offense. The king has sent me to meet your daughter. He looks for a wife and thinks your daughter most suitable. I am here to meet her and judge her character."

"My daughter? But King Salak has never met my daughter."

Ja'el silently cursed his indiscretion. His knowledge of the girl came from the secrets of magic. Now he faced an obvious question and he scrambled for an answer. *Father, where is your wisdom now?*

Morcon's answer came immediately. *A good man's reputation will precede him.*

Ja'el smiled warmly. "The king wishes to marry and your daughter's good character and reputation has spread even to Varlana. King Salak trusts you, reveres your friendship, and wants to join your house with his."

A big smile lit up the Damon's face. "Then you shall meet her at evening meal. Please allow me to show you to your room." He smiled and hummed as he limped up the staircase. As he slowly escorted Ja'el down a long hall, he regaled him with stories of the Castle's former glory.

The small modest castle surprised Ja'el. No great hall or lavish carpets, but suitably grand. Ja'el liked the Damon instantly, and hoped the meal with his daughter would go well.

His room overlooked the garden in his scry. but the misty scry did the garden no justice. Now he could clearly see a surprising variety of plants. They grew in a pattern he didn't quite understand, but it pleased the eye and he decided to investigate.

He left his room and wandered while he looked for a servant who could show him the way. The clean halls hinted at a servant's work, but he met no one. *Who runs this place? Are there no servants at all? There must be someone.*

Ja'el trailed his fingers across the dark paneling and felt the smooth, oiled surface. A hint of lemon hung in the air. Colorful flower arrangements filled the window sills and created pleasant patches of scents as he walked down the hall.

A sudden turn led him into a day room. Thick carpet, though slightly faded, muted his footsteps and tapestries lined the walls. Overstuffed chairs with bright upholstery were arranged in small groups for intimate conversations. Ja'el wondered how many secrets these walls overheard. He sat by a window for a time, but curiosity drove him out to explore.

More rooms and more halls revealed the peaceful beauty of the castle. A close look uncovered frayed edges on the drapes and chairs, worn patches in the carpet under carefully placed tables, and tiny chips and cracks in vases and china. Ja'el didn't care. He loved the plants and the colors against the rich, dark wood. *I would not leave here either, Damon Noran. This castle is close to paradise.*

He finally exited the front door and walked around to the back. All this took several hours, so he sat on a bench in the garden to rest.

The breeze cooled his face and rustled the leaves around him. The sound relaxed him. He closed his eyes and cleared his mind. The aroma of musty earth and sweet blooms filled the air. *How can flowers bloom in winter?* He opened his mouth to taste the air and a tangy sensation in his throat made him think of lemons. He lifted his hand and felt the breeze through his fingers. To the right he touched soft, fuzzy leaves; to the left a thorny briar. *Such variety. This is like every Damon's garden in one place. Did she do this?*

He sat still and let the sensations of the garden wash over him. An hour passed before he finally opened his eyes.

A pair of big, green eyes stared back at him. "I thought you dead"

Ja'el jumped. Hunkered down on a bed of moss, he saw a freckled face topped with untamed red hair. Clothes hung loosely around a long, skinny body. Arms and legs seemed to angle out in all directions and a boy's head tilted to the side as he studied Ja'el.

"You so still, I thought you dead."

"And now you know I am not. Who are you?"

"Nobody. But ma calls me Caleb."

"Well, Caleb. What do you know about this garden?"

"I know all to know. I can name all plants and things and tell what most do. You want know things; I tell you. I just about to tell everybody about dead man in the garden, that how much I know."

With a twinkle in his eye, Ja'el stood, stretched, and reached out his hand. "A man once told me 'Never refuse knowledge from a wise one.' So, how about you show me around this garden of yours?"

Caleb returned a very serious look. "I don't hold a hand I don't know. I told you mine. You tell me yours."

So, there's a garden code of honor. "I am Ja'el, come to meet the Damon's daughter."

"Antania? Oh, she fine." Caleb gave Ja'el an impish grin and grabbed his hand. "Now this here, where you sat, …"

For the rest of the afternoon Ja'el learned all about the garden. Caleb showed him the climbing tree, the hole in the wall, the squirrel nest, even the secret fort.

Ja'el stood before a monstrosity of scrap wood and burlap hidden inside an overgrown pyracantha near the back wall. "This is impressive."

"I built." He led Ja'el through a labyrinth of rooms that ended at a little used gate. It leaned precariously against a rotten fence. Caleb beamed a smile at Ja'el as he gingerly opened it.

"I made myself."

"Caleb, how long did it take you to build your fort?"

"Long time. Gathered wood and nails, borrowed hammer. Long time."

Ja'el admired his tenacity. *There is more to this boy than meets the eye.*

"Caleb, what do you know about the plants in the garden?"

"Antania does plants. I do forts."

His mother's voice called out from the castle and Caleb darted inside. Ja'el went to his room to wash for dinner.

Antania. What a lovely name. Queen Antania. Queen Antania. Rolls through the teeth like honey. People could love a queen named Antania.

A bell rang from downstairs. Ja'el set off down the hall for dinner.

* * * * *

Noran waited in the dining hall with his daughter. "King Salak is a good man, but I don't understand this proposal. I'm not comfortable with this, but it's a king's request and will be difficult to refuse."

"You say he is a good man."

"Yes."

"Well, it seems a gift from heaven. Father, we can't go on like this; living on a thread. I'm almost too old to marry. If I don't make a good match soon, we will lose everything."

"There is more to life than castles, Antania. We would be happy in a cottage with a garden."

"You are Damon. Your leg has weakened you, but you are Damon. You are good to your people. They need you to protect them."

For the moment, Noran gave up. "You sound like your mother."

"There's nothing wrong with that."

Ja'el's entrance interrupted them. Noran smiled.

"Ja'el, there you are. Antania, meet our guest, Ja'el from Varlana."

She turned and beheld the most handsome man she ever saw. Dark hair framed a gentle face with bright, intelligent eyes. The belt on his robe drew her attention to his full shoulders and slim waist. Her breath caught in her throat and her hands began to tremble. "So nice to meet you, sir."

Ja'el couldn't think. The misty scry did not prepare him for her natural beauty. Her soft red dress complimented her long, wavy hair. Her voice sounded like the dulcet strings of the lamar. Ja'el's knees began to shake and he lost his tongue. He smiled and bowed his head.

Noran watched all of this and grinned. Then he rang a small bell. "Let us all sit down and get to know each other."

Ja'el held the chair for Antania. Her hair smelled like jasmine. When his hand accidently brushed across her arm, he felt her soft skin and his knees began to give way.

"I must apologize. The trip has exhausted me more than I knew and I must retire. Antania, we will talk tomorrow." Ja'el almost ran from the room. His head spun faster than his heart pounded. *What trickery is this?*

He stumbled blindly through the halls. After he made two wrong turns and entered three wrong rooms, he finally fell into his bed in confusion. Closeted in his room, Ja'el recounted all his father's wisdom for help. "The head must rule the heart or a man loses who he is." There, finally a good one. He lay on his bed while he pondered his reaction to the girl. *Did she spell me? Yes. She must have.* He searched his mind for a defense. Tomorrow he would be ready and she would not upset him again.

* * * * *

"Well, my dear child, it seems you have made an impression."

Heat rose in Antania's cheeks. "Father, I only said 'Hello.' I hardly think I impressed anybody."

"Even so, Antania. He will choose you, if not for the king then for himself."

She pondered her father's words against her feelings. *No. This is too much. I will walk the garden tonight and in the morning life will be normal. Peace must reign the day.*

* * * * *

The king's council convened at the request of Kalaren, the head of the Merchant Guild.

"My king, robbers attack the supply wagons headed toward Varlana."

Salak pointed his staff at his Captain. "Tobin, you must send guards out to police the roads."

"Yes, my king, but my forces here at the palace will be weakened. May I have your permission to recruit more men for Varlana?"

The king waved his hand in the air. "Yes, of course. Do what you must, just round up these thieves. Varlana must prosper."

Janell pushed the subject. "Kalaren, are there any descriptions of these men? Do they wear distinctive clothing or colors?"

"No, general. They wear black and cover their faces. They say nothing, so we don't even know what region they are from."

"They are thieves, that is all we need to know," said the king. "Tobin, let me know as soon as you have dispatched them."

"Yes, my king."

CHAPTER 4

THE KING'S OFFICIAL BUSINESS

As the sunrise spilled through the window, Ja'el rose, washed his face, and put on his official robes. They actually looked like all the others, but he felt more official in this particular one. He cleared his throat, took a deep breath, and marched to the dining hall as he recited today's mantra. *I am an official of the king on official business. I am an official of the king on official business. I am an official of the...*

Antania turned from the buffet as he entered and his mantra deserted him. "We have fresh fruit today and oatmeal. Please, help yourself."

As Ja'el filled his plate, he wondered at the food. "How can you have fresh fruit in winter?"

"We have built a greenhouse here. Light always shines and fruit and vegetables grow all year round."

Ja'el thought about the lean seasons in Varlana. "I must see this greenhouse."

"I can show you after morning meal, if you like. Do you feel well enough?"

"I am quite recovered, thank you."

They ate in awkward silence.

He seems so gentle and wise for a young man. Is he kind? Is he married? She glanced quickly in his direction and shyly smiled.

She is finely featured. Good manners. I wonder if I take her away from a lover? I cannot imagine a young woman so gentle and sweet without many admirers. He looked up from his plate and caught her eye. She smiled and he ducked his head to eat. *I am an official of the king on official business.*

She sighed inwardly. *Why is this so uncomfortable? Might as well get straight to the point.*

"Antania, tell me about your life here at Evan Castle."

"Father says you are here to interview me for the king. Does he really want to marry?"

Her directness surprised him and he choked on a strawberry. "Yes, he is determined to have an heir. He also wants an appropriate queen to rule with him. (*Uh-oh*) I mean, a beautiful woman whom he and the people can love." *What is happening?* He must regain control of this conversation. "Tell me about Caleb."

The radiance of her smile filled the room. "He is a special child. The son of our cook, so he thinks he knows plants." She giggled. Ja'el was transfixed by the sound. "He only wants adventure in the garden while his mother works."

"I enjoyed his company yesterday. I feel I know your garden very well, from the climbing tree to the secret fort."

"He showed you the secret fort? He must like you very much."

Ja'el's confidence grew at her approval. "Are you the gardener?"

"I suppose. Since Mother died it has fallen to me. But I love the dirt and the challenge."

Ja'el remembered the scry. "Yes, locusts can be incredibly challenging."

"You saw one? I thought I caught the last one. Where is it?"

"No, no. Not in your garden. I…I saw one on the road to the castle." He silently chided himself for his carelessness.

"Good. Peace must reign the day. Are you finished? We can see the garden now."

He rose from the table and followed her to the garden. Her dress swayed softly as she walked. The smell of roses hung in the air behind her. He admired the way her hair shimmered each time they passed a window. *Stop that! I'm an official of the king on official business. I will not be distracted again.*

When they reached the garden, he moved in front of her and asked questions as they walked. The plants steadied him. Her answers proved the depth of her knowledge and quickly he became absorbed in herbal discovery.

The greenhouse amazed him. "How do you keep everything so healthy all year?"

"We heat with this compost in the winter and cool with water in the heat. My mother designed the system so all the plants could stay lush. 'Happy plants grow peace,' she used to say." She offered him a peach.

"So big!"

"The greenhouse holds in moisture which is good for everything."

"Oh!" Juice spilled down his chin as he took his first bite, but Antania held a clean rag. They laughed as she gently wiped his chin. Their eyes met and for a long second they gazed at each other. Ja'el tore himself away. *I am an official of the king on official business.* He remembered his thoughts of the greenhouse at morning meal.

"I'd like to build one of these greenhouses for the king's palace. If it's successful, maybe we can build more for the populace."

"Father keeps the plans in his study. I'm sure it will be no problem for you to see them. It would be our joy to help you build a greenhouse in Varlana."

He looked at her and smiled. Her beauty took his breath away. *Back to the plants. Back to the questions.* But he'd already made up his mind. She would be queen. Her beauty and intelligence surpassed all others in Umberlan. She must come to Varlana. *King Salak will be pleased.*

Day after day he grilled her about every aspect of her life, her ideas, and her experiences. She gently probed him about his past, his father, his role at the palace. By the end of the week no secrets stood between them.

One day he joined her as she walked to town.

"Have you ever known a life outside of Evan Castle?"

"No, and I don't really want to. I've always lived here and would happily die here but my father is anxious to marry me off. You came just in time."

Ja'el flushed and turned away to examine plants along the road. "I don't mean to pry, but are you spoken for?"

"No." She sighed and skipped forward to walk backwards in front of him. "I have never been in love. My heart belongs to my mother's garden." She laughed and tripped on a stone. Ja'el quickly reached out, grabbed her arm and pulled her to him to prevent her fall. She relaxed into his accidental embrace and he held her a bit too long.

The smell of her hair...

The strength of his arms...

He let her go and they walked to town in silence.

* * * * *

Noran approached his daughter carefully.

"You and Ja'el are spending many hours together. What do you think of him?"

She pulled herself out of the chair and paced the room. "Father, I believe I'm falling in love. How can it happen so fast? I don't even know this man. It's very confusing."

"That would be falling in love."

"What happened with you and mother? Did she love you right away?" She returned to her chair.

"I've told you many stories about her, but here's one I've saved for just this moment. When we met, my insecurity and awkwardness usually drove women away. But she saw something in me no one else did. She came alongside me and stood by me through my mistakes and I grew to love her more than myself. When I asked her to marry me, she agreed. I believe now she didn't love me right away, but knew love would come. I can't explain it, but by the time you arrived in this world, your mother and I forged a relationship stronger than love and I evolved into a different man. No matter how it starts or ends, love changes you. You must be careful who you choose to walk with."

"I have been chosen for the king. Hasn't my choice been taken away?"

"You always have a choice, Antania. The choices you make in the next few days will set your future. Do you want to be queen?"

"Yes and no. I want the power to help people, but my heart wants Ja'el."

"Tell him of your love. Give him the choices he seeks. You will walk your futures together. It's only for you to decide how."

* * * * *

The days filled with happiness for Ja'el. When he wasn't with Antania, he walked with Caleb. They explored the land around the castle and

Ja'el shared his illustrated herbology books with the enthusiastic boy. They both lost track of time while they searched the books for pictures of the local plants.

"What this one?"

Ja'el flipped through the pages. "It is Omdilla Pontus; helpful for upset stomachs or dizziness."

Caleb started to eat it, but quickly spit it out. "Ehck! Why anyone eat that?"

"It says here when you boil it in water and add honey it is not so bad."

"I choose upset. What this?"

Ja'el spent many afternoons with Caleb, and he began to understand the intelligence behind his halting speech. He never repeated a question. If he asked about the same plant, he only wanted to learn more. *I have been looking for an apprentice. I wonder...*

Ja'el settled into a comfortable schedule at Evan Castle. He spent his mornings with Antania ("on official king's business") and afternoons with Damon Noran or Caleb. His heart and mind felt peace for the first time in a long while.

Time passed and his responsibilities started to weigh on him. Every time he thought about his duty his heart sank. *She is for King Salak, not me. She is for King Salak.* He fought with his emotions until his thoughts turned to Jakfa. *He must not rule. She is the future of Umberlan.* "A man's destiny is bigger than a man's desire." His father's voice made him resolute. *Umberlan must be first.* He finally asked Noran for Antania's hand on behalf of the king.

"You have grown close to my daughter, Ja'el. Is this what you believe she wants?"

"I came here to find a woman worthy to be queen. Antania certainly qualifies."

"Then, if she is in agreement, I give my consent."

"The wedding is planned for summer. Will you be able to travel then?"

Noran's face fell. "I will not. I can barely walk now and I'm afraid everyday my leg is more painful. I do not share this with Antania and I would appreciate your discretion."

"What does your healer say?"

"There is no healer at Evan. Antania provides salves from the garden, but I'm not improving. I fear I will miss the wedding."

Ja'el stared in shock and shame. He should have paid attention to Noran's suffering. He assumed Noran benefitted from a healer's care. Antania's father should not suffer. He mentally rolled up his sleeves. This situation would change.

"I will take care of you for now. I have seen plants in the wood to relieve your pain. Tomorrow Caleb and I will make you effective treatments."

"You mustn't. I'm afraid I will never be able to repay you."

"I do not ask for payment. The king will not be happy if you do not attend the wedding. It is for him I do this."

Ja'el strode out of the room intent on the immediate future. He sent word of Antania to the king. They would arrive in a month. The nuptial plans could begin immediately. *That should send Jakfa reeling.* He couldn't help but smile. Then he turned his mind to the local plant life.

In the evening he found Antania in the garden. The peace she felt among the flowers and plants gave her the courage to speak of the future.

"What is he like, King Salak?"

"He is honorable and majestic. His heart is full of compassion for the people. He will be a good and kind husband."

She sat quiet. *Can I speak of love?* She dug deep into herself to summon up the courage to tell him of her feelings for him. It came to nothing and only filled the quiet with tension.

Ja'el's eyes darted away from her. His discomfort made him blurt out, "I would like to draw a picture of you to send to him. I am not a master, but I can send him a good likeness. Would you let me do this?"

I'm a coward, but at least we'll be together for a while. "Yes. I'll meet you here in the morning. The light will be good."

"Thank you, Antania. I will see you then." He left her to her thoughts as his mind filled with face. Deep into the night he imagined the best angle and pose. Long after he made up his mind, he kept her image in his thoughts.

* * * * *

She sat in the darkness and absorbed the peace of the garden. *How I will miss this place. Mother, I have always felt your presence here. Will you be in Varlana?* She didn't think so and it hurt to know she may never see her beloved garden again.

Tears lined her cheeks as her heart turned to Ja'el. *Such a beautiful man. Does he not know my heart? Can he not see my feelings? Why can't I find the words to tell him? Why must he give me to the king when he can have me for himself?*

Footsteps interrupted her thoughts and she slowly rose to turn and face the joy of her father. *I have never been in control of my life. My choices are not my own. In this land, a woman follows where a man leads. That rule changes when I am queen. A small consolation, but something to live for.* She met her father at the base of the stairs.

"Ja'el is going to help me with this leg of mine! He says I should be well enough to travel by the wedding! Oh, to see my sweet girl married to the king! I can imagine how beautiful you will be."

They climbed the stairs as he shared his vision of her future. She barely heard him as she thought about the women of Umberlan free from oppression.

Noran made plans. Antania made plans. Ja'el made plans. Hardly an eye closed in sleep for all the plans in the air.

* * * * *

The king's council room filled with concern. Damons and merchants talked over each other to get the king's ear.

"Five wagons this month."

"The robbers are getting violent. They beat my drivers."

"Supplies are dangerously low, my King."

"The roads to the north and south are too dangerous to travel now."

"TOBIN," Salak's voice boomed off the walls. "Why do these robbers still exist?"

"My king, they seem to know where we are. When we patrol north, they work south. When we patrol near the city, they strike farther out." Tobin let his words hang in the room. The implication vibrated in the air, but he would not be the one to say it.

Kalaren said the obvious. "Are you implying there is a spy among us?"

"I can't say for certain. But all the evidence points to it."

Once again, the room erupted. And once again Salak shouted for quiet.

"Tobin, what about wagons from the east? Is Gailen able to protect his roads?"

"Yes, my king. He works for you. Wagons from the east arrive safely."

"Good. My brother always did know how to keep the peace. There is your answer. Reroute all supply wagons through Gailen's lands to the east."

Janell had stood silent, his tight fists hidden behind his back. He could hold his tongue no longer. "My king, this decision will make Varlana totally dependent on Gailen's protection."

Salak turned on him, his eyes squinted and his mouth in a line. "And your suggestion is to keep losing supplies to these robbers? Shall we ignore the truth right before us? If Gailen's roads are safe it is a credit to his troops and his loyalty to the crown. We will use the eastern route. I'll hear no more about it." He turned away from Janell and smiled. "Tobin, you will continue to patrol to the north and south. Maybe you'll get lucky and capture some of these criminals." He stood to address the room. "I have an important announcement to make."

Salak paused for effect.

"I am getting married. My bride will arrive within the month and soon Umberlan will have an heir to the throne. Turn your attention to this celebration, my friends. There will be joy in Varlana and Umberlan!"

The council stood in confusion. They couldn't process Salak's words in the light of their distress. A pall fell on the room and Salak began to frown. Suddenly, Tobin raised a cheer and it seemed unwise not to join in. Congratulations rippled through the council as everyone left the room. In the hall outside, faces tinged with worry walked silently to their rooms.

King Salak stood alone. *Tobin will capture the robbers or Gailen will if they dare work on his lands. My wedding will be a grand celebration, bigger than the*

Telling, and the people will be pleased. They will love Queen Antania and she will give me an heir. Then all things will be settled and we will live in peace.

With a self-satisfied smile he strode from the room.

CHAPTER 5
THE ART OF ROMANCE

After morning meal, Ja'el found Antania in the garden.

"Did you eat breakfast? We might be here a while."

"I'm fine. Where do you want me to sit?"

He moved her to the bench and unpacked his paper and charcoal. "You'll have to hold your pose. No moving."

She stuck out her tongue and he laughed. "Very attractive. Try another."

She threw her nose in the air with a huff. "How about this? Do I look sufficiently aristocratic?"

"Your little nose will never get high enough to convince me."

Eventually, they settled down and Ja'el began to draw. He started with her hair and the scent of jasmine filled his mind. He worked to bring alive the shimmer of light and soft curls around her ears. He loved her small nose under her big eyes. He took his time. The proportions must be perfect. Her lips closed over perfect teeth. The charcoal caressed her image as her face began to appear.

Every so often he would reach out and lift her chin to the light or turn her head for an angle. The touch of her soft skin on his fingers electrified and soothed, like lightning and silk. He finished much too soon and decided to draw another.

She sat as still as she could. The charcoal scratched on the paper and she wondered what she looked like to him. He looked at her for long stretches of time before he returned to his drawing. She liked his gentle eyes on her. She found herself lost in those eyes and felt a tug of disappointment when he turned his attention to the paper.

Then he cradled her chin to adjust her pose. She felt the touch of his fingers long after he returned to his work. She closed her eyes to breathe in the moment and heard him shuffle his papers.

"Are you finished?"

"No. Just a little longer," and he tenderly turned her head. *Draw me for eternity. I could stay in this moment forever.*

Time floated by while they lingered with each other. Duty and honor began to fade in the heat of emotions between them. And then...

"Here you. We going plant hunting? What you doing?"

Ja'el put down his charcoal and showed Caleb the picture. "What do you think? I'm sending it to the king."

Caleb studied the image and the woman before him. "Good. Now, let's go."

"Wait. I want to see the picture."

Ja'el gave Antania his second drawing; simple, but accurate. Her face didn't betray her disappointment and she returned it without comment.

"Caleb, come with me. I need to put this away and get my plant book." He carefully picked up his papers and they trotted off into the castle.

"Where are they going, I wonder?" Noran frowned. He had come to see the portrait. "Is he finished?"

"Yes. It's an adequate likeness. The king should recognize me when I arrive."

"My, aren't you enthusiastic. You have chosen to be queen, my dear. Every woman in Umberlan will envy you."

She smiled and hugged him. "I am happy," and she left the garden to hide in her room.

* * * * *

For the better part of the afternoon, Caleb scrambled over the countryside to find all the plants on his list. He brought each one to Ja'el who examined them carefully before he put them in his bag. Ja'el's bag filled to the top and they returned to the kitchen. Ja'el pounded, grinded, and mixed for hours as Caleb watched with fascination.

"What they do?"

"When I'm done, all these plants will help Damon Noran feel better."

"It magic, right?"

"No, but it is amazing. You can learn all of this, you know."

"How?"

"If your parents approve, you can come live with me in Varlana and I will teach you."

"How far Varlana? How long to learn? How old I to come?"

Caleb's mind whirled with questions, but Ja'el stood to go. Noran needed attention.

"We will talk with your mother tomorrow. I must go to Damon Noran now."

Caleb didn't hear him. He dreamed of adventure in Varlana.

* * * * *

Ja'el found Noran in his study. The big desk stood empty since Noran could not stretch his leg under it. He had moved his work to a side table next to an armchair with a stool. As Ja'el examined his leg and began to apply the compress he made, they talked. Noran liked Ja'el. Their easy conversations always satisfied them both. But tonight, hard truths would be faced.

Ja'el began. "This leg needs constant attention. You must hire an attendant to make more salve and tincture. Make sure he travels with you to Varlana. You will still need help."

"Ja'el, stop assuming what you cannot see. We have no servants here. Devonshire is the poorest town in Umberlan and I refuse to tax the people beyond their meager resources. We use the little extra we have to hire local people to cook and clean. Everything else we do ourselves."

"But...it cannot be."

"Ja'el, I am not lying to you. If our poverty is unacceptable to King Salak, you may withdraw your proposal."

"No. It is not..." Ja'el took a breath to calm himself. "It is not right for the queen's family to live this way. When I return, I will advise the king to grant you a royal stipend. Please, make me a list of your needs and I will make sure they are supplied."

Surprised by Ja'el's generosity, Noran could only wonder. *He must love Antania already.*

Ja'el racked his mind for any reason to provide for Noran. "And...I will not take advantage of your generosity. I will pay market price for the plans of the greenhouse."

"Now *I* say 'No.' Let the plans be a wedding gift to the people of Varlana. I will not accept payment for them."

They negotiated for a few more minutes until plans solidified. Then the subject turned to travel plans.

"Antania and I must leave in two days, but I will hire an attendant for you before I go. Be strict about applying these treatments and you should be strong enough to travel in a few weeks. I will not let you miss your daughter's wedding."

"You are a good man, Ja'el. I'm happy you're the one the king sent to my daughter. I feel I can trust you with her well-being." They smiled at each other and said good-night.

When Ja'el returned to his room, he retrieved the drawings of Antania. The first he put aside. The second he needed to finish tonight to send to the king tomorrow. He filled his inkwell and sharpened his quill. Every line must be carefully traced before the charcoal smeared. Finally, he completed his work and set it aside to dry. He reached for his first drawing.

Carefully, he laid the portrait on the table and stared at it again. She seemed to lift off the page and breathe. He traced her hair and the scent of jasmine returned to his senses. He felt the softness of her face as the quill moved over her cheek and chin. His heart churned with desire at the perfection of her lips. Every line took him back to the garden with her. This portrait he claimed as his own. Her life would be shared with another, but the essence of her would live for him here.

He finally left the picture to dry and tumbled into bed. *Antania* became a song he sang in his heart as he drifted into sleep.

CHAPTER 6

THE POISON STONE

Gailen's son roamed the empty palace halls. Umberlan filled with radical changes and the king's council erupted with anger and fear at every new report. He lowered his head and smiled. Jakfa enjoyed the news reports. His father's revenge came closer every day.

Only a baby when Salak took the throne, Jakfa still knew the story well. Blood did not change the enmity between Gailen and Salak. They agreed on an uneasy truce when Salak stole his throne. As a consolation, he made Gailen Damon of Castle Chimaya, the richest province in Umberlan. For the past two years, Gailen used those resources to secretly recruit an army and plot against the king.

Father's the rightful heir. When we take the throne, Salak will be disgraced and father and I will be the heroes. This wedding farce will never be.

Their army grew while the robberies took their toll. *People are angry. They'll welcome a change in leadership.* The perfect time seemed close.

His thoughts were interrupted by quick footsteps. "Jakfa, I have news," said a quiet voice behind him.

He turned to find one of his loyal palace spies. "What?"

"Ja'el is gone. He rode away from Varlana packed for travel."

Jakfa's lip curled in contempt. "When?"

"Right after the king's wedding announcement."

"But that was weeks ago." He grabbed the man by the collar. "Why did you take so long to tell me?"

The man curled up his arms in fear as his toes began to lift off the floor. Words tumbled out of his face. "No-one knew. He left at night in secret and it's not unusual for him to be absent from the palace for days at a time. No-one knew, Jakfa. I swear. I came to tell you as soon as I heard. I knew you would want to know."

Jakfa dropped him and turned to walk to his rooms. *Weeks. How could he have left weeks ago and me not hear of it?* He didn't trust Ja'el an inch. *What is he planning? Is it the wedding or some military movement?*

His mind spun in confusion. *Soldiers and robbers. Brides and heirs. Does he even know this woman?* The plans that seemed so settled now seemed to fall apart. *I must act first. If I kill him before Ja'el does whatever he plans, none of it will matter and we still rise to the throne.*

Spurred by this new emergency, he raced to his rooms. He must finish his letters and make plans.

The germ of a victory grew again in his mind. He shut his door and hunched over his desk while he made notes and shuffled papers.

A brisk knock on the door startled him.

"Jakfa, are you there?"

"Tobin, come in, come in. Is there news?"

The big, burly Captain of the King's Guard ducked through the doorway and entered the room. Jakfa didn't know where his great girth came from, but it and Tobin's rank made him extremely useful.

"The council's in shambles. Half of them are worried about spies and the others are afraid of robbers in the night. The king's supply trains are all routed through Frissia. I'd say things are going well."

"Have you heard any more about this queen?"

"Nothing. She's quite a mystery, but the whole town's getting ready for her arrival. How are we going to change the plan to accommodate a royal wedding and heir?"

"We're not. Tobin, I believe I have a plan. Come here and look at this."

Tobin approached the desk and looked at a picture of a rock.

"A rock? What kind of plan is that?"

"It's not just any rock. See the striations along the side? This rock is deadly in the right hands."

"*Any* rock is deadly in the right hands."

"Pound this one to powder and it can kill anything or anyone. And it's rare, extremely rare. No one would think of this rock as the source of an illness. It's odorless, tasteless, and if I am careful, I can kill the king in front of everyone and stand unaccused."

"You're going to poison him?"

"Yes. It seems an efficient way to stop the wedding."

"Then what do we need an army for?"

"To conquer Oberlan."

"First Umberlan and then the world?" Jakfa nodded and opened his mouth to speak. "Stop! Just tell me what to do."

"This rock is only found in the Aldies Mountains. I need you to secretly travel to the border and fill this bag with Striate stones."

Long into the night they planned the demise of the king. After a few hours sleep, Tobin assigned himself a long-range reconnaissance patrol, slipped out of the palace and disappeared.

* * * * *

It took another two weeks for Tobin to reappear. Once again, they met in Jakfa's room.

"What took you so long?"

"Remember how rare these rocks are? To fill even this small bag took many days."

"Thank you. Now go away. I have work to do."

Tobin left to prepare a report for the king as Jakfa wrapped a few small stones in layers of cloth. He gently laid the bundle on a grinding stone stolen from the kitchen, picked up a hammer, and hit the stones with all his might. Over and over he pounded the bundle until the stones turned to dust. Carefully, he brushed the powder into a mug and started the process again. When his arm gave out, he gathered up the mug, the stone, and the rest of the rocks and hid them under the floor.

Tomorrow he would woo the kitchen girl again. His confidence and good looks swept her off her feet. *It's almost too easy to manipulate such an ignorant service girl. I wish she didn't reek of onions and grease. I hope Father appreciates my sacrifice. There are a lot of beautiful women here I'd rather be kissing.*

Jakfa thought about their next encounter. He planned every one with precision. They stole moments of affection in the hallways when no one watched. Their secret affair made it all more exciting for her. She already loved him deeply. Very useful since she delivered the king's meals. An arm around her waist; a furtive kiss in an alcove, and she didn't see his other hand drop powder in the king's food. She would take the blame and the punishment if someone discovered the poison. If she revealed their affair, he would deny it. No one would take the word of a kitchen maid over the nephew of the king. Perfect.

He carefully planned the slow increase in the doses to give the illusion of illness without sudden, suspicious death. For the first time in more than a month, he slept like a baby.

CHAPTER 7
TRANSITION AND BETRAYAL

The next day Evan Castle saw a bustle of activity. Ja'el began to assemble supplies for the trip back to Varlana, took Caleb to forage for more plants for Noran, and sent the portrait of Antania to the king.

Antania went to Devonshire to find a suitable attendant for her father. She also hired a boy to tend the castle garden. She found it suddenly easy to get things done. *Life is easier when you're the queen.* The attendant returned to the castle with her and she brought him to Ja'el.

"This is Mortimer. He is the son of our apothecary and has agreed to care for father."

"Good. Sit down and tell me what you see." Ja'el drew back a cloth and revealed a display of plants on the table. All of them would be combined in different measure to make salves and tinctures for Noran. He grilled and trained the poor man for hours. Finally, Ja'el smiled. "You'll do fine."

Satisfied with Noran's care, he checked the packs and the horses. *They look good. Just one more thing to do.* He entered the kitchen to find Caleb with his mother and father.

"Our boy told us you want to take him away." They both scowled at him.

"He has a bright mind and learns quickly. I think he should apprentice to be an apothecary and sage. Of course, he is too young now, but in a few months when he turns twelve, if you feel he would benefit, I would love for him to join me in Varlana and be my apprentice. I am sure the king would approve."

He came up with the bit about the king a few hours ago. *Let's see if they move my way now.*

Caleb's parents looked at each other wide-eyed in amazement.

"Our boy will meet the king?"

"Yes. He will spend many hours in the king's palace with me."

He watched their eyes grow wide with pride. His father rubbed Caleb's orange locks and Caleb smiled in victory. He would travel with Damon Noran to the wedding and join Ja'el in Varlana.

Master and apprentice took one last walk together in the garden.

"I could go now."

"Yes, but Damon Noran needs your help when he travels. Mortimer cannot do it all alone."

"What Varlana like?"

"I believe Damon Noran has a picture book in his library. It is a grand place with tall buildings and finely dressed ladies. King Salak is a good king and the people love him." Ja'el tried to prepare Caleb for the sights and sounds of the city, but they only made three rounds of the garden before Caleb returned home.

He will be a handful, but I think I will enjoy it. He climbed the stairs to his room one last time and planned to get one more good night's rest before they left. A noise in the garden caused him to look through his open window. Antania slowly walked the garden path. She gently caressed each flower.

I'm excited to return home and she is saying good-bye to hers. He watched her for a long while. His heart ached because of her pain and he fought to be calm. *What I want to do is not what I should do.* He resisted the temptation to go to her and turned away from the window.

* * * * *

Antania wandered the garden for hours, She etched each plant and flower into her memory. *Mother, what will I do without your flowers to bless me? Is a queen allowed to plant and sow? How will I live without soil between my fingers?* She could not bring herself to leave the garden and she lay down on a bed of moss. She would stay awake in her beloved garden all night. Her fingers found the soft, rich soil and she breathed in the scent of her dear earth. Tears flowed freely as she fought against weariness. *Why am I so tired?* The moss felt soft against her cheek. Eventually, she could resist no more and she quietly cried herself to sleep.

Ja'el heard the rustle of her dress as she lay on the moss. The night breeze wafted her soft cries through his window while he searched his mind for a way to ease her pain. When she stilled, Ja'el stopped the chant and turned his face to the wall. He could not comfort her in the garden, but he could give her sleep.

* * * * *

Fortune smiled on Jakfa. The king suffered from a cold, nothing serious, but the healers ordered bed rest for the day. Salak bellowed his protest, but in the end he relented and arrangements were made to bring him meals in bed.

Jakfa secreted the powder in his pocket. It would only take a little, a pinch or two. He sauntered down the hall and searched for his target.

There she is. The pretty little kitchen maid with Salak's mid-day meal. She smiled when she saw him and quickened her step. Jakfa's affectionate smile hid his intent. *This is too easy.* He gently took her arm and led her into an alcove.

"Are they working you too hard, today? I hear the king has taken to his bed."

"Oh no, Jakfa. I'm alright." She looked into his eyes, so close to hers, and smiled. "You are always so kind to me."

He kissed her ear and whispered, "Put down your tray and come to me." She felt his hand slide gently behind her back and pull her to him. Her heart fluttered at his gentle, loving kisses.

His other hand slid into his pocket and pinched some powder between his fingers. "I've missed you" he murmured into her ear as he sprinkled the powder on the king's food. After a few kisses and a few more affectionate words he released her.

"I will meet you here again later, my beauty." and he walked off down the hall.

She felt she walked on air as she picked up the tray and counted her good fortune a man like Jakfa could love her.

CHAPTER 8
THE BITTERLANDS

Ja'el and Antania left Evan Castle early the next morning. A humble caravan, just two horses and a pack mule, but the whole town of Devonshire lined the streets to send her off. She smiled and waved as she called most by name.

Very royal. She is a natural. Ja'el's heart swelled with pride. *See how everyone loves her. It will be the same in Varlana. She will be the best queen in Umberlan's history.*

At the edge of town, she stopped and looked back. A wave, a sigh and her new life began.

"I hope this works"

"What?"

"I have plans, Ja'el. If I'm going to give up everyone and everything I know, I want something. King Salak better be as kind as you say. I have plans I am determined to fulfill."

Ja'el stopped his horse. "What kind of plans?"

"For the women. I want to see them appreciated for their intelligence and given the freedom to work and prosper on their own, not beholden to a man for everything. I will spend my life for them, but I *will* do it."

He believed she would and said no more on the subject. They rode in silence, each musing about the future.

Ja'el had carefully planned their trip down public roads dotted with towns and reputable inns. The good chance of unseen, inquisitive eyes helped them keep their distance from each other. Every night would be spent at an inn (in separate rooms) so Antania would be well-rested by the time they reached Varlana.

The first night they each settled in and Ja'el closed his door. He unpacked his scrying bowl, filled it with water, and began to stir and chant. The king's bedroom came into view. King Salak rested in his bed. His manservant, Terrell, waited by his side. Ja'el's eyes narrowed with concern. *Why is he bedded down so early?*

Since he left Varlana he focused on Antania and didn't scry the king. Now he wondered if he missed something important. Once again, his father's voice brought calm. "One piece does not illumine the whole puzzle." *This could be anything. I'll look again tomorrow and begin to evaluate.*

The next day Ja'el began to teach Antania about court. He gave her a picture book of sorts he created so she could memorize the faces of the important people she would meet.

"That is King Salak."

She spent some time on his page. "Is it a good likeness?"

"I am no master, but I think so."

"He's older than I thought. Is his health good? Will he live a long time after we're married? I'd rather not do this royalty thing by myself."

"What goes on in your head? Do not worry. He's fine."

She turned the page. "Who's that?"

"Jakfa, the king's nephew."

"He's very handsome," she teased. "Is he nice?"

"Watch yourself there. He is next in line for the throne. He will not be happy about the king's marriage and, when you have a son, he will be your child's enemy."

She stared at Ja'el and looked for some clue he teased her, but found only seriousness and severity. *What am I getting myself into?* She summoned up the courage to turn the page.

They stopped in Sherling for mid-day meal and then headed northeast to avoid the Bitterlands. All afternoon she learned about the Damons, their families and their allegiances. Ja'el even talked about a crisis in the kingdom. These ideas seemed foreign to her. She began to regret her sheltered life. How could she navigate these murky waters? She felt wholly unprepared and moved her horse closer to Ja'el for comfort.

He saw her distress and took her hand. "You will have me to guide you. And the king will be good to you."

* * * * *

After they found rooms and settled in for the night, Ja'el shut his door and prepared the scrying bowl. The misty image showed the king in bed. Terrell fed him while Jakfa looked on. He seemed concerned, until he stepped back to leave the room. Just before he turned, Ja'el saw the smile on his face. *There is only one thing Jakfa would smile about.*

He continued to watch as the king violently vomited. Terrell wiped his brow and solemnly cleaned the mess. *Salak, what has he done to you?*

He hurried down the hall to Antania's room. Although he didn't want to alarm her, they must speed their journey and reach the palace as soon as possible. He planned the lie he would tell her.

"Antania, I have received a message from the king. We must return as fast as possible, which means we must change our route."

"What's happened?"

"I am not sure, but we must hurry. Are you willing to leave the public roads and travel through the countryside?"

"Of course. Show me."

He dipped his finger in water and drew a map in the dust on the floor. "Here we are and here is Varlana. Our original plan is the safer route east around the Bitterlands, but if we travel in a straight line instead of these winding roads, we can shorten our trip by two days. We will have to travel through this section of the Bitterlands. It will be a challenge, but if we are careful, we can do it."

"Then let's do it."

"Antania, it is dangerous. We will sleep on the ground. There will be no inns and we packed no food. There is no market in this small town. We will have to hunt and forage for food and water. Are you sure you want to?"

"I have slept on the ground before."

Well, he thought, *she does not lie there.*

"And I know what plants we can eat and which ones grow near good water sources. If you can build a fire and keep us safe, we will make it."

"Then get a good sleep. From now on, it will not be easy."

The next morning, they turned off the road a short distance from town. Antania followed Ja'el down narrow animal paths and through forests and glens. The tough beauty of the rocks and trees held her spellbound. Twice, Ja'el called her to spur her horse after she stopped to admire a view. He decided to try to distract her with conversation.

"When we arrive, there will be a great procession to greet you."

"How will they know we're there?"

"There is a signal post on a hill outside of Varlana. We will raise the banner of Evan Castle and wait for them to come to us. Your escort into the city will be impressive."

"I have saved my best dress for the occasion."

"Good. Will it be pretty in a golden carriage?"

"No! A gold carriage? How did anyone think of such a thing? What a waste of gold."

"It is not real gold, but fine golden paint that shimmers in the sun and gives the impression of gold."

"Well then, I guess I will agree to look pretty."

He filled her afternoon with tales of dances and festivals. The imagery made her dizzy by the time they found a place to camp. He laid the fire while she searched for food and water. After an evening meal of berries and mint, they talked for a while and laid down to rest on opposite sides of the fire.

Ja'el lay still until her breaths turned slow and steady. He quietly removed his scrying bowl and found a flat place not far from camp. This night he saw the king sit in a chair while he talked with advisors. He seemed animated and engaged. When the conversation ended the advisors left the room and the king slumped over the arm of the chair. Ja'el watched Terrell gently help him back to bed. Salak lay lifeless as Terrell undressed him and tucked in the covers. A side door opened and a young woman entered to take away the food tray.

Who is this? He studied her intently, determined to scry her next. He didn't hear a figure approach until a soft voice whispered in his ear, "What's this?"

He jumped and tipped the bowl over. Antania stood before him, hands on hips.

"What is this witchery you have?"

This is a problem. Could he convince her to keep his family's secret? He thought not. *Maybe I can convince her she never saw it.*

"Witchery? What are you talking about?"

"I saw the picture in the water? Who is the man on the bed?"

Ja'el realized the futility of deceiving her and remained silent as he watched her put the pieces into place.

"King Salak. He looked very ill. Is this why we must hurry? Is Salak dying?"

"I do not know. I only know what I can see, but I am concerned. It would take a lot to keep him in his bed. I think someone does him harm."

Her lips drew down. His distress worried her. "We must leave now. The moon is full, we can see."

"No. It is not wise to put the horses at risk. But we can pack and saddle the horses and leave at first light."

"Who's the young woman you watched?"

"How long did you look over my shoulder?"

"Long enough to see your scrying. Who is she?"

"You must not reveal my secret. Sorcery is frowned upon and I could lose my place at court."

"I will protect you. Now, who is she?"

She promised so easily. She must love me very much. His smile swelled with affection.

"Ja'el?"

"What?"

"Who – is – she?"

"Oh...um..." He cleared his throat. "I do not know. I have never seen her before, but a slow poison in his food would explain his weakness. I am going to scry again and follow her."

Antania brought the rest of the water and refilled the bowl. "The spring is just a short walk away. We can quickly replenish before we leave."

Ja'el stirred the water in the moonlight and an image began to appear.

* * * * *

She hummed a sweet song as she washed the king's dishes. *I wonder when I'll see him again. He's so wonderful. And we're to be married!*

She twirled around in joy and laughed as soap suds flew about the room.

"Knock, knock."

Her heart skipped a beat and she turned to smile at her beloved. She ran across the room and jumped into Jakfa's arms.

"Little Bird, you'll knock me over."

"I love it when you call me Little Bird."

Jakfa smiled and kissed her. "I can't stay, but I wanted to see you one more time today. Do you still love me?"

"Oh yes. Oh yes. I will love you forever."

"Then I will see you tomorrow, Little Bird." He kissed her once more and turned to leave. At the door he wiped his mouth. *Disgusting girl. Soon I'll be done with you.*

She sighed with joy and returned to the sink. *Beautiful man.* She looked at the suds in the sink. *Soon I'll be done with you.*

* * * * *

Antania gasped in surprise. "That's Jakfa, isn't it?"

"Yes."

"You told me he is an evil man. Yet, here he is in love with a servant girl."

"*She* is in love, but look at him closely. He does not love her. It would be like him to use her in some way to poison the king."

The misty water cleared as the vision vanished. "Is this all the evidence you have? Guesses and theories?"

"I know. But I also know Jakfa's character and the depth of his desire to be king." Then Ja'el told her all he knew about the rivalry between Salak and Gailen, their uneasy truce, and Jakfa's attempts to turn the court and the Damons against the king.

"Gailen believes Salak stole the crown from him, but his father favored Salak over Gailen and broke tradition to crown the younger son. King Salak has never been comfortable as king, but takes the responsibility seriously. Gailen and Jakfa want power. They would rape the land and kill the people in endless wars to gain more and more land. As long as King Salak lives, they have only the power he gives them. They are forced to pay homage to their king or they will lose what little power they do have. Gailen and Jakfa live for the day Salak dies and Jakfa takes the throne. Now do you see why Jakfa will be your son's enemy?"

"I am afraid. Who can I trust? Will Jakfa try to kill me?"

Her fear collapsed his self-control and he wrapped her in his arms. "No one will harm you while I breathe."

They stood quiet and still for a long time. Overcome with love and concern, Ja'el lifted her chin and gently kissed her. "Not while I breathe." They lay down on the soft earth. Enfolded in his strong, lean arms, she listened to the heartbeat of the man she loved. Still and content, they lay together until the sun broke the horizon. Silently they rose. Ja'el packed the last of the supplies while Antania restocked the water. Then they turned their eyes toward Varlana and rode toward the Bitterlands.

✻ ✻ ✻ ✻ ✻

The sun rose high when they reached the edge of the Bitterlands. The air beat down hot and dry. Low thorny scrub bushes dotted the brown landscape. Oppression hung heavy in the atmosphere.

"This is the most desolate place I've ever seen. What happened here?"

"This used to be green and lush. We are actually riding in an old river bed. But when the capital moved to Varlana, the king rerouted the water for the city's population. The farmers left and the land fell into ruin."

"Why would the king do such a thing?"

"In the time before Damons, when kings ruled cities, the king of Varlana controlled most of the north-eastern lands. He formed an alliance with the kings in the northwest and they began to conquer the rest of what is now Umberlan. He married a woman from Varlana and, to please her, made it the capital. To sustain the new capital, he diverted all the water for miles around to the city."

"Is that a love story or an evil plot?"

"It is so long ago, you can decide. All we know is what we see. The Bitterlands are a blight in Umberlan."

Ja'el spurred his horse to a faster pace. There would be no place to camp until they left the Bitterlands behind them. The unrelenting sun beat down. Ja'el fought to keep his eyes focused. Antania slumped in the saddle. By late afternoon their water ran out.

"How much farther? I see no signs of water anywhere."

"Keep looking. We have a long way to travel. Stop talking."

The sun beat on them until evening, but the dark of night offered no relief from the heat. It emanated up from the rocky ground and hung in the air. They tossed and turned in a vain attempt to find a cool spot to rest.

The next morning broke early. Their bones ached from the hard ground and their mouths were dry as the dust that clouded up around their feet when they stood. They saddled their thirsty horses and began again.

"We must find water today. The horses will not last to the end if we do not."

"*I* won't last either. Ja'el, I'm feeling sick."

"Look for water, Antania. Stay alert and look for water."

A few minutes later Ja'el heard a weak, "There" and followed Antania to a rocky outcrop. Small plants grew green among the stones and they searched until they found a trickle of water falling over a worn ledge. Ja'el waited while she drank. Then he carefully filled whatever he could to carry water to the horses.

Filled with guilt at her selfishness, she stopped him. "Let me finish this. You drink."

They rested by the little stream while the horses drank. With the water bags filled, they mounted and began again. The rest of the day brought constant heat. The next day held no relief. Waves rippled up from the ground and caused them to see vague images of what they desired. Their mouths swelled with dryness. Their bodies ceased to sweat. Spasms rippled across the horses' exhausted muscles.

Suddenly, Antania shouted, "There," and she spurred her horse to a gallop.

"No. Antania, stop!" Ja'el watched helplessly as she forced her horse beyond its limit. He dismounted when her horse fell and neither got up.

"Antania!" He ran, even though he knew it wasted energy. She moaned beside her dead horse. Her voice cracked out, "There was water. I saw water. Where is the water?"

Ja'el stood silently and regretted their rash decision. *There is still a day to travel out of this God-forsaken land. She cannot go on like this. We may not make it.* He scanned the landscape in all directions. The sun baked everything. No trees or buildings offered shelter, only cracked earth and low rocks.

He sighed down to his bones and retrieved his knife. He skinned her horse and made a lean-to for shade. Then he built a small fire and cooked some horse meat.

"Eat, Antania. The blood and fat will sustain you." He heard his horse lick at the body of his dead companion. He never looked. He didn't want to know.

When the sun set, Ja'el helped Antania on his horse and walked beside her as they stumbled toward Varlana. Twice he thought his horse would fall. Once Antania began to drift to the side. She collapsed on Ja'el's shoulder which broke her fall, but forced his head to slam against the saddle. Dazed and confused, he fell, she fell beside him, and they ceased to move.

Ja'el felt a hand on his back and a low voice said, *"You will not die today. Rise."*

A warm strength infused his body and he opened his eyes. A man stood over him and offered his hand.

"You are not wise to cross the Bitterlands here, but I will help you. Come."

Ja'el forced himself to stand. Together, they gently draped Antania over the saddle and began to walk. The longer Ja'el walked with the man, the stronger he felt. His thirst seemed to melt away and his muscles relaxed.

"Why did you choose this path?" the man asked.

"It is the shortest way to Varlana and the king is in need."

"It is the shortest distance, but a longer trip."

"I do not understand."

"You have lost a day in your struggle to survive." Ja'el's eyes grew wide. *"Don't worry. The king lives and you will arrive on time, but if you are to succeed, you must consider your path."*

"You are talking of more than the king's health. What do you mean?"

"How are you feeling now?"

"I am much better."

"Good. One hundred paces ahead is a farm. There you will find water and food. Rest, but don't delay."

Ja'el strained his eyes against the heat to see the farm and when he turned to ask the man to point it out, the man had vanished.

He patted his horse as they continued to walk. "I am seeing things that are not there, old friend. Let us hope the farm is real."

Soon he came to the edge of the Bitterlands and found the farmhouse. He led his horse into the gate as his body gave way and he slumped to the ground. *It is true. What happened to me?*

The horse smelled water and trudged into the yard. Ja'el joined him at a trough and drank deeply the cool, clear water inside. Then he carefully slid Antania to the ground and helped her drink. He found a ladle, filled it with water and held it to her lips. "Swallow it all. One more swallow. Come back to me, Antania. You must live or I will die." Frantically he worked to revive her. Finally, she opened her eyes.

Tears spilled out of his eyes and onto her cheek. "You live, my love."

"Stop Ja'el. You're wasting water."

He held her to himself and rejoiced. He rocked and kissed her until she pushed him away.

"I am weak, Ja'el. We both need to eat. Is there food here?"

He searched the deserted farmhouse and found some old fruit and a jar of dried meat. The horse found hay in the barn. They ate and slept all that day. By the next morning, their strength had returned enough to continue. They stripped everything off his horse except the saddle and left their packs in the barn. Then Ja'el and Antania both mounted his horse and they rode out.

All day they rode across green fields and enjoyed a cool breeze.

"This is heaven."

Ja'el held her closer. "Yes, it is."

They rode in silence and just enjoyed the nearness of the other until the sun disappeared over the horizon. The soft earth under a great mulberry tree invited them to camp. Ja'el made a small fire and Antania found water nearby. They drank their fill and lay down exhausted.

"What if we skip evening meal and have a good morning meal? I'm too tired to forage."

"I will offer no argument. Sleep well. We arrive in Varlana tomorrow." Ja'el saw no reason to scry tonight. There would be no more to learn and he wanted to believe the promise of the man. He would soon see for himself. He lay on his blanket and stared at the dark sky. The fire could wait a little while.

It wasn't long before Antania slept and Ja'el slipped away to gather firewood. She still slept when he returned to build the fire. All day, the memories of the night before had tormented him. Now, in the blanket of darkness, the intensity of his love strengthened and he wanted to be beside her. He built the fire and forced himself to put it between them to keep his desire at bay.

The fire warmed the edges of the cool night air as Ja'el pondered the king's danger. *I can make a tincture of Bloodswart to purge his body, but is he strong enough to bear it? Lemon water would be gentler, but may not be strong enough.* He considered every cure he knew and made his decision. The king would begin to recover tomorrow or he would be killed in the attempt. He didn't doubt Jakfa's reaction to his return. There would be a struggle, but Ja'el determined to win.

Lost in his thoughts, he didn't hear the rustle of fabric as Antania approached him. She sat cross-legged beside him, her dress a mess.

"Ja'el. Are you awake?"

"Yes. Why have you come so close? This is not wise. We enter Varlana on the morrow. Do not tempt fate like this."

"Ja'el, I want to speak with you *because* we enter Varlana so soon. I will not have this chance again."

"What would you say?" Ja'el steeled himself and sat up to face her.

She squared her shoulders. "You must know my heart is entirely yours. I will marry the king to please you, but if you want me, I will forsake my vow and be yours."

Ja'el's heart came alive and broke in the same moment. "You are to be queen. Our love must be second to our duty to the king and Umberlan. Do not test me. I am not strong enough to resist you."

He rose and moved to the other side of the fire.

She sat still for a long time and then rose to join him. "You are right. I am for the king."

Ja'el bowed his head. "My queen."

She ran her fingers through his hair and felt him shiver at her touch. She touched his cheek and looked into his eyes. "Why do you always look down when you say 'My queen?'"

The dam of self-control broke and Ja'el's emotions burst out. "I have loved you from the first moment I saw you. The scent of jasmine and roses in your hair haunt my waking hours. Your beautiful voice and soft lips invade my sleep. I am only alive when I am with you. The thought of never touching you again is too heavy to bear and those two words demand we stay apart. I must say 'my queen' but I will not meet your eyes to do it. My heart breaks every day. I will survive only because I saved a piece of you for myself." He showed her the picture he kept close. "This is what I drew of you in the garden."

She stared at it for a long time and then gave it back. She watched as he carefully secreted it among his supplies. "You loved me even then as I loved you." She took his hand and pressed it to her cheek. "We have wasted time, Ja'el, and now we only have a few hours left."

All restraint disappeared. Their kiss lit up the night sky. They melted into each other's arms; each kiss more passionate than the last. She gasped in pleasure as his hands moved down her back to caress her thighs. "I love you. I've always loved you." she whispered in his ear. But his father's voice rang out in the other. *"Your duty to your king must outweigh your own desires."*

"Father, what am I doing?" He pushed her away and crumbled to the ground in shame. "Leave me alone, Antania. Do not touch me. We must stop this madness or it will destroy us."

She knelt beside him. "No!" He scrambled to put the fire between them again. Again, she stayed still for a long time and then lay down. Ja'el tried to concentrate on the wisdom of his father, but her presence constantly distracted and pulled at him.

Antania's heart filled with the vivid memory of Ja'el's touch, but the sting of his rebuke kept her still. They lay awake in silence, afraid to speak.

The silence continued the next day as they rode to Varlana. It gradually became a little easier between them, less uncomfortable, as they began to fix their minds on the palace. The sun moved into afternoon when Ja'el stopped the horses on top of a small hill. "There it is. Varlana in all its glory."

"It's beautiful," she managed to reply.

With the city in sight, Ja'el felt settled. He turned to her and smiled. "We will survive, my love. I will watch over you."

"While you breathe?"

"While I breathe."

He raised the banner of Evan Castle and they watched the procession approach to welcome the new queen.

CHAPTER 9
THE KITCHEN MAID'S FATE

Ja'el watched as Antania carefully arranged herself in her golden carriage. Her radiance glowed even through her nervous smile. He bowed his head, "My queen." She remembered his declaration the night before and it comforted her. The procession started in all its state to usher in the new queen.

Ja'el mounted his horse and raced for the palace. His weary horse complained, but he drove her mercilessly. He urged her to gallop ever faster even though she began to foam from the mouth and sides. *Come on, girl. Give me a little more. We're almost there. The king's life is at stake.*

Through the streets of Varlana they flew. The horse's gallop echoed off the walls of the buildings while Ja'el cried for the people to give way. He didn't stop at the palace gate, but pushed his horse right up to the palace steps.

He threw the reins at a stable boy and grabbed his supplies as he shouted directions.

"She has worked hard. Walk her, brush her down and feed her. Put my pack outside her stable untouched. I will be down to inspect your work, so make sure she is comfortable and rested."

The stable boy hurried off to comply. He recognized Ja'el as a favorite of the king. This horse would receive the best.

Ja'el raced through the halls to the king's chamber. "Out! Everyone get out now." Salak's simple food steamed in silver dishes on his lap. Ja'el hurled the dishes across the room. "My king, you must spit out everything in your mouth." The servants stood in stunned silence. "OUT. GET OUT."

They stumbled over themselves to rush out the door. Ja'el had suddenly reappeared a mad man.

Alone, the king wearily studied Ja'el. "What's come over you?"

"I believe you are being poisoned. Forgive me, my king, for taking so long to return."

He applied compresses to the king's feet and hands. "These will help draw the poison out. My king, there is more we must do, but the treatments are difficult for the body to absorb. The next few days will be hard for you."

"Cure me, Ja'el. I cannot die today."

Bloodswart then. Ja'el prepared the potion and the treatments began. No one else but Terrell attended the king. Ja'el's scry revealed the tender care he gave Salak and he trusted him. He stood guard while Ja'el emptied buckets of vomit and waste. Several times a day they changed bed linens and compresses stained with dark excrement. Terrell burned all the used linens and bandages. The king ate no food and drank only lemon water and potions supplied by Ja'el. After four days, he looked better.

"You're killing me, Ja'el"

"I am glad you are feeling better, my king."

"Will I make it to my wedding?"

"You will eat food on the morrow and we will see."

"Have you discovered who did this to me?"

"I analyzed the puss on a few compresses and it indicates a rare poisonous powder from ground Striate rocks. It would have killed you in a few more days."

"It seems you arrived just in time."

"I am not so sure. Striate can have lasting effects; weakness, pain. It depends on how much of the poison has settled in your bones. It is impossible to remove it all."

"I am the king. I order my body to health. Help me out of this damn bed."

Salak sat in a chair for the rest of the afternoon. Terrell draped robes around him and Ja'el allowed a few visitors. They would report the king's improved health and stop the rumors of his deathbed.

Still, two weeks passed before Salak managed to leave his room, however, he continued to gain strength. In the mean-time, he hosted short meetings with government officials in as much "state" as his bed chamber would allow.

* * * * *

Jakfa paced his rooms in anger again. *He's a meddling fool. The plan worked until Ja'el came back.* His audience with the king showed him his failure. *He's looking so much better,* he thought with a scowl. *How did Ja'el know? And who is this mysterious woman?*

He remembered the procession. The whole city lined the streets to see their soon-to-be queen. No one could doubt her beauty, but she looked overwhelmed by it all. His spies knew almost nothing about her. *A small woman from a small province. Evan Castle at Devonshire. Who even heard of it? Leave it to the king to choose a woman from the poorest region in Umberlan.*

His thoughts returned to her insecurity. *There's possibility there.* He would inquire after her. Maybe she could be turned.

His attention turned to more immediate matters. Tobin arrived and the two sat at the desk to plan. Ja'el's quiet investigation into the attack on the king threatened them greatly. Ja'el suspected the kitchen girl and Jakfa wanted the inquiry to end with her.

He lifted a small bag out of a drawer. "This is what's left of the Striate you brought. I need you to slip it into her possession somehow."

"I don't slip in or out of anywhere. I'm the guy who gets noticed everywhere he goes. Do you know how hard it is for me to 'slip' out of town? And this is a big place!"

"Then who do you trust who's smaller than you?"

"My brother's son, Rolof, will help me. My brother is one of those peaceful men, but Rolof likes to fight. I'm teaching him against his father's wishes. He can keep a secret."

"You have a brother?"

"Yes. He's married with two children. I also have a sister with a family. We grew up…"

"Yes, yes. How wonderful for you. Here's what I need you to do…"

They planned and schemed long into the night. The kitchen maid lost control of her life by the time they wrote the last line.

*****

The castle was turned upside down as the guards searched for the poison. The guards found the powder under the mattress of a kitchen maid, the very girl who delivered the king's food. She was taken to the dungeons to await trial.

In the dark, she cried until her eyes dried out. Her mother crept down the stairs to see her while the guards slept.

"My child, what have you done?"

"Mama, I didn't do anything. I don't know where that powder came from."

"Oh, my girl. What are we going to do?"

"Tell Jakfa what's happened. He won't let anything happen to me. Tell him, Mama. He'll save me."

Her mother left and sent several messages to Jakfa before and during the trial. He never answered. She wondered if he received them.

Every day she watched as her daughter's life grew shorter. The angry judge didn't care about her innocence. Someone had to pay for the attack on the king and her daughter was chosen. When she was sentenced to hang, her mother brazenly strode through the halls of the palace looking for Jakfa.

She spied him entering the dining hall and ran to grab his arm.

"Master Jakfa, you must do something to save my girl. Will you let your Little Bird die?"

He spat on her face and wrestled his arm out of her grip. "What have I to do with your daughter, woman? She's a filthy scullery maid and you are not allowed to enter these halls. Guard, beat this woman and bar her from the palace."

He entered the hall and thought no more about it. She was taken away and never seen again.

At the end of the month the whole city turned out to see the traitor beheaded. Jakfa stood at the front of the crowd. She caught his eye and silently pleaded for mercy; for the sake of their love. He pulled a dead bird out of his pocket, dropped it on the ground and turned his back. When her head thumped into the basket, he grunted in satisfaction. *Done.* Now he could pursue the queen.

* * * * *

Antania arrived at the palace with high hopes. She stepped out of the guided carriage and her guides moved her quickly through the halls until, with a flourish, they whisked her into her rooms. The door shut. She stood alone in the middle of the room and turned in slow circles while she stared at a most magnificently beautiful place.

Heavy gold drapes lined the big windows and shimmered in the afternoon light. Delicate couches complimented petite chairs attractively arranged for conversation. The ceiling featured a massive depiction of beautiful women entertained by exotic creatures. She curled her toes into the soft, luxurious rug under her feet.

How much more can there be?

Four doors invited her to explore. The first opened to reveal a modest room for her attendant. *I wonder what I'm supposed to do with an attendant? Maybe I can make this my plant room? There's plenty of light.*

The second door opened to the bath. She saw a big tub lined with soft linen, a water bowl and jug, a fireplace, and a smaller door on the opposite side of the room. In it she saw some sort of chair with a big hole in it. *Who sits here?* She closed the door in disgust and moved on.

The third opened to a smaller room much like the first. A collage of portraits of the queens of Umberlan graced the ceiling with empty spaces for more. *I wonder if I get to choose where my picture will go?* The couches and chairs here proved softer and more comfortable than those in the first room. She tried out each one and settled on a favorite. *I will read here.*

On the other side of this room stood the fourth door. It revealed her new bedroom dominated by a massive bed. Thick pedestals supported a canopy draped in silk and lace. It draped over the sides like lush moss on a tree. She climbed the steps and dove into the mattress. Big downy covers wrapped themselves around her as she sank into the softness.

She luxuriated in it for a while until she panicked. *How am I supposed to get out?* She tried to sit up, but the bed swallowed her. She bounced. No good. She tried to rise to her hands and knees, but only sank in deeper. In fact, everything she tried sank her deeper until she collapsed into uncontrollable giggles. Finally, she rolled herself over the side and landed with a plop on the carpet. This made her laugh out loud until her stomach hurt. *Ja'el did say life would be interesting.* She tried to compose herself when she heard the door open.

"My queen, are you all right?"

Antania looked up to see a pretty young girl with a face full of concern. She wore a dress of fine linen, but modest design. Her beautiful blonde hair crowned her head in perfectly arranged braids.

"Yes, I'm fine. Who are you?"

"Master Ja'el sent me to attend you." Antania frowned. *Has he had time to do this? I've only been at the palace a few hours.*

"He said you may not believe me and I was to say, 'While I breathe.'"

Now the queen-to-be smiled. "What is your name?"

"Belinda."

"Belinda, have you ever attended before?"

"My queen, I have attended the Lady at Trawliff Castle."

"So, you know what's expected of you."

"Yes. I have moved my things into my room and will do as you say."

Antania didn't know what to tell her. She'd never seen an attendant, much less knew what Belinda should do. Of course, she couldn't confess it. *This is difficult.*

"Why don't you tell me things you've done before and I will tell you how I feel about them."

This surprised Belinda. The queen seemed not to know her place. This familiarity led to danger and as she began to explain all her required duties and chores, she remained standing and formal. Belinda knew how to hide her true feelings. She played this game well.

She impressed Antania with the list of her skills. *But why is she so willing to be subservient?* She decided Belinda would be her first liberated woman and set about to befriend her.

"Sit down beside me, Belinda, and let's talk."

"My queen, it is not good for me to find myself equal to you in any circumstance." *There. Now she knows I will not be so easily trapped into punishment.*

Antania sighed. *This will be harder than I thought.* "Then what do you propose to do? Will you show me around the palace?"

Belinda looked at the floor. "My queen, you are not to leave until the king sends for you. He must meet you first. Then he will present you to everyone else." *How does she not know? What kind of test is this?*

"So, I am trapped in here until the king recovers." Her plans to explore the palace and begin to know the strange politics here were now in shambles. This stopped her before she started.

"Yes, my queen. But *I* can go out. I can bring you whatever you like: food, deserts, animals, games, books. Whatever you desire." She probed for information. *What game are you playing?*

"How about some news of the king and Master Ja'el? Can you bring me that?"

"My queen, I can tell you now what I know and then gather more if you like."

"Tell me what you know then."

Belinda began with Ja'el's dramatic entrance at the palace steps. In her quiet way she spun a good story and kept Antania entertained by her insights. When Belinda told of Ja'el's tirade in the king's rooms, Antania laughed out loud. Belinda lifted her eyebrows and quickly looked at the floor.

"It's only funny because the king lives. Ja'el is so composed. I can't imagine what everyone thought of the mess he made."

She laughed again and this time Belinda joined in.

Belinda considered herself an excellent judge of character. In fact, she met all kinds of characters. But she had never met a woman so sincere. She actually enjoyed their conversation and forgot her place. She sat in a chair. When she ended, she leaned back in satisfaction. Horrified, she realized her breach of etiquette and jumped up.

She is good. I've never been trapped so quickly before. Every Lady found some reason to punish "their girl" on the first day. They felt it established authority and proper respect. For many years Belinda avoided the whip. Now she steeled herself for the inevitable.

Startled by her sudden jump, Antania asked, "What's wrong?"

"My queen, I have dishonored you. I am compliant."

"What do you mean?" *This is like speaking a foreign language.*

"I will comply with whatever punishment you choose for discipline. I will learn to know my place." *Humility sometimes lessens the sentence. I hope she's as kind as she appears to be.*

"Why do you give me so much power over you?" *Is court life so cruel? I can't function like this.* She decided to create her own court rules. *Might as well start now.* "Belinda, I come from a place where there are no servants, only people who help each other. I am not like the other women you have worked for. I won't punish you for being yourself."

Belinda stood silent, unsure of her next move.

"I will require your honesty and discretion. I will expect you to treat me with the respect a queen deserves. However, you and I will come to respect each other as friends. If not, then you must go."

"My queen, I do not know how to do what you ask." She decided to leave some options open in case this, too, became a trap.

"And I must learn how to be a queen. It looks like we're both in the same predicament."

Belinda smiled. This woman *was* kind. She began to let down her guard and relax.

Antania sensed the change in her. "So, we are agreed?"

"Yes, my queen."

"Good. Now, I would like you to show me how to get in and out of this bed."

For the next few weeks Antania and Belinda grew comfortable with each other. Belinda put her wiles to work and collected palace gossip to keep her queen up-to-date, especially about King Salak and Ja'el. Antania got her education after all.

Belinda borrowed some palace maps from the library for Antania to study. She discovered Antania's desire for a garden and arranged for pots, soil, and flower seeds to be brought to the rooms. Her duty required her to please the queen. Her pleasure urged her to please her friend.

One morning Belinda entered the rooms with a pretty yellow envelope for Antania. "It's an invitation, my queen."

Antania's eyes lit up. "Am I finally leaving these rooms?"

"No. The king recovers, but is still bedridden. However, the king's nephew, Jakfa, has requested an audience with you this afternoon. I hear he's handsome."

Now her eyes narrowed. "What does he want?"

"I have no idea, but it would be unwise to refuse him. He is the king's nephew and an important man."

"Tell him I will see him, but only in the front room and you must be there, too."

"Of course, my queen." She hurried off to give the reply.

When she returned, she held another envelope. "A letter from the king's quarters."

Antania recognized the script on the front. *Ja'el.* She tried hard not to run when she turned to her bedroom and told Belinda not to follow. The door closed and with shaky hands she opened the envelope.

My Queen,

I hope Belinda is a good attendant for you. I chose her from among many with the hope she will please you. She is capable and sincere. I know you will watch over her as is your duty, my queen.

The king recovers well. I have not forgotten your isolation and soon he will come to you. I hope to accompany him myself, but other concerns may draw me away. I have told him of you and he is anxious to begin a new life with you by his side. Impress him with humility and kindness.

Do not forget the lessons learned on your journey to Varlana.

While I breathe,
Ja'el

Between the lines lay the real message. *He is looking out for me. He loves me. He remembers our nights together.* Hungry for his presence, she traced his words with her finger. For an hour she held the letter and read it again and again. Finally, she carefully slid it back into the envelope and hid it in a drawer. She steeled her heart and left the room. Jakfa would arrive soon.

* * * * *

Belinda helped her arrange herself on a couch near the door and stood at her post behind her. When Jakfa entered the room, he could only advance a few feet before their presence stopped him. Antania looked unhappy to see him.

"My queen, the king sends his regards."

"Thank you, Jakfa."

An awkward pause filled the room while Jakfa, who had planned to introduce himself, wondered what to say next. The queen's expression remained severe.

"He requests your patience while he recovers. He has not forgotten you and will come to you as soon as he is able."

Antania almost snorted at his drivel. *What a sniveling, conniving...* "Thank you, again, Jakfa. I never doubted the king's regard and look forward to meeting him." She could be civil, but she didn't have to fawn over him. She remembered what happened to the kitchen maid and wanted to hit him. The fabric on the arms of the couch stretched as her fingers dug in. "Is there more you wish to say?"

Ja'el must have turned her against me before they arrived. I will not sway her in time. "No, my queen. I will tell the king you will be happy to meet him." As he bowed to leave, he cast his eye on Belinda. She smiled and her face flushed when their eyes met. *Ah. I must learn of her. She could be useful.*

When the door shut behind him, Antania slumped back on the couch with a grunt. Belinda gazed at the door.

"He is as handsome as they say."

"He is handsome, but handsome can hide evil. I don't want you near him. He is dangerous."

Belinda heard the talk about Jakfa, both good and bad. *You can't walk two steps in this place without hearing his name.* She formed no opinion, but now she thought about his most handsome face and warm smile. To please her queen she held her tongue, but he intrigued her and she hoped they would meet again.

CHAPTER 10

BELINDA BEGINS A DANGEROUS GAME

Just two days later she got her chance. Belinda was sent to the kitchens for the queen's evening meal and now she waited in a side room for the tray to be prepared. She mused about what games she could play with Jakfa when he entered the room. She quickly decided to start with the shy innocent girl routine.

"Oh. I'm sorry. I will wait outside." She rose to leave.

"No, no. Please don't go. I'd like a little company right now." He sat down with a serious expression, lost in thought.

Belinda observed his pose. It seemed contrived. *Could he be playing with me, too? This might be fun.* She waited quietly for a few seconds, and then, "What are you thinking about?"

He sighed.

Oh please, don't be so obvious.

"I am worried about the king."

"He seems happy to me. What is wrong?"

"He picked this woman sight unseen. She is beautiful and seems sweet-tempered, but what do we really know about her?"

You waste no time pumping me for information. What's your game? She raised the stakes a little. "Do you believe she means to harm the king?"

Jakfa realized he'd moved too fast and backed off. "No. I just want to make sure he's happy."

Lighten this up or I'll give myself away. She smiled and raised the pitch of her voice ever so slightly. "I think she's just wonderful. She smiles at me and treats me kindly. She acts just as a queen should."

"Yes," said Jakfa. "And her companion should also be as sweet and kind as you."

He flashed her a smile designed to make her swoon. She managed to flush her cheeks a little and looked shyly down into her lap.

"I must go, Belinda. But I hope we meet again. I have enjoyed our little chat."

He gallantly bowed and left the room.

Belinda reviewed the encounter. *He is practiced. A very calculating man. It will be a nice diversion to match wits with him. He is royal, after all, and will grow tired of a servant girl. But while he's attentive it'll offer me some entertainment.*

The next day they encountered each other again. Jakfa strode down the same hall Belinda used to return to Antania's rooms. He accidently bumped her and knocked her a little off balance.

Jakfa gently took her arm. "Are you alright? I'm so sorry. Are you hurt?"

"No. I'm fine. Don't worry." She gently removed her arm from his hand.

"Are you sure? I can't believe how careless I was. I couldn't live with myself if I injured you."

Goodness. He's actually fawning over me. "I'm quite recovered, thank you."

"May I make it up to you?"

Aha. Now he reveals himself. "There's no need."

"I'm going to market tomorrow. Please come with me."

"I have my duties for the queen."

"I will assign the best of the maids to attend her."

"I don't know…"

"I hate to go by myself. You would be the perfect company. It's an hour of well-deserved fun and I won't take no for an answer. We'll go while the queen takes her nap."

Belinda stood silent and shyly blinked her eyes.

"I will meet you here at mid-day." He bowed and gently kissed the back of her hand before he strode away.

Well, maybe I can get a new hat out of this. She smiled as she returned to her queen.

* * * * *

The market bustled with activity. The sheer variety of wares made Belinda's head spin. She thrilled at the sights and sounds. Jakfa showed her exotic fruits and vegetables, beautiful silks from far-off lands, and talking birds with brightly colored feathers.

Jakfa remained by her side all day. Relaxed and attentive, he watched over her and entertained her. Twice Belinda began to succumb to his charms and she pulled herself up short. *Don't you forget the game, girl. He's not falling for you. Don't you fall for him.*

Her head on straight, she played this game with him well. She did get her new hat and he doted on her every word. *He's good, but I'm better.*

At the end of their time together, she felt him watch her as she returned to her rooms in the palace. *So far so good.*

CHAPTER 11
⌐ A LONG-AWAITED MEETING ⌐

Ja'el finally pronounced the king healthy and Salak dressed to meet his new bride. Terrell tried to fasten his regal clothes while Salak bounced with anticipation.

"Terrell, must you button every button? Skip a few. No one will notice."

"My king, I know you are anxious to meet her, but you must be perfect so she will admire you. Eight more buttons and then your shoes."

Salak groaned. "Ja'el, you must come with me. I insist. I will not argue with you anymore. You steady me."

Ja'el sighed and accepted his fate. "I will accompany you." *But I don't know how steady I will be.* The king's care had consumed him. He had seen no one but Terrell since his return. He orchestrated it. His seclusion had kept him away from his greatest weakness.

She didn't answer his letter, but no surprises there. Any answer would have raised suspicion. *I will be near her again.* His knees turned into jelly. *I will get through this.* "Strength of character conquers the impossible." *Thank you, father. You never fail me.*

King Salak watched Terrell fasten the last buckle and he jumped up. "Let's go. She's waited long enough." And off they went, Ja'el's dread and Salak's excitement.

* * * * *

Belinda woke Antania at sun-up.

"It's today, my queen. Your isolation ends today. The king will be here in a few hours."

Antania grunted in frustration as she tried to get out of bed. Eventually, she reached out to Belinda for help. "How can you love a bed and hate it at the same time?" She fussed her sleeping gown back into place. "I hope you know what to do. I've never met a king before."

"The king has allowed three others to help prepare you. We all wait for you."

"You sound very formal today."

"My queen. It is the day you meet the king!"

Antania sighed and gave herself over to Belinda. She endured the milk and oil bath, the perfumes, the lotions, and the hour it took to dress. They braided and curled and pinned her hair. She bore it all until the plumes and live birds arrived.

"What are you going to do with those?"

"They are for your hair, my queen."

"This is ridiculous. Take them away. I will suffer no more and I will not have birds tied to my hair. If he doesn't like me, I will return home, live quietly and die a pauper.

The birds and plumes left the room in a hurry and all the maids fussed as they arranged Antania in the most throne-like chair in the room. Finally, with the stage set, Belinda stood two steps behind her and the other servants left.

"He will be pleased at your beauty." she whispered. Antania hoped so. She had planned and waited for this moment for weeks.

She heard a bustle at the door and a herald entered. "My Lady, King Salak, the king of Umberlan."

In strode Salak, and Antania waited a moment for effect. When their eyes met, she slowly rose and bowed gracefully before him.

"My king," she said in a soft voice. The sweet sound hung in the air like the scent of perfume. Her skin glowed with health. Her hair shimmered in the soft light of the room.

Salak couldn't breathe. He stared in admiration at her form bowing before him until Ja'el softly cleared his throat.

"My dear, rise before me. I must see your face."

Antania rose and locked her eyes on the king. If she moved her eyes Ja'el would fill her gaze. Her heart pounded not for the king, but because *he* waited in the room.

Salak took her hand. "We will walk in the gardens and talk. I must know you and you me. Then I will present you tonight and all of Umberlan will see the beauty of their queen."

She smiled and they walked out the door. *Freedom. Sweet freedom.* It felt so good to be free of her rooms she took no notice of the empty halls. The king took her arm as they walked to the gardens.

Ja'el fell in behind and instantly regretted it. The gentle sway of her walk took his mind back to Evan Castle. *This will not do.* He turned to Belinda beside him.

"How is life with the queen?"

"She is so kind. I know of no other woman who will make such a good queen."

"Yes. Are you adjusting to palace life? The king's court is very different than a Damon's entourage."

"It is different, yes." Her thoughts turned to Jakfa. She enjoyed this little adventure, but he must remain her secret. "I have made friends."

They entered the garden and the scent of jasmine filled the air. Ja'el excused himself and moved off in solitude. Belinda stood just inside the garden entrance. Enough for propriety, but far enough away to give the king and Antania their privacy.

* * * * *

Ja'el found a bench in a lonely part of the garden and sat in stony silence. His mind raced with memories of her touch, her kiss, the night spent in embrace. He thought his desire gone, but now it flared up in flames too violent to ignore. He loved her so fiercely he knew there would never be another for him, and now he watched her walk with the king. His tortured heart swung from happiness to pain. The two people he loved most in the world pledged themselves to each other, and he paid a great price for it.

* * * * *

Antania fought for control, all her senses keenly aware of Ja'el's presence in the corner. But she couldn't allow this first encounter with the king to be ruined by distraction. She turned her back to Ja'el and faced Salak.

"Your garden is beautiful."

"I understand you are a gardener."

"I tended my mother's garden after she died. I have always loved the scents and beauty in a garden. It is where I feel the most alive."

"And are you happy in this garden?"

"I am happy in any garden."

"Then this shall be yours. Do with it as you wish. I give the gardens of this palace to you."

Antania beamed with joy. "If this garden is truly mine then forgive me, my king. I must indulge a joy I have been denied far too long." She drove her fingers into a flower bed and pulled out a handful of soil. She closed her eyes, raised it to her nose, and breathed in the odor of earth. Peace began to reign the day.

When she opened her eyes, she saw the king chuckle. "You have gotten a little too close to the earth, my dear," and he brushed a fleck of soil from her nose. They laughed as she cleaned her hand on a towel.

All afternoon they walked the garden together. Ja'el watched their pleasure with each other as long as he could, then he left the garden with Belinda in tow.

"Wait for the queen in her rooms. I will wait for the king."

Belinda strolled through the palace on her quest and marveled again at the beauty of this palace. Suddenly, halfway to the queen's rooms, Jakfa appeared. "Belinda, my beauty, why are you walking alone?"

She smiled, but continued to walk. Jakfa fell in beside her. "Where are you going in such a hurry?"

"King Salak and Queen Antania are in the garden. I am to return to her rooms and wait for her."

"She is not queen yet."

"She will be, there is no doubt." Belinda's pride at Antania's success beamed through her smile. "He's quite smitten with her and has already given her the gardens as a wedding gift. Umberlan will finally have a queen."

"The king is taken with her then?"

"I believe it happened when he first saw her." She took on the persona of a childish maid. He seemed to like that one. "You should have been there, Jakfa. Magic danced in the air. Love is a wonderful thing."

Idiot girl. How long must I listen to you drivel on about love and flowers?
"Your description is much better than reality." He took her hand and led her to an alcove. "Will you join me in the library? There is a book of poems I want to read to you."

"I can't, Jakfa, although I want to. I must return."

"She will be with the king for hours. A few minutes with me will not be noticed." He softly kissed her fingers.

"Jakfa, don't be angry, but I must go."

He held her hand and forced her to wait until he felt her discomfort. Then he kissed her fingers again and let her go. "I will never be angry with you, Belinda."

He's too easy to play with.

She fits in nicely.

She walked toward her duty as he plotted her demise.

CHAPTER 12
THE ROYAL WEDDING IS ANNOUNCED

With the formal announcement of the royal wedding, the city became a beehive of activity. Courtiers kept merchants busy with special requests. Damons began to arrive in gilded carriages. Ja'el received word Damon Noran, Mortimer, and Caleb would arrive a week hence and he began to prepare his home. He ordered one robe for Caleb in advance. He would have to be measured for the rest. Ja'el moved his things into his father's bigger room and cleaned his old room for his new apprentice. He also found accommodations for Noran and his entourage, paid for by the king's stipend which started the day after the garden walk. *Antania will be queen.* Salak wanted nothing to go awry.

Ja'el greeted Noran when his carriage reached the city gate.

"Ja'el. So good to see you again. Come. Join me in this fine carriage and show Mortimer and me your fine city."

Ja'el climbed in the carriage. "Where is Caleb?" Suddenly, he heard a "Whoop" from above. "Caleb! Get in here now."

When Caleb settled in the carriage, he gave Ja'el a sheepish grin. "I have never seen anything like it. I going… I am going to like it here."

Ja'el raised an eyebrow at Noran.

"Damon Noran teaching me to speak right. Varlana a big town."

"Oh well. We've made some progress, but you'll have to take over now."

"How is your leg? Are you comfortable?"

"Mortimer is my lifeline. I feel wonderful."

"If you need supplies, Mortimer, ask for me. Maybe I'll send my new apprentice to make deliveries."

They arrived at the palace and several footmen greeted them.

"Mortimer, always walk two steps behind Noran, but never let him out of your sight. You will share rooms, so the treatments will not be interrupted. Caleb, you will stay with me at my house."

"You don't live in palace?"

"No. We must be free of politics. It is not far. Get your bag and come."

Antania waited for her father just inside the doors. Through the window, she saw Ja'el and Caleb turn and walk away. *My father is here and my wedding is next week. This has gone too far to falter now. I must let him go.* She waited as her father approached. He swaggered up the stairs with ease. When he reached the top, she emerged to hug him.

"Father, it's so good to see you. How is the garden at Evan?"

"Not wasting time for news, are you? The garden is beautiful. You are beautiful. Evan castle is beautiful. Are you doing well?"

"I am fine. The king is a wonderful man. He has given me the gardens here as a wedding gift!"

"Ha. He found the way to your heart." They laughed together warmly as they entered the palace.

"Now may we rest in our rooms or do I meet the king first?"

"Salak will greet you tomorrow. I convinced him to let you rest today."

"Thank you, Antania. I'm excited, but weary. Show me to my rooms."

King Salak smiled. He had secretly situated himself on the balcony above the entrance to witness Antania's reunion with her father. *You can learn much about your new bride in a moment of reunion.* He grinned at Morcon's voice in his head. *Welcome advice, old friend.*

The encounter on the stairs confirmed everything he already believed about Antania. Her heart shone good and true. She would be a wonderful queen. Satisfied, he returned to the palace to prepare for the wedding.

* * * * *

Damon Gailen arrived later the same day. His great grey horses and enormous entourage created quite a stir as he approached the palace. Salak waited at the entrance.

"Brother!" Salak gave Gailen a bear hug.

"Salak, are you ready for the big day?"

"More than ready." He looked behind his brother to the beautiful woman waiting in the carriage. Her smile beamed as she sat radiant in her dress of red silk and gold inlay. *She must be a new one. She looks happy.*

Salak never knew why his brother's women always grew sad. *Maybe it's because he calls them all Ingrid.*

"Ingrid, come and meet the king."

The new Ingrid stood, unsure how to exit the carriage without help. A palace footman hurried to her aid. She stumbled out of the carriage and flounced up the stairs.

"My king." Her clumsy curtsy annoyed Gailen. He quickly took his brother's arm and turned his back to her. She fumbled with her skirts and tried to rise.

"I trust my rooms are suitable."

Salak signaled to the footman to help Ingrid and then turned to his brother. "I have given you the entire lower floor of the west wing. It is most luxurious. You will like it."

It's your rooms I'm after. I wonder if the new queen will like the name Ingrid. "I'm sure I'll be fine. Tell me about this woman you are to marry."

King Salak talked of Antania all the way to Gailen's rooms. By the time Salak left, Gailen needed some quiet. His brother agitated him. *He patters on and on. No girl will be your salvation, Salak. The crown will still be mine.* He unpacked, lay on the big bed, and contemplated the plans underway.

Soon Jakfa arrived. "Father, it's good to see you. We haven't talked face-to-face in many months."

Gailen smiled, "How do you like the new queen? Is she yours yet?"

"There's bad news there. Ja'el turned her against me before I even met her."

"No. I did not raise you to fall back at the first obstacle."

"And I did not. Her attendant, Belinda, is quite taken with me. I have access to the queen through her. I believe Belinda is ready to be turned."

"Good. How goes the king's recovery? I hope he suffers the aftereffects of Striate poisoning. You showed some genius there, Jakfa."

"He's still a little weak, but grows stronger every day. Antania is a balm to him."

"I came here for war, and you're giving me hearts and flowers. What is this?"

"I leave the war to you. You leave the palace intrigue to me. The king's reliance on Antania just makes my position with Belinda better for us."

They sat at the desk and Gailen leaned back in his chair.

"The stranglehold on Salak's supplies is proceeding to plan. All the king's supplies are now routed through my region. The day of the wedding they will be reduced by half. In three months, they will slow to a trickle. In eight months, the shortages in Varlana will be severe and we will prepare to attack."

"Eight months is a long time. What if Salak finds another route? What if he puts it together?"

"There are no other routes. Tobin's closed them all. As for Salak, isn't it your job to keep him in the dark? You're the master of showing a lie and making it truth."

"We should take advantage of the celebration. Bring your elite force in now; quietly, disguised as celebrants. We can billet them all over Varlana. We can hide half our forces in the forests and towns all around. The other half will wait on your lands until word is sent. When we rise, King Salak will be forced to draw his soldiers back to defend the palace. Half our army is plenty to secure Varlana while it's defenseless. We'll surround the palace until the other half of our army arrives. Then we overwhelm him and take back the crown."

"No. It's too soon. We will triumph, but we must be patient. Moving an army secretly in a country as small as Umberlan is a challenge and takes time. Damons Matoki, Endar, and Arbak are with us, but Endar and Arbak live on the other side of the Bitterlands. We can't move an army from there. Matoki's border with Varlana is small. It falls on us to move the bulk of our forces. We must plan carefully and move stealthily. Don't let your ambition cloud your judgement and give away the game too early."

"How are we going to secure the city?"

"Don't forget Tobin's new recruits. He sends men loyal to Salak to guard the roads and I send him Chimaya men to take their place in the palace. They will fight for us when the time is right."

"Should we move the water back to the Bitterlands now? It will increase our ability to approach Varlana with superior forces."

"No. It would also show our hand. When Varlana is denied its water supply, there will be no hiding our intentions. We will wait."

"You sound like Ja'el with his father's wisdom."

"Morcon's wisdom kept our hands tied for many years. Don't forget that. It's fortunate his son is young for a sage, but he learns quickly. Morcon always anticipated me and Ja'el seems to be developing the same talent. Don't worry. We won't wait long."

They stayed together for hours and planned the next eight months. Then they turned their attention to Belinda.

"You should test her. Too much rests on her allegiance to you."

"What do you suggest?"

After a few moments thought, Gailen replied, "Ask her to harm the queen in some small way. Wait until after the nuptials when the queen's attention is turned away from her and she feels abandoned. Her heart will be drawn to you. You will have more power over her then."

Jakfa absorbed this idea. "Yes. I will do it. I suppose it's time to move our relationship forward. I just haven't quite figured out how to untangle myself from her. Maybe I'll kill her in the Palace coup."

"Just don't leave any loose ends."

They slowly smiled at each other. "Father, we will rule Umberlan soon."

"And then Oberlan will be ours as well."

CHAPTER 13
⌐ TO HEIR IS HUMAN ¬

Salak and Antania married in the garden. Flowers filled the air with heavenly scents. Spices hidden within the flowers tickled Ja'el's nose with cinnamon, clove, and nutmeg. Caged birds sang in anticipation and then flew free when the happy couple completed their vows. The crowd outside the palace cheered wildly when they saw the birds fly into the sky. Then all eyes turned to the balcony where King Salak would present his bride.

A glimpse of Antania's white dress silenced the crowd. Suddenly the couple emerged. Antania looked ravishing and the crowd burst into cheers.

King Salak raised his arm to silence the people. "Good citizens of Varlana, behold your queen. God has favored this union with good rains and crops all across the land. Before you and all that is holy, I decree this day my heart belongs to Umberlan and Queen Antania. Choose this day whom you will love."

The people roared their approval. Flags of every color tossed into the air. Even the wind seemed to celebrate as it rippled through the silks and banners draped from every balcony. Antania smiled and waved, overcome with their reaction. After a time, the king escorted her back into the palace and they walked arm-in-arm to his rooms.

Varlana celebrated well into the night. The next day it started all over again. The people believed this wedding ushered in a restoration of better times, of life under a king *and* queen who brought good things to the people. The people ate and drank to excess. Good crops meant pockets filled with plenty.

*****

"Caleb, stand still. Your robes will never be ready and then I will have to send you back home."

"Why I need robe?"

"You are now part of the Damon of Varlana's house. You must dress accordingly."

"I don't like wearing accordingly."

Ja'el chuckled and ruffled Caleb's red hair. "Like it or not, it is what you will wear. One day I hope you will be proud to wear these robes."

The tailor left to sew the final hem and promised to return within the hour. Ja'el sat with Caleb at the table.

"I have a surprise for you today."

Caleb sat and stared. The last surprise made him feel like he wore a dress. How much worse would the next surprise be?

"We will go to the palace when the tailor returns."

"Are we see the king?"

"Not today, but we are going to see a wise man who has taught there for many years."

"Taught?" Caleb's frown went down to his chin. "School?"

"Yes. But not just any school. I have secured you a place in the palace school. Only the smartest children go there."

"I not smart."

"Oh yes you are. You are the smartest boy I ever met."

"They not like me. I like be with you."

"I like *to* be with you, too. You will still live here with me. We will still study together. But you need to know more than just this life. It will be good for you to experience the palace from a student's point of view as well as a sage's. My father did this for me and now I do it for you."

The tailor arrived and Caleb changed into his official robes. They walked in silence toward the palace. Caleb realized he needed to grow up fast. No more forts in the garden. He walked into manhood just like Ja'el did before him.

Up the grand steps they rose and turned to the right. When they entered the classroom, students greeted Caleb with respectful looks. On his tall frame the robe made him look regal. *Maybe this not so bad.* He sat down and opened the book in front of him.

* * * * *

With Caleb safely deposited in school, Ja'el turned for home.

"Ja'el. It's good to finally see you."

Antania's voice stopped him in his tracks. He slowly turned to face her. "My queen. I am likewise happy to see you. I see you are dressed for the garden. Is it doing well?"

"Come and see. I made some new plantings you may like."

She walked by him to the door. Reluctantly, he followed.

The garden greeted them with bright sunshine. She led him to the back wall where he saw a new flower bed. Their complete privacy made Ja'el uncomfortable.

"I have planted jasmine and roses here to climb the wall and bloom sweet when warm weather returns."

Why does she toy with me like this? He didn't like this change in her and his anger boiled to the surface.

"Why would you choose those plants? Do you wish to constantly torment me with memories of love?"

She gasped and dropped the trowel in her hand. His face, his tortured face broke her heart. She fought back her tears.

"Ja'el, I choose to love you forever. These flowers are a testimony of that love. There is nothing more I can do to tell you every day how much I love you. If they are a torture, I will pull all of them up right now."

She picked up her trowel and began to dig and tear at the plants. Ja'el stayed her hand. "My queen, stop." He gently turned her back to himself. "I will also love you forever. The torture is the knowledge you love me and we cannot be together. I am sorry I did not understand. Leave them to thrive."

He kissed her forehead and ran from the garden. His self-control hung on a thread and he didn't trust himself any farther.

Antania's eyes followed him out of the garden. She sat on the edge of the flower bed for a long while to gather her composure. Unconsciously, she dug her fingers in the earth, grabbed a handful and brought it to her nose. The scent of rich soil calmed her and she rose to return to the palace. *I can't do this.* But she thought of her father and the people of

Devonshire. *I must do this.* She fought back tears as she resolutely entered the castle. Her mother's face came to mind. *Peace must reign the day.*

* * * * *

Three months after the royal wedding, King Salak sat in state and faced his council. Minister Talaene wrung his hands.

"My king, supply wagons have slowed to a trickle. Our resources are almost gone and now the water supply dries up. You must talk to your brother and find out why he is not letting our drivers through."

General Janell spoke next. "His army slowly moves toward the city. Damons Endar, Arbak, and Matoki have aligned with him against you. My king, it is time to face the truth. Your brother works against you to take your crown. You must call the war council."

Salak threw his hands in the air. "I can't believe Gailen would do this to me. Why?"

Ja'el finally spoke. "He has always wanted your crown. You cannot deny it any longer. It may be too late now, but you must call the war council and defend the city."

"Why? The king has waited too long. There is nothing anyone can do. We must flee the city before we lose our lives."

"Kalaren, settle yourself." Janell tried to restore order in the room. "We have time to mount a defense. I have not been idle while Gailen schemes. We have troops garrisoned with Damons Vorailyn and Elios. They are still loyal to you, my king. You have an army at your disposal."

Salak sat silent. Ja'el leaned in to whisper in his ear. "My king, you must respond. Let General Janell make plans with the army and open your treasury to the Merchant Guild. That will keep the peace for now."

The king stood. "General Janell, do what you think best to move the army against … my brother. Talaene, I know our stores are low, but the people must not suffer. Open the king's treasury and allow Kalaren to distribute our goods under your supervision. Tobin, you must open the northern road for wagons. Use all the guards you need to accomplish this. Our city must not bow to my brother's siege. This council is closed. Send word. The war council will open in two days."

* * * * *

Tobin left the council and moved quickly through the palace. When he reached Jakfa's rooms he knocked and quickly entered.

"Tobin. What are you doing?"

"I'm sorry, Jakfa, but I have news."

"Go on."

"The king has opened his stores to the city and Janell announced his army at Castle Solis and Castle Trawliff. The king has called a war council in two days. He has decided to move against you."

"Finally." Jakfa laughed. "He's taken so long; I doubt this change of heart will affect our plans at all. What task has he assigned to you?"

"I am to clear the northern road. Janell knew of Matoki's loyalty to you. They know they have lost the eastern and southern route."

Jakfa clapped his friend on the back. "Perfect. Let a dozen wagons through, then close the road again. They'll be convinced you are loyal. Send me word as soon as the last wagon passes and I will send assassins to kill your men. Make sure the guards loyal to you separate themselves from the king's men, or they will lose their lives as well."

"The thirteenth wagon will deliver the bodies. Varlana will shake in terror then."

"Then you send the best of the men loyal to Salak to find the murderers. Salak will agree to it. He will feel honor bound to seek retribution. You can fill their slots with men loyal to my father. Your timing is crucial. Make sure all of this takes two months."

"It can take a month to fight skirmishes with 'the robbers.' Will Gailen send orders for them to return to him?"

"Yes. I will send word to Father today. Keep me informed, Tobin. It's close now. Everything is important."

Tobin turned and left.

* * * * *

Ja'el turned away from the palace entrance to spend time in the garden. He felt her presence there and, although it pained him, it also soothed him. He sat next to the jasmine and rose bed to think. His mind filled with treachery and denial.

Salak waited too long to face the truth and now, with Gailen's troops on the move, Ja'el feared an effective defense would be impossible. His mind spun with dread, but the scent of jasmine turned his mind to Antania and, once again, his heart swelled with emotion. He didn't hear footsteps approaching.

"Ja'el, what worries you so?"

Without thinking, he took Antania in his arms and kissed her. She melted into the moment and the world stopped spinning. Then, as suddenly, he pushed her away.

"I am so sorry, my queen. I was not thinking. I will leave you."

She took his arm. "No. I like you when you're not thinking." Her heart raced and she needed to be near him for any reason, just be near him. "Tell me what worries you so."

He gathered his thoughts. "We are going to war. Gailen openly moves against the king and we are not prepared to meet him."

"What is the war council doing?"

"As much as they can. We are moving fast, but Gailen is calculating and ruthless. He has worked for this day for many years. General Janell has made some plans, but I fear there is not much we can do." Suddenly he took her in his arms again. "Antania, I cannot think because all of this puts you in danger."

"But the king talks of an heir. Won't a son solve everything?"

"Are you pregnant? Has he been able to couple with you?"

"No. Not yet. Do you know why? Am I so abhorrent to him?"

Ja'el smiled and dared to gently stroke her cheek. "I doubt it. I believe the poison earlier this year disabled him temporarily. He will recover soon."

"So now what happens?"

"It is up to the king. Be careful, my queen. You are not entirely safe here."

"I will live while you breathe, Ja'el."

"While I breathe, my queen."

They kissed in the twilight and lingered as long as they dared. She returned to the palace. He left by the back gate.

* * * * *

Four months after the happy nuptials, Ja'el found himself alone with the king again. Salak's extreme agitation forced him to pace the room. Many times, they talked of the king's physical crisis. Every cure Ja'el tried, well-known and experimental, failed.

"What is wrong with me, Ja'el? I have tried night after night. Antania is beautiful and I desire her, but my body is dead. Your cures are not working. What has happened?"

"I am afraid, my king, you suffer from one of the lasting effects of Striate poisoning."

"Lasting? You mean I will be unable to … for the rest of my life?"

"I do not know. It may be in a few months or years your vitality will return to you. I expected you to be healthy by now. I am sorry I have no cures left to offer you."

"A few years! My spies tell me Gailen's army approaches Varlana. I don't have a few years. Maybe a few months. There must be an heir or Gailen will seize power."

Ja'el sat silent for a moment. "A royal pregnancy will not stop him."

"Of course, it will. He would not dare harm the queen, a woman of such delicacy. An heir will stop him in his tracks."

Ja'el sighed inwardly. Salak pinned all his hopes for a peaceful solution on Antania's pregnancy and a son. *Now, his health may finally force him to face the truth.*

The king slowly turned to face him. "You found her, Ja'el. This has become your responsibility. I have thought this through and have decided. You must give me an heir."

Ja'el's head shot up and he sat in stunned silence. Salak offered him his heart's desire.

"You are young, but I trust you. You know Antania. She appreciates your friendship. *You* sleep with her and give me an heir. We will tell the kingdom it is my child. It will have to be done in secret, of course. Maybe you can meet in the garden shack late at night?"

"My king! What you are saying is madness. I will not do this. The queen belongs only to you." *How will we function in the same palace after a night together?*

"I need an heir. Think of it as tactical strategy. You don't have to love her, just stand in for me in this."

"It will never work." *It will work only too well.*

"Why? Are you unable, too? I thought a young man like you…"

"No, no. I just cannot think of her that way." *I think of her that way every day.*

"Then don't think of her. Think of someone else. How about her attendant? She's a pretty thing."

"My king, stop!"

Salak's eyes narrowed and his shoulder's rose. "Are you defying an order from your king?"

"You are going to *order* me to couple with your queen? It is not done."

"Not having an heir and fighting a war with your brother is not done. She must become pregnant. Who else can I ask?"

Ja'el fought with his desires. *I want her, but not this way. I cannot have her and then give her away.* He sat silent in indecision. Salak glared at his defiance and Ja'el suddenly realized his future hung in the balance. "You are not going to give up on this, are you?"

"Ja'el, I need this. An heir is the only plan I trust to stop Gailen and Jakfa. I trusted your father more than anyone and have grown to hold you in the same regard. If I must, I *will* order you to do it."

"I do not think an heir will stop your brother."

"Yes, it will. He will have to acknowledge my son and all this will end."

Ja'el tried again. "What if she will not have me?" *I will die if she will not have me.* His heart swung like a pendulum and he couldn't focus.

"This is for Umberlan. It's not a question of wants, but one of duty."

"This is too much for me right now. Let us talk tonight about this."

"I will wait a few hours, but no more. Settle your mind on this, Ja'el. I must have an heir soon."

* * * * *

When the king approached Antania about it, she plopped into a chair.

"It is your duty to provide me an heir and Ja'el has agreed to help me."

"Salak, what you are asking me to do…" *is what I want.*

"We have tried together. Ja'el says my infirmity may last a few more years. In any other circumstance we could wait, but Gailen's army is approaching the city. An heir will make him withdraw."

"So, this is for king and country," *and my joy and happiness.*

"No other reason. You never have to see him again."

Antania's heart leapt out of her chest. "For you, Salak, I will make this sacrifice."

"Ja'el says your time of conception is approaching again. We must make plans."

"I think Ja'el and I can make those arrangements. Do you really want to know?"

Salak smiled and kissed her. "Make me an heir, my queen."

She danced into her room after he left, filled with too much happiness to express. Yes, yes, yes. She would gladly make this sacrifice.

CHAPTER 14

HEAVEN, HELL, AND A TRIP TO MARKET

Belinda almost bounced as she walked. Antania's schedule left her free for the rest of the day; the garden and then directly to the king's rooms. Belinda wouldn't be needed until tomorrow. She planned on a leisurely afternoon in the library. She and Jakfa met there to talk and kiss. His calculated and careful affection convinced her he didn't really care for her, but she thoroughly enjoyed it for now.

He's the king's nephew and I'm a servant girl. The attention is nice, but soon he'll be fascinated with someone else. She almost wished his attention would wane. He kept pursuing her and, although she enjoyed his attention, they had played this game too long and it started to bore her. *Still, he is handsome and for now...*

She remembered the queen's warning. Lately, she saw moments of subtle cruelty, but she knew how to handle it. She enjoyed his deep voice and handsome face. *I hope he reads me poetry. I have all afternoon.*

She entered the library to find it empty. A little disappointed, she resigned herself to wait. As she perused the shelves, she found a book half-way out. The title interested her. She sat down to read.

The pages told of a man's travels. The first chapter described him, his connections, his job, and his favorite pastime. She felt she knew him well when she started chapter 2. She turned a page to reveal uncomfortable pictures of naked women and men. *There's a new one.* Belinda read on, fascinated and repulsed.

Suddenly Jakfa appeared over her shoulder. She snapped the book shut and hid it under her skirts.

"My, my, Belinda. What are you reading?"

"I don't know. It wasn't shelved right and I got curious."

"What did you think of it?"

Is he leering at me? Did he leave this book for me to find? She decided to put an end to the conversation.

"What kept you?"

"I wrote a letter to my father. I don't write him as often as I should. When I get the urge, I indulge it." He brushed her hair from her neck and kissed her. "I have missed you. Can you stay with me for an hour?"

"I am free all afternoon."

"Well, maybe we can have two?" He found her favorite book of poetry and sat down beside her.

She buried her book in the cushions and sat on it. *Why did I say all afternoon? Now I'll have to sit here for two hours.*

He smiled and opened the book. *It's time to move this forward, Little Bird.* He began to read.

The sound of his deep voice relaxed her. Belinda closed her eyes and lay back on the couch. Too late she realized he stopped reading. His arm wrapped around her; his lips covered hers. His hands began to wander. *I should have known. My job's not worth this.*

She shot off the couch and turned to face him. *What is his game? No royal would woo a girl like me. He'd just take me and move on.* She wondered if this game should end.

"Jakfa, don't toy with me."

"Is that why you keep me at arm's length? You think I'm using you?"

"You are the king's nephew, next in line for the throne. What do you want with someone like me?"

Finally, an opening. I'll test her now. "Yes, I am next in line for the throne. And when I rule, I will need a beautiful queen beside me. I want *you* to be my queen."

She didn't believe a word of it. But he approached her in earnest and took her hand.

"Belinda, marry me." *I can't believe she's forced me to go this far.*

"I don't know what to say." *I can't believe he's gone this far.*

"Say yes." *Say you love me and you'll do anything for me and we can stop this charade.*

Now she knew how much danger she faced. He made no declaration of love, just tempted her with a crown. She didn't want to be queen, but to spurn him could mean his wrath and her ruin. Cornered for the first time in many years, she forced herself to continue to play.

"I never thought of myself as a queen."

"All the people will love you. Servants will grant your every wish. The finest clothes and jewels will be yours every day. Songs will be sung of your beauty." *How much longer do I have to say this trash?*

She struggled to think, to buy some time. *The naïve routine might work.* Belinda began to strut and prance around the room. "I will be the most beautiful woman in Umberlan. Men will swoon at my feet." She pretended to be convinced. "Jakfa, when will you be king?"

He smiled. *I've got you now.* "As long as King Salak has no heir, the throne is ours. Is the queen pregnant yet?"

"No." *I don't like this turn.*

"Then we can insure our future, my queen." He watched her closely. She frowned as she put the pieces together. *Good, Very good.*

So, he uses me to harm the queen and gain the throne. No wonder he was so persistent. Now she determined to know more.

"How?"

Jakfa removed a vial from his pocket and gave it to her. "Every time the queen returns from the king's rooms, put a drop of this liquid in her morning meal. It will prevent her from conceiving."

"And then the king will have no heir."

"Yes, my beautiful Belinda"

"Will this hurt her?"

"No. She won't even know."

Belinda rolled the vial in her hand and watched the milky liquid. It held so much dark promise: her life destroyed and queen to an abusive king. She looked away from the man who would destroy her life if she refused. *I'm completely caught. There's no way out. I must betray my friend or sacrifice myself.* Then she put the vial in her pocket and turned to Jakfa. *I have to get away from him and think.* She forced the words out of her mouth. "I will do it."

He pulled her close and kissed her. Then he squeezed her tighter and drove his tongue into her mouth. Belinda pushed him away.

"Jakfa, it is too much." He scowled. She changed her tone. "You are too handsome and I am too happy. We will rule together forever." She skipped out of the room and shut the door. *What an evil man.* She took a deep breath, composed herself, and walked down the hall.

Jakfa watched her skip from the room. *What a stupid girl.*

* * * * *

The same morning Antania rose early and dressed modestly to work in the garden. She walked outside with her shears and trowel and began her gardening rounds. The servants and courtiers knew to leave her alone on her garden mornings. When she entered, they left. *Peace must reign the day. Especially this day.*

She forced herself to slowly meander to the back gate and opened it to the fields beyond. One quick look behind her, *No one there,* and she slipped through. She ran through the field to the edge of the forest and found the abandoned cabin hidden in the trees.

Ja'el had arrived a few hours before and transformed the run-down shack into a comfortable hideaway. He rose and bowed his head as she entered, "My Queen."

Antania's voice shook. "Can we dare to believe this is really happening?"

On the floor lay a soft bed of furs and blankets and Ja'el motioned her to sit. He could hardly breathe. He needed some calm. "We have all day and night. Let's talk a while."

Unfettered by current circumstances, they talked as though they sat in the garden at Evan Castle. Ja'el told her of Caleb and his studies. She spoke of transitions and court politics. They opened themselves totally to the other and realized how much they missed these intimate moments.

"Tell me why you drew two pictures of me in the garden."

"I poured all my love into the first. My hand almost moved by itself. Every line breathed life for me. I look at it and remember our morning in the garden and how beautiful you are. I will never part with it."

He reached out to touch her cheek and she kissed his palm. Suddenly, his arms surrounded her. Their kisses awakened every dream of love and filled them with desire. With trembling hands, they undressed each other, touching, exploring. Antania's soft skin set Ja'el on fire. When he lay his body on hers, she wrapped herself around him and drew him into her soul. They lost themselves in ecstasy until their bodies could take no more. Breathless now, they lay quietly on the blankets.

"I love you. How can I be queen without you?"

"You are my queen now" He kissed her. She combed her hand through his hair and pressed him closer. They began again, slower and more deliberate. He wanted to know every inch of her. He lingered where she felt the most pleasure. Her desire rose to a fever pitch until he could wait no more and once again, they felt the joy of the other.

She collapsed on his chest and he held her so tight she thought she would break.

"I can't let you go. Not now. I am fire. I am wind. I am thunder."

"You are squeezing the life out of me."

Ja'el released her and smiled sheepishly. "Are you hungry?" He rose and crossed the cabin to his pack.

She marveled at his body. Muscles rippled under his perfect skin. His broad shoulders complimented his slim waist and his long, perfectly shaped legs. *To have such a man love me. Why has fortune smiled on me?* Her body began to burn again as she gazed at him. Twice they had traveled to heaven and back and the sun still hovered high in the sky.

Ja'el returned with bread, cheese, fruit and water. They ate and talked long into the night, although they frequently stopped for more trips to heaven. Exhausted, they fell asleep in each other's arms a few hours before sunrise.

The sun broke through the cabin walls and hit Ja'el in the eyes. He woke and lay still for a time. Antania's body warmed him. His fingers gently traced her arms and shoulders. She stirred, rubbed her eyes, and sat up. The blankets fell away from her body and Ja'el filled with desire once again. He pulled her to himself one last time.

An hour later they could wait no longer. Antania kissed him gently.

"Is our time gone so soon?"

He hugged her tightly and closed his eyes. But the sunlight grew brighter and they resigned themselves to the day. They began to dress. Too soon she finished. Ja'el caught her hand as she reached for the door.

He kissed her again. "While I breathe." She smiled and lay her head against his shoulder. "While I breathe." She tore herself away and left him alone again.

Ja'el sank to the floor. How could it have ended so fast? He dressed to go, but stayed in the cabin. He lingered in his vivid memories until Caleb found him.

"Master, are you well?"

"Yes, Caleb. Just a long night." He began to gather his things. "Are you ready for your studies?"

"I read. I think so."

Ja'el took a deep breath and walked into the sunlight. Life must continue.

* * * * *

Belinda stared at the vial all night. The milky liquid contained her future. *My next decision will shape the rest of my life. What happened? When did this game catch me in its trap?* She thought about Jakfa's little cruelties. *I should have seen it coming.* He held her hand a little too long and too tight. He smiled at others' misfortune; a forced kiss against her will, and that book… she fell for a stupid book. Anyone else couldn't have pulled it off, but Jakfa's blatant attempt at seduction almost worked. *Jakfa's more of an artist than I give him credit for.* She didn't even realize his plan until almost too late.

She found a little consolation in his choice of her. At least she understood this game he played. He'd have conquered someone else by now. But still he scared her. He had revealed his intention; access to the queen. *It makes sense. He's spent far too much energy pursuing me.* But to dose the queen with this…whatever it was, could not happen. She could stop this, but at what cost?

She went to bed, but hardly slept and by morning she knew what to do. She couldn't trust Jakfa to stop at just one plot and she didn't know what else he planned. It would cause her dismissal, but now she must pay for her selfish indulgence. The queen's life hung in the balance.

The door to the queen's rooms quietly opened and shut, but Belinda didn't hear.

* * * * *

Belinda didn't hear Antania's entrance which made her glad. She needed more time alone. The soft sheets on her bed looked inviting. She undressed and crawled into bed. Her skin still tingled with sensation, and memories of the night before brought her ecstasy once again. *This is ridiculous!* She rolled over and willed herself to sleep.

A few hours later Belinda entered, opened the drapes, and picked up the clothes dropped on the floor.

"My queen. It is time to rise."

From out of the pillow came, "What's so important about today?"

"There is much to do today."

"Nothing until I bathe. I must have a bath." Antania could not face the court with the smell of Ja'el's musk still on her body.

Belinda sent for morning meal and drew the bath. Antania slowly sank into the warm water. It comforted her and soaked the intensity of the night away, a bittersweet experience. Eventually, Belinda sent all the servants away and they both sat down for tea.

"Now, what is so important?"

"My queen, I must make a confession and tell you some painful news."

Antania took a slow sip of tea. "Belinda, I am in a wonderful mood today and I don't want it spoiled. Measure how important your story is to me."

"It is life and death."

She observed Belinda's face draw down in concern and her hands tremble. *Did she sleep at all last night? What terrible thing does she know?*

"Speak to me, Belinda. Your distress is concerning."

Even though Belinda pushed Antania into this conversation, now she hesitated. "I'm afraid. To tell you what I know I must also tell you secrets about myself, things I've kept from you. I believe this may be our last conversation."

Memories of the night vanished. Antania carefully laid her hands on the table and leaned forward. "Talk now, and leave nothing out."

Over the next hour Belinda confessed her relationship with Jakfa. She described her cavalier attitude and the trap she found herself in. When she finished, Antania sat still and studied her tea cup.

"So, he plots to kill my child. What else does he plan?"

"I don't know, my queen. This is all he revealed to me."

Silence.

"Belinda, we can use your indulgence to our advantage. This game you played is dangerous and now I ask you for more."

"My queen, I disobeyed you. I understand the punishment and will leave the palace today."

"No. You must stay. I need to know more about Jakfa's intentions toward the king."

"You want me to spy for you?"

Antania studied the table as she sat still as stone. "Yes. Consider it your penance. Tell him you are dosing me and convince him you are entirely his. He'll reveal his plans to you, if only in an unguarded moment."

"I'm not sure I can control him." She wrung her hands in agitation.

Antania met Belinda's fear with calm. "Let me help you. I will not leave you to do this alone. We will plan every encounter and I will protect you. It is my duty."

"I don't understand. Why are you helping me?"

"Belinda, we're friends." Antania reached for her hand. "Friends don't abandon each other. You hurt me, but I'll forgive you. You're too valuable to me. I've grown to love you as a sister."

Belinda dropped her head in her hands and wept. Antania could have sentenced her to death. She could have banished her from the palace in disgrace and left Belinda to a life of poverty and prostitution. The list of punishments she could have inflicted ran long and the palace would have approved. But Antania chose to put herself at risk to help her. Such mercy, never offered to her before, engulfed her in gratitude. She responded as only she could. *I give you my life, my queen.*

* * * * *

The king sent for Ja'el just as he and Caleb settled in to review the next ten pages of plants.

"Don't worry, Master. I study. I fine."

As Ja'el left, Caleb savored his good fortune. The market started yesterday, but Ja'el set him on a delivery out of Varlana. It took him all day and most of the night. He completely missed the first market day and thought his studies would deny him the second. Now he suddenly found himself free.

As soon as Ja'el disappeared around a corner, Caleb bolted out the door. He knew the plants. He studied them diligently. Now he turned toward the sights and smells of the market. Laughter, arguments, bartering, conversation of every kind floated past his ears. The bright tents over merchants' stalls decorated the street and filled the air with excitement. Adventure could always be found on market day.

His pocket jingled with two weeks of pay and now he strolled the street in anticipation. The first vendor he saw sold the biggest apples he'd ever seen. He eagerly bought one and ate it down to the core as he wandered. *I wonder how he grew it so big and juicy?* Suddenly, a commotion started behind him.

A street urchin ran toward him holding one of the big, juicy apples. *He stole it.* Caleb couldn't blame him. They looked irresistible. The palace guards chased the boy who ran with all his might to escape.

"Stop! By order of the king"

Caleb stepped in front of the boy. His robes, though just an apprentice, made him an official of the king and he must help the guards. The boy stumbled into him and Caleb leaned down to whisper in his ear. "Give it to me, now." The apple appeared in his hand and he slipped it into his pocket. His grip on the boy tightened as the guards drew near. Caleb did his best imitation of Ja'el.

"What has this child done?"

The guards calmed down when they saw their prey in Caleb's grip.

"He stole an apple. He will be whipped for his crime."

"You cannot punish a child for an unproven crime. Search him now and show me this apple."

The guards manhandled the boy, even shook him upside down, but no apple appeared. When they finished with him, he wriggled back to Caleb's side. The biggest man narrowed his eyes and said, "Maybe you took it from him."

Caleb pulled his hands from his pockets and raised them up. On the way he slipped the apple down the back of the boy's shirt. "Search me and you will find nothing."

The guards backed up a step. He wore the robe of the house of Damon of Varlana. They grumbled, threatened the boy and left.

Caleb looked down at him. "What your name?"

"I'm called boy."

Caleb learned of the seedier side of Varlana from Ja'el. He knew something about the life of a child called "boy". *Ja'el gave me new life. Maybe I do same for boy.*

"I not always here to save you. Come to healer's house tonight. You must change."

The boy looked at Caleb in awe and swore he would be there. As he watched the boy walk away, he smiled in satisfaction. *Where more adventure?* he thought as he walked down the street.

He found a vendor who sold oddities and wandered in to explore. Shrunken heads on ribbons, strange carvings of fat men and many breasted women, rugs in so many colors it all made his head spin. Then his eye fell on a rare sight.

"What that?"

"That, my son, is a rare thing indeed." The vendor spun a tale of exotic places and strange customs. Caleb stopped listening. He recognized the wood from Devonshire, but he couldn't tear his eyes away from the image. An ornate braided pattern encircled a picture of a warrior queen, beautiful and fierce in her leather armor. She held a bow and arrow. Her strength seemed to leap from the carving.

"How much?"

They haggled over the price, and Caleb spent almost all his money by the time he left with his prize. He would have to discover her identity. For now, he safely tucked her inside his robes as he made the turn to explore the other half of the market.

114

The smell of fresh bread and meat pies enticed him, but Caleb forced himself to turn away, determined to save the rest of his money for something more important. His stomach growled to keep him company as he meandered down the opposite side of the street toward home.

He heard loud braying and laughter in front of him. A crowd gathered around a traveler who had tried to push a heavy purchase into his cart. The weight of his cargo tipped the back down to the ground and now his mule waggled his legs in the air. The mule's complaints filled the market, exceeded only by the guffaws of the small crowd gathered around.

"A man's greed will lead him into foolishness." Morcon's sayings popped into his head more often now. He moved forward to help.

"Need help?"

The man turned to see a tall, lanky boy crowned with bright orange hair. The robe of the Damon's house impressed him a little, but Caleb's small hands hinted at slim arms. He didn't look strong, but this boy seemed to be his only volunteer.

"Hold this up." Caleb moved in to stabilize the load while the man picked up a handful of hay and moved to the front. He held up the hay to the mule and let her have a few bites. Then he deliberately dropped in on the ground in front of her. Now she struggled to descend and finish her meal. He hurried to join Caleb at the back.

"Push with all your might, boy." They inched the load forward and the mule slowly approached the ground. Soon the mule happily chewed on the hay. The problem remedied, the seller asked his name.

"Caleb, apprentice to Master Ja'el."

The man's eyes widened. "Well, Caleb, apprentice to Master Ja'el, I am Jacob, the seller and buyer of…things. I am in your debt."

Caleb smiled and shook his hand. *What I do with debt?*

"Tell your master you helped me. I'll see you soon." He led his mule away and Caleb crossed the street.

He stopped to buy another apple and paid the vendor twice the price. Then he returned home. *I love market day.* He smiled with a sigh and opened his books.

* * * * *

Ja'el entered the king's rooms to find him enthroned in state. Salak sent Terrell out and set his face in a smug grin.

"How did it go last night?"

"My king, the sacrifice is completed."

"She is beautiful in every way, isn't she?"

"Yes. I managed to overcome the situation. I believe we succeeded. In a few days we will discover my effectiveness." Ever since he and Antania planned their rendezvous, he planned how he would answer the king. Now it seemed absurd.

The king took no notice. "Good. It's settled. Now, let us plan." He turned his attention to war. Ja'el could hardly keep up with him.

"Gailen's army grows, but he still only has four Damons behind him, but of the five loyal to me, Damon Noran has no resources and Notok is trapped between Arbak, Endar and the Bitterlands. He is evacuating his troops out of the country on the southern border, but they will take too long to arrive here."

Salak's fingers moved across a map of the city. "Janell moves troops here and here to defend the city, but also plans strategic defensive positions outside Varlana. My head is spinning. What do I do next?"

"What of Tobin and the King's guards?"

"He will be in charge of palace defenses. His men will defend the gate, the entrance, and the garden wall. Barricades rise up everywhere and all the windows are blocked with anything they can find."

"He will need to post guards throughout the palace in case Gailen's troops get through."

"Tobin and Janell are working together on the defenses. I trust them to succeed."

"My king, I am no military tactician, but preparations move forward. It seems things are going well."

"Going well?" Salak's fist hit the arm of the chair. "My own brother seeks to take my crown. His forces should be behind me, but are before me ready to attack. Damons loyal to my father and this family now desert me. How is this going well?"

Ja'el blanched in the face of Salak's anger. *Father, help me.* He planted his feet and faced the king. "A man must face the life before him strong in resolve and with no regrets. Gailen shows his true colors. You must show him the strength your father saw in you when he made you king."

Salak's fist came down again. "I do not want to, but I *will* fight him. Gailen will know the gravity of his decision to defy me. The war council meets again, Ja'el. Walk with me."

They left his rooms together. The intensity of Salak's anger washed Ja'el of all thoughts of the previous night. They entered the council ready to further their plans for war.

One week and all would be in place. They could not delay. Even on rations, the food supply dwindled dangerously. Rumors of war turned to fact as the citizens watched the army and the guards prepare. Refugees lined the roads to leave the city.

Damon Notok's troops would not make it in time and Janell sent word to hold. If they conquered Gailen, Notok would join them to hold the city. If they failed, Notok and Damon Noran would take the troops north to Oberlan.

Spies inside the city reported Gailen's troops hidden everywhere. They planned to slowly and quietly build their numbers until they could attack from within. Janell made a plan to rout them out and a detail left with orders.

Everything seemed in order. Gailen's plans would fail.

* * * * *

Ja'el left the council and pondered the morning all the way home. He found Caleb at the table, his face in a book, and sat down opposite him.

"Tell me about your day."

"I study and study."

"It is market day and I left you alone. Tell me about your day."

Caleb gave Ja'el the apple he saved for him and entertained him with his adventures. The boy's rescue impressed Ja'el.

"What are your plans for him?"

"I thought I pay him for chores here. I have enough to give him a little."

"A good idea, but you do not have to sacrifice your pay. I will give you the money for him, but you must teach him Morcon's ways while he works."

"A fair trade. I accept."

The examination of the medallion came next.

"Caleb, I think this is Adonna, the warrior queen who lived at Langley Castle many generations ago. A rare find indeed."

"What can you teach me about her?"

"Not much, but there are a few books in the royal library. The next time we go to the palace, we will find them."

Ja'el sat up when Caleb mentioned the seller's name.

"Jacob? Did he drive a brown and black mule?"

"Uh-huh."

"Did he have a red moustache?"

"Uh-huh"

"Jacob's in town. Did he say where he slept?"

"No. He just say tell you he here."

"Caleb, try again."

"No. He just…said to tell you.. .he's here."

"Good." Not many knew of his father's friendship with Jacob, the smuggler. Ja'el remembered their mutually beneficial dealings. Now Jacob inquired after him. *This could be very timely. But first things first.* "Now," Ja'el opened the book, "tell me about the forests around Varlana."

* * * * *

A soft knock on the door interrupted their evening meal. Ja'el winked at Caleb as he opened it to reveal a scrawny, dirty child. *Caleb, leave it to you to find the worst case.* "Welcome child, to the healer's house." Ja'el left to pour a bath.

"I came like you said."

"Good. First thing is give you a proper name. What you want to be called?"

From the back of the house came, "Caleb, again."

"What do you want to be called?"

The boy stared blankly at him. Caleb waited. Caleb sat down and left the boy standing. He turned to the fire and filled a bowl with stew. It sat on the table and filled the room with savory smells while Caleb waited and the boy licked his lips.

"What is your name?" He added a spoon and poured a glass of water. "Pick one. Any one. But it must be you who defines yourself." He stood in front of the boy, stretched as tall as he could and waited.

"Robin?" came a weak reply.

"Well, Robin, how would you like a bowl of stew?"

CHAPTER 15
⌐ WAR PLANS ¬

Three weeks later Antania found herself retching again. *How much longer does this last? Ja'el, your child doesn't like me much.* She smiled as she wiped her mouth. *I never thought sickness would make me happy.*

She read Ja'el's note one more time. *We must meet today.* He didn't set a time or place, so she arranged to meet him in the library. Belinda met Jakfa there a little while ago and Antania didn't want them alone too long. Jakfa pushed Belinda more and more, so she would use this as an interruption and give Belinda relief.

She picked herself up and began to dress. *I can't leave her alone with Jakfa too long.*

* * * * *

Belinda and Jakfa met almost every day. She began to dread their time in the library. She learned nothing new and at every assignation he became more aggressive. He laid claim on her and wanted his "rights."

She adopted the "I'm innocent and we must wait until we're married" routine, but it wore thin. He believed her devotion and now he no longer respected her. She had fooled him completely, but now he expected things from her she didn't want to give. The thought of his hands on her made her cringe.

But here they sat in the library again, in another secret tryst. He started with gentle kisses and she gently resisted, but now he was in a frenzy. He panted hard and grunted like a pig.

He grabbed her in a tight embrace. "I will have you, Belinda."

She pushed against his hold. "My king, please respect me."

Do not test me, girl. "Am I your king?"

"Yes, Jakfa." He started this game several weeks ago. It began playfully with imaginary throne rooms and great dances, but now he demanded more. Her demure answers usually assuaged his emotional outbursts, but today they inflamed him.

"Then I order you to submit to me." He threw her violently on the couch and tore open her dress. He stared at her nakedness while he fumbled with his laces. She lay still, afraid to move.

Suddenly, they heard voices outside the door. Her torn dress and fear made his intent plain. In a panic, he scanned the room for escape. He grabbed her arm and pulled her behind the big drapes, his back to the shuttered window. He held her back to his chest and slapped his hand over her mouth. She could hardly breathe in his iron grip. They stood still and silent as someone entered.

* * * * *

Ja'el ushered Antania into the library and they both scanned the room carefully.

Good. They're gone and Belinda is safe. Antania turned to Ja'el.

"What is so urgent, my love?"

Jakfa stiffened and his grip tightened. *She has already cuckolded the king. His reign is weaker than I thought.*

"I have just come from the war council. All the Damons loyal to the king will move their forces and meet to the north of Varlana. In one week, we will attack and root out Gailen's army. His revolt will be over before it's begun."

"What about his army to the east?"

"It will take them two weeks to reach us. By then it will be over, but until then it is not safe here. You must leave the palace, Antania. Our child must not be harmed."

Jakfa's grip tightened until Belinda's teeth cut her lip. Her heart sank as Ja'el betrayed her. If she left this library alive it would be an act of God. Her mind raced to find a story Jakfa might believe.

"I will visit my father. Devonshire should be far enough away."

"Good idea. I will send for you when it is over."

They kissed and cooed at each other before they left. When the door shut, Jakfa released Belinda and slapped her to the floor.

"My queen has betrayed me."

"No, Jakfa. I dosed her when she visited the king and he hasn't sent for her in a long while. I didn't know she and Ja'el..." *Please believe this lie and find me useful. I must leave quickly.*

He considered her answer. It made sense. *Maybe she's not lost to me, yet.* He decided to keep her and gently helped her from the floor. "My beautiful Belinda." His voice oozed with warmth and tenderness. "I am so sorry. My desire took control. I can't believe I did this to you." A tear gathered in his eye. "Please forgive me. I will never hurt you again." He gathered her in his arms. "Oh Belinda, Belinda, my beautiful queen." He kissed her softly and looked into her eyes until she managed a smile. Mollified, he began to pace around the room.

"We have to move quickly. One week is not too soon, but it will be difficult. I can mobilize the army in Varlana in two days. We can lay siege to the palace until the rest of the army gets here like we planned. We'll just start in two days. Yes, I think it will work."

He took Belinda's hand and led her in a dance around the room. "We will be royalty by the end of the week. You will be queen, my beauty. Queen of all Umberlan." He practically flew as he led her around the room one more time. "I must plan." He spun her out and watched the tatters of her dress swirl. "Your dress is beautiful. You must wear it for your coronation." He kissed her and then breezed from the room.

Belinda shut the door behind him and stood alone; her dress torn beyond repair. She couldn't leave the room without a change of clothes. *He thought me beautiful after he ruined my clothes, bruised my cheek, and humiliated me. And now he wants to parade my degradation in front of Varlana at my coronation.* Trapped in the Library, she considered what she learned. Panic replaced humiliation. Urgency overcame shame. Antania must be told. She plotted while she waited.

Eventually, a maid entered to dust the shelves and Belinda sent her to bring a dress. When the maid returned and she changed, she tore her ruined dress into rags and burned them in the fireplace. Never again did she want to touch it.

Antania waited for her when she returned. She greeted Belinda with a big smile and sparkle in her eyes. "Belinda, I have great news!"

Belinda wasted no time with small talk. "I know it all. The war council, the invasion in one week, and your trip to see your father."

"But how…"

"Jakfa and I heard you in the hall and hid in the Library before you came in. We heard it all. My queen, your plan is uncovered and Jakfa will move against the city in two days."

"Two days! We can't be ready in two days…"

"You must tell the king and I will go to Ja'el. We cannot operate in secret anymore and you must not create suspicion. Jakfa knows of you and Ja'el now. You aren't safe here. Does the king know it's not his child?"

"Yes. He knows all. In fact, this baby is his idea. But now we must act. Your idea is sound. I will go to the king. You leave at once for Ja'el."

* * * * *

Desperate pounds on his door roused Ja'el from a nap. His responsibilities on the king's war council, his worry for Antania, and all his daily duties exhausted him. He groomed Caleb to take some responsibility, but he still needed more time.

He pushed himself out of bed and swung open the door. Belinda's bruised face pushed past to enter. They sat down at the table.

"May I fix you a compress for your bruise? What happened?"

Belinda dove in. "The queen and I have spied on Jakfa for many weeks." She raised a hand against his reaction. "Not now. You can scold me later. He took a liking to me and I encouraged him. Just a bit of fun at first, but then he asked me to harm the queen."

"Wait, Belinda. We have guests. Caleb, Robin show yourselves."

Discovered, they appeared from behind a door, eyes lowered in embarrassment.

"Robin, you must take this coin and buy wood for the fire now." Robin scurried out the door and Ja'el turned to Caleb. "You are about to hear adult things. You are becoming a good man, but our lives will change in the next few days. You need to know what is coming, but you must tell no one. Do you understand?"

"I understand, Master Ja'el."

"Then sit here to hear the rest."

Caleb joined them at the table and Belinda continued. She left out the torn dress, but the bruise she couldn't hide. She also didn't relate Ja'el's relationship with Antania. Caleb's young ears didn't need to hear *all* the details.

"The queen is talking to the king now. What should we do?"

Another knock at the door interrupted them. A messenger called Ja'el back to the palace.

"It appears the queen has finished her talk with the king. He calls back the war council tonight. You must ready the queen to travel. I will come to you tonight with a plan. Caleb, find the seller, Jacob. Do not stop searching until you find him. Bring him here and wait for me."

* * * * *

The king reconvened his war council immediately. He refused to divulge the queen's involvement and the Damons found it hard to believe news from such a mysterious source.

"Where does this information come from?"

"How do we know it's reliable?"

Voices raised in argument and frustration until Salak pounded the table for silence. He stared them all down until a small voice from the back of the room asked the question on everyone's mind.

"Who betrayed us?"

The question hung in the air until the king responded.

"We have not been betrayed, but Jakfa's spies are everywhere and conversations are overheard. Someone's indiscretion brought us to this point. It is unfortunate. Let us not waste time with blame and spend our energy on a solution."

Through the night they planned until they finally agreed on a strategy.

The king's guards will be withdrawn from the city to defend the palace. The king's elite force will gather on the hill to the north of Varlana. When the king attacks from the north, half the guards will enter the city from the palace gate and trap Gailen's forces in the city. Caught in a vice, they would be subdued.

The soldiers east of the city will hunker down in trenches, a defense against Gailen's advance from his estate. Their numbers will be increased to hold Gailen's forces at bay until the city is secured.

After the city is secure, the guards will stay in the city to "clean-up" while the king's soldiers will be sent to the east to swell Salak's army and finish Gailen's revolt for good.

Everyone agreed with the plan. They would begin immediately.

* * * * *

Tobin left the council and went directly to Jakfa. He explained the council's decisions and strategies completely.

"This is a good battle plan. It will be hard to defeat it."

"It's only good if all the parts work. You are Captain of the Guard. What can you do in the palace to collapse its defenses?"

"I will send the palace guards loyal to Gailen into the city to swell the troops; about 100 men, but I don't think it will be enough."

Tobin paused in thought. *Where is the weakness?*

They both realized it at once.

"The garden wall" they said in unison.

"We will hide troops in the overgrown field outside the palace behind the garden. Hundreds of soldiers can wait there in ambush. Wait to station your guards there until I give the word."

"They should be able to pull it down quickly. I can do some damage from the inside to make it easier."

"Excellent. Once we have breached the wall, the palace is ours. Tobin, there is one more thing I need you to do for me."

"Sure. I've got nothing else to do."

Jakfa ignored him. "The queen plans to travel to her father to escape the battle. We will not be able to dispense with her here as I hoped. Have her followed and see to it she never arrives."

"It is done."

He left the room amazed. Jakfa asked him so casually, but he knew the seriousness of the task. It made Tobin proud to be so trusted. He knew assassins in every region, but only his best would do this job. He returned to his room and wrote a message to the most ruthless man he ever served with. Then he sent his fastest rider to Langley Castle.

* * * * *

Jakfa met with his father less than an hour later. After he shared all the new information, Gailen patted Jakfa roughly on his shoulders.

"You did well, son. There is only one more thing."

Jakfa couldn't think of anything. "What?"

"You must immediately start a rumor in the city about the attack in two days. Spread it in every bar, inn and street corner. The whole town must know in one night."

"I can use the soldiers in the city. But why? I thought we wanted secrecy?"

"Our secret is out. Now we must fight."

"With rumors and gossip?"

"Two of the best weapons. Come here, Jakfa, and let me show you something." He led his son to a battle map on the table. "What lies to the east of Varlana?"

"Our troops."

"And to the south and west?"

"The Bitterlands."

"And when the city panics and begins to flee, which road will they travel?"

"To the north. It is the only safe passage."

"And where are Salak's troops?"

"To the north. My god! The road will be packed with slow wagons and people. How is Salak's army supposed to get to the city?"

"Exactly. Between Tobin at the palace and the refugees on the north road, Varlana will fall in one afternoon."

Gailen's horrible smile filled his scarred face and Jakfa returned one of his own cruel smirks. Victory, once again, came to them. Spurred on by his excitement, Jakfa raced from the room and began to send messages.

* * * * *

The council adjourned and Ja'el drew Salak aside. "My king, we must make arrangements for the queen to leave the palace until the fighting is over."

"Ja'el, I'm surprised at you. Gailen will not reach the palace. She will be safe here." And he strode away down the hall.

Ja'el went to the queen's rooms.

"Antania, the king is sure of victory, but I am not. If Gailen overwhelms the palace defenses you and Salak will be the first to die. You must leave in disguise. We have no idea who to trust. Gailen's troops are already in the city."

Belinda chimed in. "Hannah is a friend of mine. She works in the kitchen. I can ask her for clothes. A trade for a fine dress will get us all we need."

"Belinda, you must cut my hair. It is the one feature everyone knows and I won't be able to hide it."

Ja'el's heart sank. He loved her silky hair.

"Ja'el, don't look so sad. It will grow back." A moment of levity and then they returned to business.

"Don't pack things. Hide money in your clothes. Food, supplies, clothes, these things you can buy along the way. Speed is everything. You must travel light."

Belinda worked on a list. "What about morning sickness? Is there a draught she can take to prevent it? I can't think of a bigger clue to her identity than throwing up on the side of the road."

"I will make you something, Antania."

"Thank you, Ja'el. It would be nice if you helped your baby behave." She kissed him and said, "My concern is leaving Varlana. How will we exit the city without being seen?"

"Jacob, a friend of my father's, is in town. A seller by trade. I will ask him to smuggle you out of the city. He is strong and wily. You will be safe with him."

They talked for another hour and firmed up their plans.

"Why aren't we talking of *your* escape, Ja'el?"

"My love, I must stay and help the king. I will know where you are and come find you."

They walked arm in arm to the door. Antania pulled him close. "Ja'el, I'm afraid."

"While I breathe, my love." and they kissed good-bye.

* * * * *

When Ja'el walked into his home, there sat Jacob at the table. Caleb entertained him and Robin with tales of Devonshire and secret forts. He stopped when Ja'el entered.

"Caleb, take Robin to the back and tend to the yard while Jacob and I talk." They obediently left the room.

Jacob stood. He towered over Ja'el. His thick reddish-brown hair fell to his broad shoulders. A loner and smuggler, years in the business toughened him. His thick calloused hands hung next to strong stocky legs. His beard almost covered his face with thick wiry hair.

Now his teeth shone through his beard as he grinned. "Ja'el, you have grown into an intimidating presence." His laugh boomed off the walls and Ja'el remembered the sound from many years of conversations in this room between Jacob and his father.

Jacob's voice lowered. "Your father's death is a great loss."

"Yes, but his wisdom lives on." Ja'el held up a roll of parchment. "I have been collecting his wisdom for two years. I should read some to you. It will help you reform your ways."

Another laugh filled the room. Then – "Ja'el, you didn't send your young lad away to talk of this. What is your need?"

Ja'el's smile faded into a frown of concern. "Jacob, you must convince me I can trust you." He stood rigid against Jacob's presence. "Your friendship with my father is not ours. And this cargo is too valuable to take any chances."

"You are your father's son. I owe Caleb for his help today. It is a big favor he can ask of me. No one else in the crowd lifted a hand."

"Not enough."

Jacob's brows drew together and he started again. "When your father's health began to fail, he sent for me. I vowed to keep an eye on you and help you in times of trouble. I have never broken a vow, especially to Morcon, and I won't start now. You can doubt my loyalty to you, but not to your father. Tell me what you need or I am on my way."

Ja'el relaxed. "It is the queen who needs you, Jacob. I am asking you to save the life of the queen."

"So, the rumors I've heard are true? Gailen moves against Varlana?"

"Yes, and the king believes victory is assured. I am not so confident. The queen is pregnant with the royal heir. Her life must be protected."

"I understand. What is the strategy?"

For two hours they plotted the queen's escape. Jacob explained a system of signs he used when others needed to follow him in secret. He would leave a trail only Ja'el would understand and they would meet in a few weeks. The safest plan took them north to Oberlan, since all of Gailen's loyal Damons ruled in the south. Jacob would travel little known roads and trails the smugglers used. The queen and Belinda would be over the Aldies Mountains and in Oberlan under King Ardenna's protection in two weeks.

* * * * *

The next day a delivery arrived at Langley castle. Arbak recognized Tobin's writing. *I haven't heard from him in a while.* He opened the seal.

Arbak,

The new queen of Umberlan stands in the way of our future. She carries the heir to the throne. She may travel through your region in the next few days. You must guarantee Queen Antania never returns to Varlana.

I will pay you handsomely for your loyalty.

For Gailen,
Tobin

"Tobin, what d' I care about yer revolution." he said to no one. "My bizness is good. Why should I kill some queen and jeperdize meself? O' course, he don't outright say to kill 'er. Juz don' let 'er come back. An' the money sounds good."

He thought about his business. *Royal babies. I'd like makin' royal babies. If I git 'er here, no one'll ever find 'er.* He set about to make plans and send the rider back with his answer.

* * * * *

Tobin laughed when he read Arbak's reply. "So, you want exclusive rights to her, do you?" *He may be crude, but he's wily and resourceful.* If Arbak said he would take care of the queen, Tobin knew he would. *Still, a little competition never hurt.* He left the general warrant in place, put the queen out of his mind and turned to the tasks at hand.

Gailen waited outside the southern gate. He left to meet him and complete their preparations.

When Tobin arrived, he called the guards off their post to give him a report. They stood at attention in a dark corner inside the wall while they hid their discomfort. Their captain commanded and they obeyed. Tobin drew two knives out of his cape. With one he stabbed a guard in the heart, then quickly slit the throat of the second before the guard recovered from his surprise.

He wiped the blood from his skin with a sash from the guards' uniform and quietly opened the gate. The bodies he dumped outside under a pile of dirty straw. He stiffened when he felt a hand on his shoulder, but didn't utter a sound.

"Good work, Tobin, but watch your back."

He relaxed. "My king, are you ready?"

Gailen smiled his gruesome smile. "Lead on. It's time to finish this."

Silently, Tobin fastened the gate and led his king to headquarters in the city. He helped Gailen settle in before he returned to his palace duties.

* * * * *

The next day the women cut each other's hair, Belinda's golden blonde just as memorable as Antania's silky black. They burned their locks in the fireplace. "Leave no trace of your escape" Ja'el had advised. They collected all the coins and cheap jewelry they could find, wrapped them in cloth to avoid clinks and jingles, and secreted it all away in their clothes. Hannah's clothes accommodated Hannah's big body, so their figures and fair skin hid in nondescript folds and bland colors. Belinda picked faded browns and greys, very unremarkable. They waited until nightfall.

Rumors flew through the city of the imminent attack. All the courtiers fled and the servants hid downstairs in the kitchen cupboards and closets. The palace looked deserted as Belinda and Antania slipped through the halls to the garden that evening. They found their way to the back gate and quietly left the palace. They followed the wall to the corner, turned right toward the cabin, and followed the edge of the wood. A soft grunt and a clank of a sword on armor made them freeze.

Belinda silently pulled Antania into the shadow of the trees and they waited, afraid to move. Soft sounds of hidden soldiers seemed to surround them. Soft snores suddenly rose out of the grass. Belinda squeezed Antania's arm and they crept slow and quiet through the underbrush until they found the cabin.

Inside, Ja'el waited in the dark. He put a finger to his lips and both women nodded. He chanted softly and led them into the night and through the trees to the north edge of Varlana. From there they took city streets and hurried to Ja'el's house.

Once inside, he locked the door and shuttered the windows. "We must speak softly and set no light. Gailen's army is everywhere."

"How many soldiers are in that field?"

"I don't know, but they will sleep until morning. I am concerned about the garden wall. It will not hold back an assault. When you leave, Caleb, Robin and I will return to the cabin to do what we can."

Antania's mouth set in a hard line. "Ja'el, be careful. What do you know about fighting?" She never saw or heard of Ja'el in a fight with anyone. What would he do against so many?

"I know things better than fighting. We will be alright. Let me tell you about Jacob."

He told them everything he knew about Jacob and, by the time Jacob arrived with his wagon and the horses, Belinda and Antania felt comfortable traveling with him. They climbed into a shallow box hidden under the wagon floorboards with just enough room to move a little. When Jacob replaced the boards, he stacked big, heavy sacks of grains on top. Showers of dust covered the women. Boards creaked from the weight and the scent of dirt and seed flooded their noses and scratched at their throats. The women felt helpless and afraid. Antania reached for Belinda's hand as the wagon slowly began to wind through the streets and out of the city.

* * * * *

Robin slept while Caleb watched Ja'el lay out his supplies. A wild assortment of sticks, jewelry, herbs, and exotic things lay all over the floor. He sat in silence, mesmerized by these strange boxes and bags.

"Caleb, tonight you are going to see secrets hidden in my family for hundreds of years. There are only two people in the entire country who know this secret. You will be the third. There will be no others. To divulge what you see tonight will kill us both."

Caleb remained silent. He kept his eyes on Ja'el and nodded.

"Many generations ago, magic thrived in these lands. Magic helped conquer the tribes here. It united the people into one land, Umberlan. Then one day a king rose up who didn't remember how magic helped his country. He feared magic would be used against him and he outlawed the use of it. He hunted down all the wizards and sages and killed them. It has been a capital crime ever since.

"My family chose to keep this ability alive. There has always been magic in my family, but the need for secrecy has forced us to hide, even from each other. There is no shared knowledge. I do not even know if other wizards exist. Great amounts of knowledge have been lost. What I know now is not the strong magic of wizards, but the smaller magic of sages." He watched Caleb's reaction. Caleb silently waited.

"There are spells and incantations I can weave to help the king tomorrow. We are going to a cabin near the edge of the woods by the palace and prepare to fight in the morning." Caleb's eyes grew big and he sat up, but still made no sound.

"Do not worry. We will be hidden and no one will know. I do not like what I saw tonight and I am not sure the palace will stand. If the garden wall is breached, all is lost."

Finally, Caleb spoke. "Master Ja'el, what you need?"

Ja'el smiled. "I need your support to keep me awake, and I need you to know the names of these things so you can bring them to me." He began to show Caleb all the strange things spread on the floor. After Caleb memorized them, they packed it all away.

"Caleb."

"Yes Master?"

"We may never come back to this house. If we do not come back, we will walk a long way. Gather only what you can carry and be careful what you choose."

Caleb packed the medallion of Adonna, the warrior queen, before anything else. Ja'el gently packed his portrait of Antania in the garden and his parchments of Morcon's wisdom. Silently they finished their work, picked up Robin, and crept to the cabin.

Caleb laid Robin on a bed of straw and Ja'el leaned over him and muttered another sleep spell. He didn't want him to witness the fight. Robin's slow deep breaths would continue all night. Ja'el sat in the middle of the floor and began to chant.

CHAPTER 16
THE DARK BEFORE DAWN

Two hours before dawn, Salak and his elite guard joined the soldiers on the north hill. The day before, his men tried to clear the road, but more refugees just bottlenecked behind. They finally gave up and chose to approach through unoccupied grass beside the road. It would be awkward, but not impossible. They steeled themselves and waited for dawn.

Gailen joined his army hidden in abandoned buildings near the palace. He openly stationed troops at the city gate to distract Salak from his real intent. All his pieces fell into place. Now he waited for Salak's next move.

Jakfa threw the last of the wood, trash and greasy rags into piles scattered around the throne room. *That should be big enough. Now, let's see what I can find* and he trotted off to the king's rooms.

Tobin stationed his best guards to protect the palace gate and entrance. The rest he positioned in the garden to protect the wall. *Gailen's troops will enter here. Everything must be according to plan.*

Varlana's best captain led the guards who protected the garden. Tobin watched as he posted his men strategically along the wall and checked their weapon supply. He saw troops in the field and sent two guards out to do reconnaissance. His confidence amused Tobin and he smiled. *He has no idea.* For the past several days Tobin worked in secret to weaken the wall. He left no evidence, but Gailen's troops knew the vulnerable spots. *The wall will fall quickly.*

* * * * *

The looking glass tube entertained Caleb. If he squinted one eye and looked through it, everything seemed to jump closer. He could see details on the guards at the wall, even their buttons and laces. The subtle dips in the grass where the soldiers hid became obvious gaps filled with green, black, and silver. With this, his job would be easy.

All the strange things Ja'el brought lay in rows at his feet. It fell to Caleb to report the battle changes and give Ja'el whatever he asked for. Ja'el sat on the floor near the window and faced the field. Caleb knelt beside him.

Ja'el filled his scrying bowl and placed it on the floor before him. *Can I do this, father?* He believed if he envisioned what Caleb described, he could chant over the bowl and strengthen the results. Right now, the bowl showed soldiers asleep in a field. *Sleeping spells. I wish I knew something more powerful.* "Be creative. Use what you know to solve your problems." *I don't know much, father. I hope it's enough.*

He closed his eyes, dipped his finger in the bowl and began. The more he chanted, the deeper the soldiers slept, but the sheer number of soldiers created a problem. He'd never tried this with a big group before, and he felt tired already. Would he last the day?

* * * * *

The black before dawn covered everything in eerie silence. No birds. No crickets. No leaves rustled in a breeze. Tension rippled through the air as men strained to keep themselves still, while earnest eyes scanned the gloom for any sign of movement. Even the horses felt the oppression of the dark and stood rigid beneath anxious soldiers. Death waited silently for dawn.

CHAPTER 17
⌐ THE BATTLE IS JOINED ⌐

The sun cracked through the horizon and Salak let loose his war cry. It rang across the hill and echoed in the trees. With a whoop and a yell, the north forces began to gallop toward the city. Hooves rumbled on the ground and drawn swords glinted in the early light. Two hundred men sped past the refugees and shook the air with thunderous cries of victory.

Onward they flew, their eyes cast on Gailen's troops at the gate of their beloved city. The king's valiant men vowed they would cut down Gailen where he stood. King Salak stood in his saddle and shook his sword in the air. His men tasted victory.

When the last horse roared past, the refugees on the road threw off their old coats. They ran to form a loose line across the grass. Hundreds of Gailen's bowmen now faced the backs of the Varlanian soldiers. They notched their arrows and fired a rain storm of death into the backs of Salak's red and gold. Volley after volley ripped through Salak's ranks and slapped into his soldiers, until corpses littered the ground.

"Onward. Onward!" Cries of victory became panicked yells. The elite force formed a circle around the king as they raced into Gailen's forces at the gate. The deluge of arrows stopped when the king reached the gate and the fight to gain entry began. Gailen's forces fought fiercely, but Salak finally fought through. The king lost more than one hundred men before he entered Varlana and barred the gate.

They caught their breath and tallied their losses. Drunk with thoughts of victory, Salak called for advance. His officers pleaded for him to move slowly and check houses and buildings along the way, but the king determined to press on and move the battle plan forward. Bravely they mounted and tore through the streets to defend their king as he galloped to the palace.

The horse's hooves drummed against the empty city streets. Salak rode all the way to the palace gate without a shot fired. *All Gailen's troops must be left outside the city!* He finally stopped to count his losses. His soul grieved the heavy toll, but he pushed his grief away. He felt victory in his grasp.

* * * * *

At dawn, when Salak's war cry rang out, the soldiers in the field outside the garden began to rise. Groggy from heavy sleep, they made easy targets for the arrows of the king's guard. The element of surprise evaporated and Gailen's troops scrambled for cover.

"Master, new green from north."

Gailen's numbers swelled as soldiers from the road joined Gailen's force in the field. With Salak safely in the city, the bowmen moved to their new objective, swell the troops in the field and breach the garden wall. They joined the green ranks in the tall grass and trees.

"Green shoots from trees."

Ja'el called for a talisman which Caleb hastily gave him. His chants became sing-song and Caleb saw the green in confusion.

"Green confused. Going every way. Oh! They move close."

The image in the bowl changed. A small group of soldiers crept through the trees. Ja'el sent a command and all at once they burst through the trees and ran toward the wall. Their premature charge alerted the king's guards, and they shot them with ease.

"The green down, but I see officers organizing".

The image changed again. Gailen's officers met to regroup and mount a coordinated attack. Ja'el called out for a brooch and began to chant in grunts and groans. Caleb tried to ignore him and keep his eye on the battlefield.

"Green officers arguing. Oh! Here comes another rush on garden. And another."

Ja'el sent a dozen mixed messages to Gailen's troops to expose them to the king's guards. *It's working!*

"Green split army. Half to north. Half to west. No wait, three splits, north, west, and I don't see where the rest are."

"Caleb, do not look for them. Tell me what is happening."

"North troops aim to fire."

Ja'el dipped his finger deeper in the bowl. Misty figures lined the trees and aimed their arrows at the heads of the guards. A little nudge and their arrows missed high.

"Master! Arrows from the west."

They already flew through the air. Ja'el tried desperately to change their course, but inanimate objects couldn't receive suggestions and the arrows found their targets.

Ja'el called for a charm and in a few moments two maids appeared with bandages. They set up a triage near the interior door and began to treat the wounded. Slowly, the guards lost fighters. Slowly, Gailen's forces increased. Stones began to bulge out in the wall from the weight of the defenders, but it held.

"The green moving into small groups. All approaching from different angles. The north is shooting. No! It distraction. Men move against wall under guards!"

Ja'el called for a totem and began to hum and snort. Suddenly, the kitchen maids joined the fight and rocks and flower pots began to drop from the top of the wall. Green pulled back.

Hours dragged on as the battle for the garden waged. Everything "green" threw at "red" seemed to go awry. But then the strategy changed. Gailen's army decided to split into small groups of seven or eight. A designated leader attacked a given stretch of wall any way he saw fit. Green soldiers seemed to explode into chaos, but each attack targeted a weakness in the wall and the red defenders began to be overwhelmed. Soon Caleb couldn't keep up with all the activity and Ja'el became confused.

"Just keep your eye on the garden," said Ja'el. If he couldn't influence Gailen's troops, he would concentrate on the area in front of the wall. He would have to react much more quickly, but he saw no other options.

The intensity of the fight wore on Ja'el and he began to weaken. He grabbed a talisman on his neck and mumbled a quick incantation. He felt his strength return. *But at what cost?* He would count it later. The battle continued.

* * * * *

Slowly, quietly Gailen's army began to gather in the street. They trotted behind Salak's men until they saw the palace. Then, all at once, they began to shout and drive forward.

The king's men turned to see a crowd of Gailen's men headed right for them. They quickly formed a battle line around the king and steeled themselves for the fight.

Gailen's men hit their line full force and the fight turned fierce. Sword on shield rattled through the streets. Steel on steel rang in the air. Slowly Salak's cavalry began to push Gailen's troops back. As the distance grew between the fight and the palace gates, Salak called for the palace guards to reinforce the rear.

"Protect the flanks" he yelled, and the gates opened. Hundreds of guards poured out to fill the gap and protect Salak.

We will win this day, thought Salak as Gailen's army retreated farther back into the city.

Suddenly, Gailen's men retreated behind a wall of Chimayan shields. Salak's forces attacked, but the shields did not give way. They pushed Salak's army back toward the palace while the red swords flailed in vain. General Janell called retreat as the bowmen on the palace wall began to shoot.

More green and black shields raised over the heads of Gailen's soldiers and the arrows could not find their mark. General Janell watched as Gailen's men pushed toward the palace gate and divided Salak's forces in half. Janell directed the arrows toward the rear of Gailen's troops where the shield wall showed cracks. Men began to fall. He rallied his men on the palace grounds around the gate and moved archers into position in front of it. The ornamental gate looked intimidating, but soft, shiny metal laced through the decorative iron and Janell knew it would never hold against Gailen's numbers.

Furiously, Salak's men fought to push back, but Gailen's soldiers would not yield. Steadily they moved their shield wall forward. As the wall of green soldiers neared the palace gate, the red archers stationed inside the palace grounds began to shoot through the lacy metal work. As one green man fell, another moved up to sacrifice himself. The green soldiers began to stumble over the dead, yet still they pressed on.

When they reached the gate, the red arrows flew in solid sheets. Green soldiers pressed against the gate and died from the crush of the men behind as they pushed to bring the gate down. All the dead men did not fall, but became shields for the soldiers behind. Janell called out, "Cease fire," and moved the archers back up on the wall to shoot down on the invaders. He hoped for a miracle to create a safety zone for the king.

The gate groaned and creaked against the force pressed against it. The red guards strained against their fear to run as they saw the gate bow and the hinges strain to hold. Sweaty palms wiped on leather armor. Hearts raced and lungs panted. With a groan and a bang, the gate finally gave way and they tore into Gailen's men like cannon fire.

Gailen's army poured through like a waterfall. They fanned out on either side and tried to surround Salak's men. Janell ordered a continuous volley of arrows from the palace wall. Frissia suffered heavy casualties, but their soldiers kept coming. Green and red mingled together as swords clashed. Janell's bowmen became confused and shot indiscriminately, killing friend and foe alike. General Janell saw their confusion and ordered them to turn their fire outside the palace grounds on Gailen's troops in the streets.

Arrows rained down on the green and still Gailen's army came. they loosed arrows until their arms shook. When the last arrow flew, Janell cried out, "Rally to me for Varlana!" and jumped into the fray. The bowmen drew their broadswords and followed. Gailen's force quickly swallowed them.

Salak found himself trapped among his forces by the gate. He fought his way toward the palace and met some of his elite force. They gathered around him, fought their way out of the worst of the battle, and took shelter down an alley in an old armory shack. Halfway to the shack, a stray arrow caught a gap in his armor and lodged itself in Salak's thigh. When they entered the armory, Salak collapsed on the floor, a severed artery pumped blood out of his body. Quickly a soldier applied a tourniquet to stem the flow.

"Terrell" whispered the king.

"My king, save your energy. You have lost much blood."

"Why are you..."

"I have always fought for you, my king. This is no different."

Salak smiled weakly and raised his hand to pat Terrell on the shoulder. "We beat death once. We will do it again."

* * * * *

Tobin observed the fight from the top of the entrance stairs. His guards held the front entrance to the palace. They built strong barricades in an arc at the base of the stairs. These guards and those barricades needed to hold or the palace fell. *They aren't scared enough.* He ordered them to hunker down and forced them to watch the slaughter of their comrades.

"Commander, should we charge?"

"We will hold. They will not enter here." Tobin tried to strengthen his men's resolve. He didn't want them to retreat into the palace. They could hide in there for days. *Better to deal with them all right here.*

The battle at the gate suddenly ceased. A brief moment of stillness preceded roars of victory and then a solid mass of green and black began to charge the barricade. Beads of sweat dripped on the landing as Tobin's men watched the enemy approach. Gailen's soldiers reached the bottom stair.

"Hold for King Salak and Varlana!" Tobin yelled. His men raised their pikes, yelled a war cry, and immediately crumbled under the relentless onslaught of Gailen's troops.

Tobin retreated into the palace. He didn't need to watch the slaughter. Gailen's men would follow their orders. He had more work to do.

He headed for the kitchen. All the servants gathered there to avoid the battle. They thought their jobs secure. They all swore they didn't care who ruled them, as long as they got paid.

However, when Tobin arrived, he observed two distinct groups. The women and children huddled by the pantry. The men frowned at him and continued their low conversation around the table.

This won't do. I'll have to add them to the signal.

He lit the torch in the kitchen fire and called out, "The palace has been breached, but the guards are holding. Salak's troops are on the way. I need to take you to the throne room where you'll be safe. These outside walls make you vulnerable." He *was* the Captain of the Guard, after all. They all rose to follow the man in authority. *Good. Very good.*

They trooped down the hall and waited as he opened the throne room door and invited them in. "Looters" he answered to their questions about the mess. When the servants filed in, he threw the torch into the closest pile of rags and locked the door. He tore off his red and gold armor as he strode down the hall. *Where are you, my friend?*

Tobin ignored the servants' screams as he left to find Jakfa. The flames caught the grease and dry tinder and roared out of control. Fire darted from one pile to the next unabated. Banners and silks curled back as the fire began to lick the bright fringes and consume the balcony. The servants huddled to one side of the room, but flames roared into a furnace before they could plan their escape. Smoke stung their eyes and choked their lungs as they began to fall. The heat burst the windows and shattered glass pelted the charred bodies below.

Smoke billowed into the sky and Gailen's western troops saw their sign. They began to move toward Varlana.

* * * * *

Gailen's troops quickly dispatched Tobin's men at the entrance. They ran up the bloody steps into the palace and turned to the right. They must now attack the garden. The battle wasn't over yet.

They streamed through the door and threw themselves at the palace guards. The king's guards turned to defend themselves and the soldiers in the field breached the wall. The guards and the wounded died quickly. The women they saved for sport.

* * * * *

"Master!" Caleb caught Ja'el as he slumped over. The long day and relentless battle took its toll. Now his jaw hung slack and his temples showed grey. Caleb cringed at such a rapid change in his master. He gently laid him down and picked up the looking glass. Without Ja'el's protection the garden wall quickly fell. Caleb watched as the green washed over the wall. *Master will want to know.* He cried as he witnessed carnage the likes of which he never imagined. He finally dropped the looking glass forever a different man.

* * * * *

Salak's men quietly defended the perimeter of the armory and bravely kept their precious treasure free from danger. However, they caught the attention of Gailen. He had lost sight of his brother earlier in the fight. *Have I found you again, Salak?*

"To me!" he yelled and a small group of soldiers assigned to dispatch wounded nearby moved to his side. He pointed down the alley. "We're going to find us a king. Destroy his defenses, but leave my brother to me."

They fanned out to approach the armory from all directions and began to close in. Too late to move, Salak's men saw the advance and moved inside. They could defend against a few men at a time who came through a door. If they exposed themselves in the open, they would fall to the enemy. Their lives hung on a slim hope. Five brave men drew their swords to face the attack. Terrell quietly checked the king's wound and tourniquet, picked up his sword and joined the defense.

It ended quickly. Salak's men fought valiantly. Gailen lost more men than he expected, but in the end, he sat among the bodies on the floor next to his brother unopposed.

"Salak. We are together again."

Salak turned his head to stare at his betrayer.

"Do you remember when father took us to swim at the lake? One day, you were about twelve or so, you dove underwater and your feet got tangled in the weeds. I dove in to save you. Do you remember?"

Salak weakly nodded his head. His eyes widened in fear as Gailen drew his knife. Gailen moved toward Salak's leg and gently cut away the tourniquet. Salak's life began to pump out onto the floor as Gailen calmly watched.

"I saved you because of our bond. We're brothers, you and I. Sometimes I think you forget about that." He leaned against the wall, lost in the memory. "I got to you just in time, remember? I swam with you to shore and pulled you to safety. I stayed with you then and I'll stay with you now until the end. Don't worry, brother, you won't die alone."

Salak opened his mouth, but his voice crackled and stopped. The color began to drain from his face as blood pooled under his legs. Gailen traced the edges with the point of his knife. "Father came at a run. He ran right by me and knelt by your side. Remember how he doted on you?"

Gailen's soft, tender voice ignored the gasps of his brother beside him. "I never got his attentions. I thought he would be happy I saved you, but he was so angry. Remember? He beat me again for allowing you to be harmed." A deep chuckle escaped through Gailen's wry smile and filled

144

the room. "He never beat you, did he?" Gailen finally looked at his brother's distress and tempered his voice. He gently patted Salak on the shoulder and spoke with soft serenity. "I should have let you die back then."

As Salak struggled for life, Gailen's gruesome smile widened. "I won't make that mistake again."

* * * * *

When Salak's troops on the west flank saw the smoke, they fell back to defend the city. Captain Dugan soon realized the futility of this maneuver and retreated to the woods to regroup. Gailen's forces marched into Varlana unopposed.

* * * * *

Tobin found Jakfa in the king's rooms. He stood in front of the royal wardrobe. Clothes piled in heaps all over the floor. Jakfa wore an embroidered cape and the ceremonial crown and admired himself in a big mirror.

"How long have you been in here, Jakfa?"

"What do you think, Tobin? Do they suit me?"

Tobin snorted. "Sure, your majesty. Now come with me. The fun is just beginning."

As they left, Jakfa grabbed a beautifully engraved silver tray. "I bet this has never carried royalty before." They laughed as they walked to the entrance.

The troops gathered at the front steps and waited for orders. Gailen tied one of Salak's legs to a rope and dragged his body behind Salak's own horse to the base of the entrance steps. The soldiers cheered until Jakfa raised his hands for silence.

"We have won a great victory today. (Cheers and clapping) "The usurper is dead. Long live the king." Jakfa bowed to his father and the soldiers went wild. They ripped down the red and gold banner of Varlana and replaced it with the green and black of Frissia. For more than two minutes the cheers went on. Gailen dragged his brother's body halfway up the steps while soldiers kicked and stabbed it. Jakfa carried the silver tray to the base of the stairs while Gailen scanned the crowd.

Tobin watched in silence as the scene unfolded. *Those two sure know how to put on a show.*

"Where is this traitor's sword?" Gailen shouted into the crowd.

Salak's sword moved from hand to hand in silence until Jakfa reverently offered it to the new king. Gailen kicked Salak's body over and brought the sword down on his neck. Salak's head bounced down the stairs and the crowd roared while Jakfa grabbed it by the hair and arranged it on the silver platter. Like a fountain, a red river flowed to the marble stairs. He marched to the outer gate behind his father and proudly displayed the prize. The army cheered and danced behind him. A few sullen faces of merchants and families who stayed in the city peeked from behind curtains and shutters.

Gailen smiled his terrible smile and waved to them. *They will not be safe for long.*

At the gate two pikes stood; one labeled "Usurper" and the other "Usurper's wife" Jakfa jammed Salak's head on the "Usurper" pike and the crowd cheered for another minute.

"Varlana is ours, Take your fill." Gailen yelled to the crowd and everyone ran back into the city to loot and destroy with abandon.

Gailen, Jakfa and Tobin sat on a rock while blood dripped down the pike beside them.

"Tobin"

"Yes, my king."

"You have proven your worth throughout this adventure. You are now a general in my new army."

"Thank you, my king."

"How does it feel to be king, father?"

"How does it feel to be free, Jakfa?" They laughed together as they walked back into the city.

CHAPTER 18

⌐ FUGITIVES ¬

The wagon stopped and Jacob freed Antania and Belinda from under the cargo.

"Why have we stopped?"

"Where are we?"

Jacob raised a hand to silence them and motioned for them to follow. They began to climb a small rise. He laid on the grass at the top and so they did the same. In the distance they could see a thick plume of smoke rise into the sky.

"What is that?" came a whisper from his left.

"That, my queen, is what is left of Varlana. It has fallen. There's no other reason for it to burn. You are now a fugitive, an enemy of the kingdom. Our travels will be more dangerous now."

"Varlana is gone?" Belinda wiped a tear from her eye. "Why destroy such a beautiful city?"

"Gailen makes a statement to everyone who was loyal to Salak."

Antania dropped her head on her hands, afraid of his next answer. "What do you mean *was* loyal?"

"I'm sorry, my queen, but Salak must be dead. He would never allow Varlana to burn. I believe he would kill his brother before he allowed it."

"You're right." Antania sighed a deep breath. "What do we do now? We are in need of you, Jacob. Are you loyal to Salak or will you sell us to the highest bidder?"

"I made a vow to keep you safe and I will not break it. Gailen is no king of mine. Come. We need to move on."

They scrambled down the hill and climbed back in the wagon. North. Their safety waited in the north.

* * * * *

Caleb watched over Ja'el and Robin through the night. At the start of the day Ja'el had spun some sort of invisibility spell around them and apparently it still held. Soldiers searched the woods all night and never noticed the cabin. He took the time to carefully pack, and then quietly waited while he prayed not to be found.

The fight he saw through the looking glass horrified him. Women abused and then cut open to watch their own stomachs spill on the ground before them. The agony of men tortured for sport. Soldiers cheered while their comrades kicked heads and body parts into garden pots. Caleb squeezed his eyes closed and tried to shut out the sight. He put his fingers in his ears against the sounds. His nose filled with a horrible stench as the smoke billowed into the sky.

Finally, he gave up, lay down beside Ja'el and reached for his hand. Silently he cried and willed himself to stay sane. *You will help me, Master. You will help me.*

In his exhaustion, Ja'el clasped Caleb's hand. *Yes, Caleb. I will help you.*

Caleb heard his Master's voice in his thoughts and bolted up. "Master? Are you awake?"

But it took the last of Ja'el's strength to send his thoughts. He imagined he spoke aloud. He sank into a deep sleep and could offer no more. Caleb lay beside him again, a flicker of hope appeared in his heart and he slept.

＊ ＊ ＊ ＊ ＊

Ja'el didn't stir until afternoon the next day. Robin still lay in a spelled sleep. Caleb turned him, but he didn't wake.

"Caleb, are you alright? I am worried for you."

"Master, I have seen...horrors."

"I am sorry, Caleb, but you must tell me everything before Robin wakes. If we are to survive, we must know our enemy."

For hours Caleb related the events following Ja'el's collapse. He stopped several times to compose himself and when he finished, he turned his tear stained face to Ja'el.

"Master, I want to forget these things. Can you remove them from my mind?"

148

"I can, but I will not."

"You said you would help me."

"Yes, and I am. If I take away these memories, you will have learned nothing."

"I don't want to learn these things."

"And yet, you have grown. Listen to the way you speak to me. Your broken patterns are gone."

"Are speech patterns so important it's worth this?" He balled his hands into fists and struggled to keep his voice low. "I don't need this violence to grow up. How are these thoughts going to help me clean the house or walk to the market?"

"Caleb, sit down and listen. Our life is changed forever. We cannot go back to Varlana or live in any city or town. We must hide now. We will live in rundown, abandoned homes where no one will find us."

Caleb stiffened but remained quiet.

Ja'el continued. "Slowly we will gather information. We will find what remains of the king's army. Maybe we will be able to take back the throne, but first we must find the queen and protect the heir. Do you understand the immense task before us?"

"But our lives…"

"Are dead. They died with the fall of the palace. Now we must run and hide. And your memories will help us. They will make you cautious and eventually they will steady your resolve. Our journey is going to be hard, harder than anything you or I have ever done. You need to be strong, Caleb. We both do."

Caleb reached out to steady himself against the wall. "Master, I don't think I can."

"I, also, am afraid."

Caleb's head snapped up. "No! You are never afraid."

"I have never faced these things. My father never faced these things. No one has taught me wisdom for this. Caleb, we must help each other. I will be strong for you if you are strong for me." Ja'el looked at Robin asleep on the floor. "And together we can keep Robin safe. What do you think?"

Caleb shuddered as he took a deep breath. His hands shook as he reached out to Ja'el. In their embrace, he felt the ember of Ja'el's strength and received the awful truth. Ja'el hugged him tightly.

"Caleb, I find myself thinking of you as my son. It is time I began to treat you as such."

"Master, today your words give me great comfort."

Robin began to come around and they smiled weakly at each other.

"I'm hungry," came a whine.

"Me, too. Caleb, I am too weak for travel today and Robin is too tired. Will you find us something to eat?"

Caleb found dried meat and bread. They ate and rested.

＊＊＊＊＊.

When the sun fully set and Robin returned to sleep, Ja'el unpacked his scrying bowl.

"Let us discover what happened to our friends. Are you strong enough for this, Caleb?"

"I don't know, but it is necessary. Go ahead."

They filled it with water and searched for Jacob. The trio emerged in the wagon traveling under thick trees along a disused wagon trail.

"Good. They are safe."

Next, they looked for King Salak. The grisly sight of his head on a pike at the city gate made them jump back in disgust. When they dared to look again, they saw General Janell's head perched on one side of the king and an empty pike reserved for Antania on the other. The heads of Damons and nobles thought loyal to the king kept company. Empty pikes bore the names of the men soon to be displayed, including Ja'el. After the image faded, they sat paralyzed with horror.

Eventually, Ja'el spoke. "I am a wanted man which puts you in danger as well. You are well known as my apprentice. I am sorry, Caleb. I have brought disaster upon you."

"Master, you asked me if I wanted to stay with you or leave. I chose to stay. I don't regret it. Don't you add guilt to what we bear. We will break. Besides, you know I love adventure."

"But this…"

"Master, please stop. I don't know what to say. Let's scry another. How about Damon Noran?"

He emerged in the bowl. He frantically packed the castle. Mortimer still attended him and helped with the crates and barrels. "Good. He is wise. His is the smallest region surrounded by Damons loyal to Gailen. His castle will be the first to be attacked. He has no army. Retreat is his only option."

"Master, what of the people of Devonshire?"

"You mean your family?"

"They have been loyal to Damon Noran. Will they be punished?"

"They have been in his employ which should be enough to save them. Your parents are wise enough not to let their faithfulness to Noran blind them to reality. They will keep silent and find other work."

They scryed most of the night, but discovered little else.

"Tomorrow we must move away from this cabin. It is not safe."

"Where are we going?"

"I do not know, but deeper into the woods away from the patrols. My spell will not hide us much longer and I am still not strong enough to weave magic again. Keep us packed, Caleb. Let us get some sleep before Robin wakes up."

Chapter 19
Old Friends and Dark Places

Jacob, Belinda and Antania traveled Jacob's hidden smuggler's routes, as they worked their way north toward Oberlan and safety. Antania rode openly in the wagon unless they passed through populated areas. Then she hid in the secret compartment on a bed of straw and downy blankets. Jacob stopped every so often to leave a trail of pre-arranged signs for Ja'el to follow. Their slow pace helped keep them unnoticed as they steadily advanced toward their goal.

However, their slow pace bored Belinda. This morning, she rode next to Jacob for an hour and the thick trees on both sides remained constant and uninteresting. She ran out of ways to entertain herself.

"Let me drive, Jacob."

"What? Have you ever driven mules before?"

"Mules? They look like horses and I've ridden horses."

"I said *driven*. And they're mules."

"Let me take the reins. I've watched you for a while now. I think I've got the idea."

Jacob chuckled. "You do, do you?"

Belinda scowled. "Yes." *Why is he so belligerent?* "I can do it. Go lay down in the back for an hour. What can go wrong? There's nothing out here but trees."

Since he knew this particular stretch of the road well, he handed her the reins and climbed into the wagon bed. His grace surprised her. *How can such a big man move so well?*

How did I jump back here without falling on my face? He waited a few moments and soon feigned sleep while she happily drove the wagon.

Antania sidled over to him. "Will she be alright?" she whispered.

"Millie will stop at the first distraction she sees and this wagon will stop with her. Don't worry."

Sure enough, soon the wagon stopped. Jacob listened to Belinda snap the reins and shout "Git on there," but the wagon wouldn't budge. Finally, he rose.

"Be quiet, girl. The whole nation will find us if you keep yelling."

"What's wrong with your horses? They won't listen."

"They're mules and it's in their nature not to listen. I believe you and they share that trait."

Uncontrollable giggles peeled out from the back of the wagon.

"Now *you* turn on me, Antania?" But she admitted the truth of it and joined in the laughter. After their laughs died to snickers, Belinda gave the reins back to Jacob.

"Master of the mules, have your way." She climbed into the back to keep Antania company.

She's the most peculiar woman I've ever met. At least she keeps the trip interesting. Jacob began to whistle softly as he brought the mules to heel and they started off again.

* * * * *

"Gabe! Mara!" Jacob's voice woke up Belinda and Antania. They sat up and yawned. "Gabe, what brings you out this far?"

"Hello Jacob. I see your cargo is as interesting as mine."

"Ladies, meet my old partner, Gabe and his wife, Mara." A baby began to cry and Mara reached around to pick her up. "And this is…"

"Our daughter, Megan." The women cooed at the baby together and Gabe drew Jacob aside.

"Word is the queen escaped Varlana. You wouldn't happen to know anything about her, would you?"

"These ladies are hitching a ride north. What have you heard?"

"Gailen is hungry for revenge. There's a heavy price on the head of anyone loyal to Salak's memory. Watch yourself, Jacob. Spies are everywhere."

Jacob thanked him for the warning and they each went their way. He thought no more about it.

* * * * *

After five more days' travel, Jacob became sullen and withdrawn. Twice natural disasters forced them to turn south. A huge tree fallen across the road. A collapsed bridge. And now a flooded riverbed. Jacob felt more and more uneasy. Although he tried to hide his worry, Belinda noticed his change of demeanor.

"Jacob, what's wrong?"

"We should be near Oberlan by now, but our way is always blocked. It's like someone plots our course south."

"But it can all be explained. Big storms, rotten wood, a collapsed dam. You saw the evidence yourself."

"Still, it's not natural for so many things to go wrong. Now we're forced to cross the border in the south and add weeks to the trip."

"We are safe. Let's not make trouble where there isn't any."

They left a town called Nottsville a few hours past. Antania hid in the floor under sacks of grain. Belinda rode in front with Jacob. Jacob stopped the wagon.

"You get in the back and hide in between the sacks. I don't like the feel of these woods."

Belinda scrambled into the back of the wagon. "I swear, Jacob, I'm holding you responsible for my bruises. This is tiring." She crouched behind a big box.

Jacob cracked the reins and the wagon began to move.

* * * * *

Ever since Gabe's report, Arbak had tracked the trio. His men forced them into his region and now this rider said they had just left Nottsville. He sent the word, "They're close enough. Move in." He saddled his horse and raced to the meeting.

* * * * *

After a few minutes, Belinda relaxed. She took a breath to speak, but sounds erupted all around her. She pulled a bag of grain over her corner to hide as she listened to gruff voices.

"You there, stop" yelled a voice in front.

"What are you hauling, driver?" came another from the side.

"Goods for delivery and sale in Beechwood. I mean you no harm."

"Show me your travel permissions" Another voice. *How many are out there?* Anxiety picked at her. *Jacob has done this before. We'll be alright.*

Jacob handed over the papers. "Everything is in order."

"We will see."

She heard papers rustle. Then the wagon jostled as men jumped on the back. Cargo shifted against her as sacks of grain were tossed over the side. Crates met the same fate. Soon, her crown of golden hair shone in the sun.

"What have we here?" The man grabbed Belinda by the arm and dragged her to the edge. He shouted into the trees. "Arbak, I think we've found her."

A voice echoed back. "No, that ain't 'er. But take 'er anyway."

Jacob stood and drew a sword. "You'll be backing away from us now."

The men laughed as Arbak emerged from the trees. "Yer a brave one. But yer a stupid one."

He raised a musket and fired. Jacob fell to the ground and Belinda's heart sank.

Antania strained to hear it all. Until the gun fire, her terror kept her silent. Now she banged on the wood above her. Panic led her to use her only weapon. "Stop what you're doing. I am your queen. I order you to stop this now."

Arbak approached the wagon and a terrible smile split open under his nose. He shouted into the floor boards. "I've worked hard to find ya, girl. Thank ya fer stoppin' by." His laugh ricocheted through the trees. "Good work all of ya." He tossed a bag of coin to each one. "I got it from 'ere." Arbak didn't want his hires to know his destination. "Git out a here. I c'n handle two bitches."

The men galloped away and Arbak struck Belinda. She fell against the sacks and struggled for balance. "I only got room fer one. You better run, girl." He pulled out another musket and aimed it at her head. Terrified, Belinda scurried over the side and began to run for the trees. Her mind raced as fast as her legs and, when the shot rang out, the bullet hit a branch inches from her head. The branch ricocheted off the tree, hit her head and knocked her cold. Blood oozed down her cheek.

Arbak wandered into the woods and found where she fell. He kicked at her and rolled her over. The blood on her face and her limp body convinced him she died. He kicked her once more for good measure and whistled a happy tune as he climbed into the wagon and drove away.

Antania wept at the loss of her friends. She pushed against the floor boards, but they wouldn't budge. Helpless, she waited to discover her fate. When the boards finally lifted, she found herself outside a rundown castle. A horrid man leered at her. He reached out to touch her and she slapped his hand away.

"You'll learn whose house this be soon 'nuf." He grabbed her arm and threw her out of the wagon. She struggled to rise, but he kicked her in the back and sent her sprawling. He turned her over, sat on her legs, grabbed a handful of her dress and lifted her face to his. "Yer a special one." He knocked her unconscious, threw her over his shoulder, and carried her inside.

Antania woke on a stone floor chained to the wall in a cold room, dark as the blackest night.

*****

Ja'el, Caleb and Robin moved deeper into the woods and sheltered for two nights under a gigantic mulberry. Caleb stayed with Robin and foraged near their camp for food, while Ja'el searched the area for any sign of Salak's army. He found many frightened people who fled the city, but no soldiers.

They moved their camp farther south and Ja'el searched again. Slowly, Ja'el broadened his search and gathered refugees. After two weeks, he found an abandoned campfire, but no wagons or people. The hot coals warned him of people close by and he slowly scanned the area for occupants. He saw nothing and turned to leave.

A figure burst out of the underbrush. "Ja'el?"

He froze and slowly turned. "I do not recognize you. Why do you think I am this Ja'el?"

"I am Dugan of the king's brigade, assistant to General Janell. I saw you many times at the castle."

Ja'el searched his memory and recalled a junior officer in attendance to General Janell. He remembered a happy man engaged to the General's daughter. Now tension lined his face and pulled his mouth into a thin line.

"Dugan, how many men are with you?"

"I know of at least 50 men in these woods loyal to me. More have left to find their families. We're trying to find the rest and raise an army to take back the city."

"Dugan, the most you can do now is protect the men you have. Let them go. You cannot defeat Gailen's forces with so few and raids will only bring his soldiers deeper into the woods to find and kill you. Do you know how many refugees hide here?"

"We have found none."

"I have brought some to you. Your duty now is to protect the people here. If you want to fight, fight against capture, illness and fatigue. Let their numbers increase while you always lead them safely. They will attract more and your army will rise. We must play a long game now."

"Who is leading Salak's army?"

"I believe you are."

Dugan face went blank. "But...I'm not a strategist. Officers of higher rank plan the long game."

"You are the highest-ranking soldier now. Everyone else has been killed. Do you believe you have the forces to bring victory to Varlana with the king and General Janell dead?"

"No."

"Then build trust with the people here and let your soldiers go home if they choose. When the time is right, we will call them back."

"What will you do?"

"The same. If we each succeed, we will meet again." Ja'el suddenly realized the potential of this situation. "Dugan, we must keep in contact. How well do you know your men?"

"Well enough. Some I have known my whole life."

"Then sit down and let us talk." They put their heads together and planned a communication network. Trusted soldiers received orders to go home to families across Umberlan, but the real intent was to create communication routes across the country. Dugan and Ja'el hunched over a map and decided how messages could be sent from one end of Umberlan to the other without discovery. In the end, Dugan looked at the map with pride.

Ja'el smiled at his expression. "That is how you play the long game, Dugan. Now I must go."

"We will talk again, Ja'el."

* * * * *

Noran and Mortimer closed up Evan Castle quickly. Noran instructed all the laborers to show no allegiance to him if they wanted to live. Then they packed two horses, saddled two more, and quickly rode away. They traveled in the dark of night and kept off the main roads. It slowed them down, but helped avoid the constant patrols.

They skirted the edge of the Bitterlands through Varlana and, once past the ruins, headed north to the foothills of the Aldies. Halfway there, Noran's horse pulled up lame. Mortimer examined him and found a flawed horse shoe.

"But Mortimer, we just shod the horses."

"Yes, but the smithy purposely made this one with a flaw." He walked a short distance back down the trail. "See here, your horse leaves a distinct mark for anyone to follow. I can't believe I didn't see this. Noran, we've been compromised. Who knows how close they are?"

"Then we must hurry. Unload the pack horse and I'll ride her. We can leave this one behind."

"No, it's too late. They've followed us for two days. We must separate. I'll take your horse to the west. You take mine to the north. We'll send the pack horses in the other two directions. I can lead them away from you. By the time they come back, they won't know which horse is yours."

"No, Mortimer. We must stay together. My leg is healed. We will fight side-by-side."

"You must get to Oberlan and lead the revolution. No other Damon can do it. No other Damon is bold enough or strong enough or wise enough."

"Now you sound like a sniveling girl."

"I may be, but you must go north and I must protect you. I will elude the pursuers and join you soon." Before Noran could stop him, he jumped on the injured horse and drove her into the west.

Noran stood for a while after Mortimer disappeared over a rise. He loved Mortimer like a son and now his heart beat heavy with foreboding. *Come soon to Oberlan, Mortimer. My life needs your friendship in it.*

* * * * *

Jacob played "dead" in the road for several minutes after the wagon disappeared. He wanted to be sure Arbak didn't come back. He needed time.

He figured Arbak would take both women and then he could follow and overpower Arbak before he got back to his Castle. But the shock when he heard him shoot Belinda cut him to the core. Jacob saw Arbak violently kick her several times and she didn't move. Steeling his nerves, he decided to rescue Antania first. Then they could both return to bury Belinda.

He limped into the woods to follow the road in secret. He scrambled over the wall near the gate and hurried down the drive to see Arbak carry Antania over his shoulder into the castle. Jacob began to run. He must reach the door before Arbak locked him out.

Thankfully, Antania filled Arbak's arms and he left the door ajar. Jacob waited a moment for him to move further into his house and then, silently, he slowly pushed the door open and quickly scanned the room before him.

Jacob saw a huge dining hall. This door opened near the kitchen for entertainers to enter and exit at celebrations. A thick layer of dust covered everything. *No, too white. It's flour.* Jacob could see Arbak's footprints trail across the floor.

His feet are much smaller than mine. I won't be able to walk in his footsteps to hide my own. He couldn't enter this way. He backed out of the door and began a walk around the exterior wall. He found every other access point bricked over or boarded up. The flour covered floor of the dining hall remained his only option.

Damn you, Arbak. He moved into the woods around the castle. There he stayed for days scouting Arbak's comings and goings. Except there weren't any. Almost immediately, a woman came and knocked. Arbak hustled her in and about an hour later pushed her out. Whatever happened frightened her and she almost ran away. Out of desperation, Jacob conceived a new plan. *I can use her as a shield to push through the door. No, Arbak will just kill her to get to me. And she's too scared. No telling what she'd do.* Every scenario he ran in his head turned into someone dead. *Too risky.*

A delivery wagon arrived once and left boxes on the stoop. An hour passed before Arbak quickly took them in. He used only one arm, the other held a musket ready to fire. *He'll kill me before I get within fifteen feet.*

He shook, weak from hunger and thirst. Finally, he resigned himself to the need for reinforcements and food. At least he could sabotage the wagon. He snuck into the barn, said good-bye to Millie, and rubbed grease off the wheels. *Three more runs and they'll break. I can't see Arbak getting his hands greasy.* It offered a small consolation, but if he could hobble Arbak even a little it would increase his chances of success when he came back to get Antania.

He grabbed a shovel and made his way back to the road to bury Belinda.

* * * * *

Hours after the wagon left, Belinda sat up. Her head pounded and her vision blurred. She blinked hard and rubbed her eyes, but nothing helped. Her body hurt everywhere and she searched for injuries. Just her head and a few bruises. She prepared to stand. Pain stabbed her side and caused her to gasp, which created more pain. *Broken ribs? What happened to me?*

Slowly she climbed back to the road. No wagon. No Jacob. Nothing. She stood in the road and tried to collect her thoughts. *I'm alone. Where am I? What do I do?* She tried not to panic, but a whimper escaped her throat.

"Don't worry, Belinda. I will stay with you for a while."

She jumped at the voice and a stabbing pain from her ribs answered.

Her voice shook with fear. "Is someone out there?"

A man appeared in the road. He reached out his hand. "I will help you if you let me."

"I don't know you."

"Yes. But I was sent to help you. Let me carry you a while." He gathered her up in his strong arms and began to walk. Peace surrounded him, almost like a light, and Belinda's head fell on his shoulder. She began to sleep.

Eventually, the man put her gently down along a wall next to the road. "You are going to Beechwood," he said, and then he disappeared. She stood in confusion until she heard a gate open beside her.

* * * * *

Aleese crumpled the paper in disgust. Another call to Langley. She hated Arbak, hated Langley Castle and hated herself for helping him with his "business." *Not that I have a choice.*

The gate creaked as it opened and Langley loomed over her the long walk down the drive. Arbak met her at the door and ushered her through the castle. At the top of an imposing set of stairs he lit a torch and they began to descend to the dungeons. The smell of urine and decay assaulted them.

"How many do you have now?" she asked.

"Nuff to keep ya busy. I need ya to look at a new one." He sorted through his big ring of keys and opened a door.

A strong voice called out of the darkness. "Why do you dare to hold me here?"

Another smaller, gentler voice answered from another cell. "Honey, stop that. He's gonna beat you good. Best keep your mouth shut."

Arbak moved a few doors over. "Best you do the same, girl." He slammed shut a slot in the door and returned. He entered the cell and motioned to Aleese.

She knelt beside the new woman. Her bruised face turned up and her eyes narrowed in defiance. "I have friends who look for me. You won't keep me here long."

Aleese whispered back, "It's best if you stay quiet. He might let you live if you stay quiet."

The woman turned away and tried to change position. Arbak laughed. "Git comfy, girl. Ya gonna be here til that bairn comes. Then I git to have a go." He leered at her and laughed again.

Aleese finished her exam and stood. "She's strong, but not far along. You need to keep her healthy. Feed her well and keep her warm."

"I'll feed 'er what they all git. Don't tell me how to do buz'ness, woman. Now git."

He locked the cell and followed her up the stairs. At the door he tossed her a small bag of coin, pushed her through, and slammed it behind her.

Her tears blinded her as she left the grounds. *I can't keep doing this, but he'll kill me if I don't.* Confused and distracted, she didn't see the woman in the road.

"Please. Tell me how far is Beechwood."

Aleese turned and pushed Belinda back from the open gate. "You mustn't be seen here." Belinda bent over in pain. "What happened to you?"

"They attacked us on the road. A man shot at me."

Aleese approached her. "Who? Are you hurt?" Your head is bleeding."

"I think I'm alright, but I must find my friends. A woman and a man."

Belinda slumped against the woman and slid to the ground.

"You need help. I am a midwife and know something of healing. Come home with me and let me treat you. Then we will find your friends."

She picked up Belinda and supported her as they walked as quickly as they could to a small house just outside of Beechwood. They trudged inside and Aleese dropped Belinda on a bed. She immediately fell asleep.

Lines of worry creased her brow. The new prisoner in Arbak's dungeon whispered of friends. Could this woman be one of them?

Why does this always happen to me? She couldn't get caught in the middle like this. If Arbak discovered she helped her, he would have her killed. And he could do it. She would have to go. Aleese would clean her up and dress her wound and then she would have to go.

* * * * *

After a day of rest, Belinda began to feel herself again. But she didn't remember this bed or the woman. She decided to be cautious and call herself by another name. After she tried a few she settled on Sharon, a childhood friend. Yes, Sharon from the north to explain her accent. For now, she pretended to sleep.

The midwife entered the room and Belinda/Sharon closed her eyes.

"I know you're awake. How do you feel?"

So much for pretending. She slowly sat up. "I feel better. Thank you."

"You can't stay here. As soon as you're able, you're on your way."

"My name is Sharon. Who are you?"

"Aleese. I'm the local midwife."

"Where am I?"

"Just outside of Beechwood. There's a respectable inn there and two boarding houses if you plan to stay. I'll show you in a few days when you're strong enough." Aleese dropped a bowl on the table beside the bed. "Eat this. It'll make you strong." She left the room without a second glance.

A most gracious host. At least the stew tasted good. She fingered the money secreted in her clothes and guessed she could pay room and board for a few weeks. She'd get a job if the search for Antania and Jacob took longer. She cleaned the bowl and went back to sleep.

* * * * *

A few days later found Belinda nestled in a comfortable room Aleese arranged for her. Her mind considered her situation while Aleese helped her move in. *She's a funny one. I'm glad she found me, but I'm glad to be out of her house.* Then she considered Antania's condition, and thought it a good idea to keep the local midwife as close as possible.

"Will I see you again?" Belinda asked as Aleese turned to go. "I'd like to thank you for taking such good care of me. Maybe I can buy you evening meal tomorrow? You pick your favorite place."

Aleese paused at the door while she decided if she wanted a friendship with this woman. "Dante's Tavern down the street at sunset," and she left the room.

"Hmm" Belinda said to no one. "She sure knows how to make a quick exit."

The next evening Aleese and Belinda entered Dante's Tavern. Music and conversation joined happy laughter and encircled them as they walked to their table. The serving girl approached as soon as they sat down.

"Meg, how are you feeling?"

The very pregnant young woman rubbed her back. "I don't know how much longer I can do this. This baby's getting awful big."

Aleese gently rubbed her belly. "He's fallen. It won't be long now. You send for me the minute you feel the water."

"I will." She disappeared with their order and a few minutes later the cook came to their table at a run.

"Miss Aleese. Meg is calling for you."

Aleese jumped up and leaned over to whisper in Belinda's ear. "I don't know you, but we have an emergency here. Run to my house and bring me my black bag. As fast as you can, hurry."

Belinda ran as fast as she could. By the time she returned with said bag, she gasped for breath and bent over from a monstrous stitch in her side. Aleese knelt on the floor in a closet tending Meg, who struggled in labor.

"Here. What can I do to help?"

"Does the sight of blood unnerve you?"

"No."

"Then get me some clean towels and two bowls of clean water. This child isn't waiting for anybody."

Belinda complied and they both knelt in attendance while Meg's son insisted on being delivered. Two hours later, Aleese washed the blood from a beautiful baby boy. Meg's husband arrived and when he heard the baby cry, he rushed to the closet. Belinda and Aleese backed out to let the happy father join his new family and made their way back to the table. The room erupted in cheers. Belinda became an instant hero.

"I guess we're a good team." Aleese finally smiled.

"I think so."

By the time the night ended, they ate a free dinner, Meg happily returned home to raise her new family, and Belinda took her place, gainfully employed at Dante's Tavern.

* * * * *

When Jacob returned to bury Belinda's body, he couldn't find it. He searched. Oh yes, he searched with every skill he knew, but it seemed she just got up and walked away. He found footprints back to the road, but then nothing. This shook him to the core. *Is she alive after all?*

He asked a few questions in Beechwood, but no one knew of a wounded woman named Belinda. The town buzzed about some miracle birth. He got nervous. Too many questions would make him memorable and leave a trail. He needed to collect people and supplies. Ja'el would be here by the time he got back. They would rescue Antania together and find Belinda. He left the region to start smuggling again. Soon he would return and free her.

"Hang on, girl. I'll get you out."

In a short time, Jacob's funds increased and his plans to return to Langley started to take shape. But Gailen changed the game. Now a successful smuggler needed papers and a signed agreement to give the crown 50% of the profits. Soldiers now patrolled his little used roads and forgotten routes. He was forced to comply with Gailen's demands and his profits dwindled to a trickle.

Arbak created even more restrictions. The closer a wagon got to Langley, the higher the taxes to travel. No wagons could travel within five miles of the castle. Jacob feared Arbak knew how valuable his latest catch was.

He worked steadily and bided his time.

Chapter 20
Needs Must

After Ja'el's encounter with Dugan, both he and Caleb knew to stay in the woods would bring no profit and only put the refugees in danger. They broke camp and headed north to find Jacob's trail.

"Caleb, I have been thinking about our future."

"Yes, Master?"

"You did an excellent job for me in the cabin, but I did not know enough to bring victory."

"You did more than anyone else."

"But not enough. I need to be stronger. Do you understand?"

Caleb looked at Robin and knew Ja'el didn't want to expose their secret. "Yes, but how?"

"You have an instinct for oddities. When we encounter a merchant or find a market, you and I will shop for oddities and books."

Caleb considered this and nodded his head.

"I want to shop."

"I have another job for your nimble fingers, Robin. Caleb and I need different clothes. These robes are not good, but if we send you with money people will question you about us."

"Master, do you want him to steal?"

"I am afraid so. I see no other alternative. Robin, this is only because of extreme circumstances. We will not make this a lifestyle."

"I'm ready." Robin looked Caleb and Ja'el up and down and set off to a local farm to find clothes.

Ja'el and Caleb sat in the trees beside the road. Caleb opened his mouth to speak and then shut it again. Three more times and then Ja'el spoke.

"What is it you want to say, Caleb?"

"I can't believe you did that."

"Needs must."

Caleb turned and threw his hands in the air. "I've been teaching him Morcon's wisdom. You remember him? And now you've sent him off to steal for us."

"I know, Caleb. I am appropriately ashamed."

"How come every time you use the word 'appropriately' I end up with the short stick?"

Just then Robin returned.

"Thank you, my boy. Your timing is perfect." Ja'el examined the clothes with approval. "Your eye is good. I think these will fit fine."

A few minutes later the robes vanished into the packs and a small family of farmers began to walk to the north.

* * * * *

Dugan's trip didn't start easily. Two days into their journey the patrols discovered them. Gailen's patrol attacked the civilian wagons and killed men, women and children indiscriminately. Dugan's troops fought valiantly to save them, but the attack struck fear into the hearts of the caravan. Three wounded soldiers would need care for the rest of the trip. Five families lost their lives.

They couldn't afford to stop and bury the fallen, so they wrapped them tightly in sheets and designated a "death" wagon. When they reached safer ground, they would stop and dig graves.

Dugan reorganized his army to better protect the refugees, but it spread them thin along the train. It made the travelers feel safer, but in reality, made the risk greater. He moved deeper into the forest in the hope Gailen's men wouldn't follow.

But the next day he saw his enemies circle to attack. He raised the alarm and the refugees left their wagons to gather in one place. Dugan's soldiers formed defensive lines and they readied for battle.

Gailen's men charged out of the trees and the fight began. Swords rang out as men parried and lunged. Shouts of pain from soldiers and civilians alike filled the air and sent birds to flight. The bodies of the dead and dying began to collect on the ground.

Dugan's mind moved into a kind of trance. His body moved in the familiar ducks, dodges, lunges and stabs it trained for, but he had never actually killed a man before. Wounded many, yes, but the thought of a kill repulsed him. He fought with caution.

A green soldier near-by witnessed this weakness and ran in to attack. He wore an evil grin, sure of his victory. His blade moved in a blur as he drove Dugan back into the huddled civilians. Dugan saw him turn to swipe at a small girl whose parents grabbed her just in time. His mind went blind with rage and he ran at the green soldier.

This pleased the soldier. He allowed Dugan to advance and at the last minute stabbed just short of Dugan's ribs. He smirked as he waited for Dugan's momentum to carry him onto the sword.

Dugan stepped to the side, slapped the blade away, and the sword grazed his hip. He barely noticed. He turned to meet his adversary who ran toward him. Dugan pretended to fall, and as his enemy towered over him, sliced his sword through the meat of his thigh to cut the artery.

Blood spurted out of the green uniform, but he would not be denied his kill. He turned with the last of his energy, determined to kill Dugan. Dugan also calculated the success of his strike and kept his distance. When the soldier fell to his knees, Dugan moved in and sliced off his head.

"For King Salak and General Janell." The head rolled to one side. The body fell to the other. Blood still trickled out of the leg. Dugan looked at the carnage and realized this man's death fell on his hands. His heart rejoiced at the death of another and then he hated himself. The people behind him cheered for his victory. The green soldiers retreated. The fight ended, but Dugan's battle became even more intense.

He dropped to his knees and screamed. It rose from the depths of his being, a primal thing; the sound of a tortured soul. He took a life and now life demanded a piece of him. He felt himself ripped apart and he sobbed, helpless to stop it. His soldiers gathered around in empathy and shielded him from the stares of the refugees who didn't understand, couldn't understand.

They waited for the inevitable. Finally, Dugan rose; his body rigid and face like stone. "We will leave the dead here. Say what you will over them. We can't be burdened while we run for our lives. Our pace will be fast. Put the wounded and the young in the wagons. We won't stop or slow down. We will leave now."

He scanned the battle field for a count of the dead. His losses remained small, but the list of soldiers who needed care for their wounds grew. He assigned women to tend them and emptied wagons for them. By the time they left, furniture, chests, and dead men littered the ground.

For the next day and night, they didn't stop. Dugan knew the soldiers would return with reinforcements and they couldn't hide their trail. They needed to be as far away as possible. Hopefully, they could stay ahead of their pursuers until they reached safety. His dwindling and demoralized army bent in weariness as they marched onward. Another attack might be their death.

When the pace slowed, Dugan stopped the train to rest for half a morning. Then they pushed on again. He sent scouts behind to track Gailen's progress. At first good news, but in only two days soldiers appeared.

Dugan left command of the train to his junior and took twelve archers to confront the patrol. When they calculated their pursuers' route, they hid themselves behind trees and waited. They notched their arrows at the sound of the march. When they came in sight, Dugan gave the signal to draw.

He let the forward soldiers go past before he gave the order to fire. Then again. Then a third time. The last of Gailen's men turned in disarray when Dugan's troops sprang from the trees. Most of the green soldiers lay dead. The rest they finished off quickly. This time Dugan's men survived unharmed and no enemy escaped.

"Leave them. We must move." They left the dead for Gailen to bury and rejoined the wagons.

"I believe we'll make it now," he reported to his junior. The refugees received this good news with relief, but they kept up the pace to insure it. No more soldiers threatened them, but in the foothills large animals stalked the group, hungry for their supplies and children. They climbed higher and the temperature fell until they reached a snow line as they crossed the top of the Aldies Mountains.

Snow never fell in the balmy plains of Umberlan and the bone chilling cold caught everyone by surprise. The snow slowed them down, but

Dugan pushed relentlessly. Their relief waited down the other side. The snow lay so thick it reflected what little moonlight reached the ground. Dugan took advantage of this and traveled all night. By mid-afternoon the next day the snowfall turned to flurries and the ground began to clear.

They pushed on until nightfall when they made camp. They built big, warm fires and took stock. Four of the wounded soldiers succumbed to the bitter cold. Men moved the bodies into another wagon and now the unused wagon they broke up for firewood. They would bury their friends when they reached warmer ground. Right now, the rest of the refugees needed to survive the night.

By the time Dugan guided his company through the Northern outpost and into Oberlan, he led battle-hardened, but exhausted men. The road followed a river until it emptied into a lake. There they made camp, buried the dead, and allowed themselves to collapse.

Chapter 21
Journey to Madness

The job at the Tavern suited her. She met almost everyone in town and made friends easily. But no one knew of Antania and Jacob. They just disappeared. Of-course, Belinda didn't know who robbed them on the road. She really didn't remember much at all which made questions difficult. She also didn't know who she could trust, and the wrong question might bring her trouble.

Her frustration grew. She must escalate; pick someone and pressure them to find out what they knew. She set her eyes on Aleese and bent her mind to it. She and Aleese grew closer as they tended the local women. She provided a fount of information about local medicine, but didn't help with Belinda's search. However, she observed Aleese, once every week, take her bag and keep a mysterious appointment. Belinda decided to discover where she went.

The next night, Belinda waited in the dark outside Aleese's house and, like clockwork, Aleese emerged and turned to walk away from town. Belinda followed quietly about fifty paces behind. After a time, she saw her enter the gate where they first met. She slipped in behind her and observed her enter a side door in a rundown castle. She crept down the lane hidden in the tree line until she hunkered down and waited close to the castle.

An hour later, Aleese emerged and plodded down the drive. Belinda followed and announced herself at the gate.

"Aleese, what is happening here?"

Aleese sprang into the air with a yell and ran through the gate ahead of Belinda, but Belinda quickly caught up to her.

Aleese turned on her in fury. "What are you doing on castle grounds?"

"I followed you. I'm sorry. I'm curious about this appointment you never let me help with."

"Your curiosity will get you killed, Sharon."

"What's going on in there?"

"I won't tell you. Stop asking."

"Then tell me about the castle. Is it the Langley Castle I've heard about?"

"Yes. It's run by an odious man named Arbak. Before him, his father ruled. Kanane, an equally odious man."

"Is Arbak married? Do you attend his wife?"

"In a manner of speaking. Stop this. I won't talk of it anymore." Aleese began to cry as she ran into her home and slammed the door.

Belinda waited a while and then knocked softly before she entered. She found Aleese in her favorite rocking chair. Belinda made them both a cup of tea and joined her by the warmth of the fire.

"I didn't mean to upset you, but now I'm concerned. What tortures you so much?"

"Sharon, if I told you it would put you in danger, too. Please don't ask me anything else."

Quietly Belinda waited. *How can I get her to open up to me?* She doubted this opportunity would return. When Aleese began to relax, Belinda spoke again.

"Aleese, I'm your friend above all. I have kept your secrets. I hope I've earned your trust. Maybe it's time I trusted you."

Aleese turned away from the fire to face her. She waited.

"My name is Belinda Cordone. I served as companion to Queen Antania before Gailen's forces destroyed the city. We traveled with a smuggler, trying to escape to Oberlan. Now I know someone sabotaged our route and forced us to travel farther and farther south until he attacked us not far from here. He captured the queen and left the man and me for dead. I search for her, Aleese. Is she at Langley Castle?"

Aleese's eyes widened with every sentence. *This is the new woman's friend and the prisoner is the queen.* This realization burst the dam of her defenses. Arbak must be stopped. She told Belinda about the women in Arbak's dungeon and his hold on her. He forced her to be complicit in his dreadful business.

174

Belinda's empty tea cup dropped to the floor. "We have to get her out of there."

"There is no way to get her out. Arbak stands over me while I examine his women. He escorts me down and back out. And he would kill us both if I brought you with me or he discovered you there."

'There has to be a way."

"She is lost to you."

Belinda suddenly stood. "No. I owe her my life. I *will* find a way. Can you give her a message?"

"I can try."

"Tell her you know me and I am here for her." She left the house deep in thought.

* * * * *

This dark nightmare never ended. Antania saw no sun, no moon. Time lost its meaning. Every once-in-a-while the woman would come into her cell and examine her. The last time she spoke with the horrible man who fed her.

"This one is carrying twins." Then she left, the door slammed shut, and the darkness descended again.

At first, she used her chains to pull herself up and stand hunched over. It relieved the ache in her bones against the floor. But now her belly grew too big. She couldn't maneuver around the chains to stand. She sat day after day, turned this way and that, but the pain became unbearable and she cried constantly.

Memories of her mother's garden and her beloved Ja'el kept alive her threads of sanity. *So long ago. So far away.* She took a deep sniff in a doomed attempt to smell any trace of earth or vegetation. The pungent odor of urine and dust burned her throat. She coughed and gagged and spit, but the odor consumed her senses and she began to cry again. *I will never see the sun or feel the earth in my fingers.* Her soul finally broke free of hope. *I will not eat. This must end.* The babies became her enemies. They prevented her from standing and forced her into deeper and deeper pain. *I will kill us all.* She smiled at the thought of victory.

All at once, the cell filled with a warm glow. Antania covered her eyes against the light, but a gentle hand took hers and she looked into the face of a smiling man.

"I have come to tell you freedom will be yours again. Do not give up."

Hysterical laughter bubbled up into her mouth. "Look at me. There is no hope here. Go away."

He sat beside her and moved her into his lap. It didn't seem possible, but his body was warm and comfortable. A silver thread appeared in his hand. It glowed with peace in the darkness around them. He sang a soft lullaby as he planted the thread in her mind and the pain in her body melted away. He rocked her until she could almost smell the mint and moss of her mother's garden.

The clank of the turning lock disturbed her dream.

"Peace must reign the day," he said and then he vanished. Darkness closed over her once again.

In came the woman to examine her. Antania turned her face away. *If you're so concerned about these babies, take them now and leave me be.* The woman leaned over to whisper in her ear.

"I have met Belinda and she is working for you." Then the woman left.

Belinda? Will she bring my freedom? The darkness closed in and another voice whispered in her ear. *Another life. Belinda is no part of this endless suffering. It's just another torment. I won't remember. I won't,* Hope faded in this place. Starved. She laughed at the image of a bony body called hope. *You go back to your corner and meet your fate. The fate of us all.* Death lingered and waited in the darkness. Antania mused to herself as she imagined all the ways hope died; all the ways she could die. What else was there to do?

* * * * *

The babies in her womb felt a vague sense of danger and reached for one another. They only knew each other. They clung together, constantly touching, always aware of the other; one identity together.

Their minds joined and sought comfort from the other. The fear and panic they felt melted away as they rested in each other's love. Peace began to reign in the womb.

* * * * *

Antania began to calm. *I can hold on. There is still hope while he breathes.* She didn't understand where these feelings of comfort came from, but she embraced them like a lover. *I will hold on. I will.*

* * * * *

"I told her your message, but I couldn't wait for her answer. She is not well."

"What do you mean? Is she sick?"

"Not physically. I've seen it before. She's going away in her mind. She needs something to hold on to or she will go mad. Maybe your message will be enough."

Belinda winced. "How soon will she deliver?"

"It won't be long now. Twins."

"Twins! We can't let Arbak sell them." She paced the floor. Then she suddenly stopped and pounded the wall with her fist. "This is impossible. I can't believe there's nothing we can do."

"Arbak has been selling babies for many years. He's smart. We can't get the better of him."

Belinda's frustration boiled over and she turned on her friend. "You did this. If he didn't have you, he wouldn't have the business. You keep him selling. You are just as guilty as he. Don't talk to me about what we can't do. You just want to keep getting paid."

She slammed the door on her way out and ran home. Sometimes the game got too hard and someone got hurt. This time Aleese took the punch. She didn't know how to fix it and right now she didn't care. She threw herself on her bed and tried to plan Antania's escape. In the end, she admitted maybe Aleese knew what she talked about. Antania's escape seemed impossible. *I've failed you, my queen.* She closed her eyes and turned her face to the wall.

Chapter 22
A New King

Varlana's glory turned to desolate ruin. Gailen's men rampaged for a week. They raped the women and girls foolish enough to stay, looted and burned every house and merchant, and killed for pleasure until they got bored. The citizens who managed to flee the city hid in the surrounding woods. Tobin volunteered to round them up, but Gailen stopped him.

"They are soft, used to luxury. Let them suffer for their selfish loyalty to a king who asked nothing from them. Eventually, they'll die and the wild animals will have food. We shouldn't waste time on them."

For days Gailen's soldiers searched the woods for Salak's men. Dugan and his troops fled, but they still found and killed a few confused stragglers. They discovered a cabin by the garden field and burned it down like the palace.

They destroyed the water system. Rivers and streams flowed again through the Bitterlands and began to nourish the thirsty land.

"In a few years this will be farmland again. Enough food for a great army. Jakfa, you must recruit farmers. Promise them free land for one harvest."

"Father, can we afford to give all this land away?"

"Listen to what I say closely. Promise them free land for one harvest."

Jakfa contemplated his father's statement. "Then after the harvest there will be crops to tax. All the work and expense to begin production falls on their shoulders. Their success becomes ours. If they fail, we lose nothing."

Gailen smiled and patted his son on the shoulder. "Yes, Jakfa. You figured it out nicely." Suddenly he slapped Jakfa's face. "But you must understand these things faster. I don't have time to explain everything to you."

By the time Gailen left Varlana, piles of ash replaced the palace and the grounds around it. The beautiful banners and silks that survived filled soldiers' bags for sweethearts and wives at home.

Gailen, Jakfa, and Tobin surveyed the damage from the north hill.

"Varlana never looked so beautiful, Jakfa."

"It's as it should be, father."

"Tobin, have you sent the messengers?"

"Yes, my king. By tomorrow night every town and hamlet will know the traitors of Umberlan. The price for the Damons is high. Who will be able to resist such a purse?"

"I will return to fill those empty pikes, but from this moment the capital of Umberlan is Castle Chimaya and Tenebray."

* * * * *

Tenebray stood bigger than a town, but not quite a city. For many months, Gailen planned to make Tenebray Umberlan's new capital. He built many homes and buildings which stood empty for months in anticipation of his victory. He expanded the marketplace to accommodate twice the merchants which dwarfed the modest number who sold on market day. The citizens didn't complain. Complaints brought deadly force, but they wondered why their Damon wasted so much of their taxes on useless space.

Now Tenebray began to grow. Soon the market burst at the seams, every building filled. New construction began on a formidable city wall. Property inside the wall increased in value and sold to dignitaries and the richer merchants.

Citizens who lost their homes and businesses created a crude collection of shacks just outside the city gates. They hung onto the threads of their business until Tobin destroyed their neighborhood and forced them to go. Like a band of refugees, they packed their meager belongings and trudged away.

Gailen cracked down on free enterprise. He'd set his sights on Oberlan and needed to expand his military force. So, he hoarded the resources of Umberlan. All businesses now operated under licenses sold by his Damons. Taxes and bribes filled his coffers. If the Damons added some for themselves, he didn't mind as long as they gave the lion's share to him.

Each Damon received orders to raise an army. Men of a certain age found themselves conscripted to serve an indefinite period of time.

Damons also added their own taxes to pay for their armies and improvements to their castles. The population felt crushed under the excesses.

"North," the oppressed people cried. "North to the Aldies." The Aldies Mountains became the way to freedom, and the roads into Oberlan began to fill with Umberlan refugees. Gailen created guard posts along the northern border to force them back. He made it illegal to travel into the mountains, unless you carried the correct papers. With the roads closed, many people lost their lives in an attempt to cross the harsh mountain range on the animal trails. Others paid handsomely for smugglers to carry them across. A man with a wagon and the right papers could become rich very quickly.

Gailen recruited smugglers who reported movements to him. They split their profits with him and traveled across the border without cargo checks. If a smuggler's name did not appear on Gailen's payroll, he disappeared and guards seized his cargo. Gailen tied Umberlan tightly to his purse strings and the army began to grow.

CHAPTER 23
TREASURES IN AN OLD CHEST

For days the trio followed the trail left by Jacob. Caleb and Ja'el took day jobs as they moved. Soon they saved enough coin to buy a pack horse. Now they could pick up their pace.

When they reached a town, they would stay for a week or so while they replenished their resources. Ja'el often hired on as a scribe or a farm-hand. Caleb usually found work for himself and Robin at the local stable or smithy. This earned enough coin to rent modest rooms. They all took long baths and turns in the soft beds.

Every market day, Caleb and Robin would explore. One day, Caleb discovered a new tent of oddities. He roamed around and scanned the merchandise and purchased a charm. When Ja'el returned he showed him his prize.

Ja'el snapped in a breath. "Caleb, where did you find this?"

"An old seller in the market today. His whole tent ran over with this stuff."

The sun hung low in the sky; the market had closed for the day.

"Did he have books, too"

"Yes, in the back. But they're old and musty. Some in pieces. I saw no value in them."

"It is not the look of a thing that gives it value. Robin, stay here. Caleb and I must walk."

Robin hated those words. It meant Ja'el and Caleb went off to do grown-up things without him. He sighed and slowly scanned the room for entertainment. Nothing. Completely bored, he wandered down to the kitchen in hopes of a snack. His young mind knew Ja'el meant stay in the building, not just the room. The kitchen smelled heavenly and the cook liked him. He smiled as he skipped down the hall.

* * * * *

Ja'el hoped they'd find the oddities trader still in town. If he could find him, maybe some after-market trades could be negotiated.

"Take me to this tent, Caleb. I must talk to this man."

"It's here, at the end."

No tent appeared, but a loaded wagon stood near the spot. Ja'el approached and a voice shouted out of the darkness.

"You there. Get away from my wagon."

"Sir, I am interested in a purchase from you. I worked through the day, but I hope you want to make more money now."

"Well then, what are you looking for?"

"My son says you have old books. I am a scribe and collect old books and manuscripts. Might I have a look at yours?" He jingled the money in his pocket.

The man quickly pulled out a box from his wagon. "You're in luck. They're right on top." He opened the box. "There you are. Come take a look"

The twilight made the titles difficult to see, but Ja'el found three worth a read and paid the man handsomely for them.

The money energized the merchant. "Anything else you want to see?" He shifted his weight back and forth in anticipation of another sale.

"No, thank you."

"I'll be back in two markets," he called to their backs as they walked away.

"Master, what are they?"

"Our path to victory. I did everything I knew to save the palace, but I did not know enough. Everything I know will never be enough. We must learn of wizardry and magic, Caleb. It is dangerous and no one must know. It will also be hard to keep this from Robin, but we must."

"What are you going to do?"

Ja'el's eyes were wide with anticipation. He held a book out and softly rubbed the cover. "Learn, Caleb, learn and practice. When we return to the battle, I will be ready." He held them to his chest. "We must search every town we come to for prizes like these books."

He gently opened a book to show Caleb the pages. "See this script? See how it almost dances on the page?"

Caleb stared at the letters. "No. It's just a book."

"I will teach you what I know and we will see if you have the gift. You have a good instinct for charms. I believe there is more to you we have not discovered."

Caleb marveled at Ja'el's excitement and hardly kept up as Ja'el strode to their rooms. When they returned, they found Robin happily asleep in the bed. Caleb wiped the crumbs off Robin's chin and sighed.

"How can a boy eat so much?"

"He is growing. I seem to remember another hungry boy not so long ago."

They laughed together as they settled in for the night. Caleb slept while Ja'el read by lamplight until dawn.

CHAPTER 24

⌐ THE PRICE OF FREEDOM ⌐

Pain everywhere. No part of him avoided the intense squeeze and, for the first time, he felt fear. *Every bone will break if this doesn't stop.* This radical change hurt him. Helpless, he hoped for freedom.

What happened to the dark and warm? His whole life he lived in the cozy place with "the other." They moved together, intertwined, bonded by their shared experience. Until this pain.

Now the other vanished. Violent forces pushed him down a very narrow way, barely wide enough for him to get through. He couldn't breathe, arms locked to his side. Panic began to rise in him. *How much longer?* Waves of pressure propelled him on until, suddenly, he breathed air for the first time and his entire world would never be the same.

Antania lay on the floor and moaned weakly. Aleese knelt on the floor in front of her. Belinda's outburst made her face her shame and guilt. Maybe this woman could be her redemption. She moved near Antania's head and pretended to wipe her brow. "Stay still," she whispered. "He will think you're dead and take you out of here."

Aleese shook with fear. *What am I doing? I'm not the brave one.* For a year now she watched the death toll of this hellhole rise. *Please, let me save just one.* She wrapped the newborn in an old towel and waited. The second baby wasn't delivering. She stood and lied.

"It's a boy. There's no more and this girl won't last another hour."

"Are ya sure? I been waitin' for twins. Can't sell jes one. What's I s'posed to do with this?"

"Your filthy business I don't care about. My work's done. Pay me and make your decisions by yourself."

"You mind your mouth, missy. Don't forgit I can ruin you." Arbak handed her the fee and looked at the woman on the floor. *She's no good no more. Better put her out.*

Aleese escaped the dungeon cells, stole some blankets, and ran out of the castle. Hidden behind some trees, she watched Arbak bring the wagon around and load the bodies inside. *Stay in there, little baby. Just a little while longer.* She followed at a distance until Arbak stopped near the castle's outer wall and began to unload his gruesome cargo. He dragged the woman across the wagon floor and dumped her on the ground. He kicked her off the side of the drive and she rolled out of sight. *Oh no. Can a baby survive this?* Every bone in her body wanted to run out and save her, but Aleese forced herself to wait for the wagon to leave.

* * * * *

Antania would do anything to escape. For months chains locked her to the wall and forced her to live in her own filth. The horrid man leered at her every time he entered. Twice he talked of rape. Once he licked his lips as he touched her. Helpless in her chains, fear became a constant companion. Her only relief was the memory of the strange man who came to comfort her. Now she believed he was a dream.

In the darkness of her life, she pushed her memories away and existed in the grey mist of denial. She tried to hold on, but lost the battle. The pain of labor only woke her to harsh reality. No more tears fell on her cheeks. All her emotions blended into nothingness. She turned into a dead woman breathing.

And now this woman called her back. A flicker of hope caused her to cooperate. The man unlocked her chains for the delivery. To lay down brought blessed relief. *Maybe...* She rolled on her side to hide her breath and lay still as death. The man left. The open door tempted her. *I could run away.* But she didn't know what waited on the other side of it. She imagined all sorts of horrible things. Then another pain slammed up from her womb. The woman said play dead. She grabbed the life-line, stayed on the floor and tried not to breathe.

His shoulder cut into her stomach when he carried her out, but still she remained limp. Her head hit the floor of the wagon hard when he hefted her in, but she breathed fresh, cold air. Her limp body showed no sign of life. She heard her baby cry nearby. She remained still. Pain wracked her body again, but she filled her mind with the only hope-filled words she knew. *I must not move.* She fought a gasp as the pain hit again. To save herself and her child, she drifted into hopelessness again.

188

* * * * *

Arbak grunted at his foolishness. This young one could have made seven or eight more before he used her up. And royalty, too. A heavy loss to the profits. Maybe he'd better start fires to heat his dungeon. Women and babies died too often this winter.

He took her to a mass grave near a break in the castle wall. If anyone found the bodies and traced them back to him, his whole business would be exposed. But this particular ravine crossed an animal path. Hungry carnivores learned quickly where to find an abundance of food. He grinned. *Nature and me got an agreement.*

* * * * *

When the wagon stopped, Antania felt herself dragged to the edge and dumped on the ground. Every bone in her body erupted in pain. When he kicked her down a hill she rolled with no resistance and stopped with a jolt. The wagon moved away. Still she didn't move. The woman didn't direct her, she didn't know what to do.

She felt something walk up her arm and something else crawled across her face. She opened her eyes and saw a dull pair of blank eyes look back. A beetle walked across those dusty dead eyes and she bolted up to find herself on top of a pile of bodies. Dead women all. Skin, like jelly, fell off bones. Beetles, worms and a million other bugs crawled everywhere, even her own legs, arms and hair. Gnaw and bite marks riddled the corpses.

She stood in shock and the weight of her feet caved in the skull she stood on. She fell face down in the muck of a decomposed stomach. Her worst nightmare come true. *I have passed from one hell to the next.*

Her mind broke. When she opened her mouth to scream it filled with flies. When she fought to escape, the bodies rolled and broke underneath her and she fell back again. Each reach for escape resulted in a slip back into the pit of death. Every failure shattered her psyche a bit more.

Aleese heard screams of panic from the ravine and began to run. She saw the woman trying to scramble out.

"Take my hand. Here, over here."

Aleese pulled with all her strength and the woman finally emerged. She moved erratically, like an insane thing. Aleese stared as Antania began to stomp her feet and tear her clothes to ribbons. When she stood naked, she began to pull out her hair in great handfuls. Suddenly, she doubled over and let out a long wail.

"Your baby's coming. Hang on, don't move." Aleese caught the baby before it hit the road and the afterbirth fell with a splat right after. She cut the cord, wrapped the baby and put her in her medical bag. The woman shook in the cold night air, blood streamed down her face and legs.

Aleese kicked the ruined clothes down the ravine and covered the woman with blankets. "It's all right. You're with me now. The bad man is gone. It's all right." She picked up her bag and slowly led the woman down the drive.

* * * * *

Unaware of events behind him, Arbak pushed the wagon on. *The big church with the do-gooder priest. I'll dump the live one there. What'm I s'posed to do with it?. If he lives, I c'n come back and git 'im. Some heirless puff will pay a pretty penny for 'im.*

* * * * *

Noise. Cold. So cold. Sounds muted in the dark and warm now pierced his ears. *Where are you, my other?* No answer. Half of his identity just vanished. He squirmed against the tightly wrapped blanket around him and tried to reach for her. But he lost the battle and finally gave in to sleep.

He didn't wake up when his mother and sister tumbled down a ravine outside the castle. He didn't wake up while the carriage drove miles away to the church. The bitter cold overcame him while he lay on the church's doorstep, and death began to woo him into never-waking sleep.

CHAPTER 25
A MYSTERIOUS CHILD

Gennie woke to the sound of a wagon at the parsonage door. She slept light and couldn't ignore the squeaky wheels. Once again John worked late somewhere in the bowels of this house, so she rose to investigate. She opened the door to an empty street, but the bundle on the doorstep made her heart sink.

"John." Gennie's voice echoed down the stone halls, but her husband didn't answer. She took a deeper breath and yelled again, "Father John. Someone left a baby outside"

She wrapped him inside her sweater and ran to the parlor. The big fireplace blazed up when she added a log and she gathered a few more onto the hearth to keep it burning. Exposure to the night's bitter cold might settle into this poor baby's lungs. He wheezed pitifully and she inched her chair dangerously close to the fire.

Oh, what a sweet thing. She held him close and slowly rocked. *Who could have done such a thing?* Babies on her doorstep didn't happen anymore. She and Father John put their dreams aside and committed to a life-time of raising someone else's children. They gave up children of their own and taught their parish the value of a child's life. Now a new generation had grown up and knew how to celebrate a birth. *Whose baby is this now?*

Gennie ran through the list of possible mothers she knew. *No. This child is not premature and none of the local women are ready to birth. Who is she?* While she pondered this new situation, Father John entered the room.

"These old bones don't jump up in the middle of the night anymore." He stared wide-eyed at the bundle in her arms. "What have you got there?"

"Someone left a baby on our doorstep. She's so adorable. Do you think it's starting again?"

John panicked. *A baby on the doorstep? I can't do this again.* He fought for control. "So, it's a girl then."

191

"I haven't checked, but she has to…" Gennie interrupted herself as she peeked under his blanket. "Hmmm. Well, *he's* the cutest thing I've ever seen"

"No note?" he asked as he sank into an armchair near the fire. "Any clue to his identity?"

"Nothing. Just this old ratty blanket. I've been thinking about potential mothers in the neighborhood and there's no one who could have given birth tonight." She jumped out of the chair. "Here, you hold him while I get some water to give him a bath. He's a mess."

Father John held the weak infant. *God, what are You doing? I'm past the age of family.* He remembered the attitude of mothers who so easily gave up their babies to die so many years ago. *Is it worth finding his mother? Will she care for him if he's returned to her?* Legitimate questions with no answers.

Gennie returned with a roasting pan and a kettle of water she hung over the flames to warm.

"You look like you're going to cook him." he snorted.

Gennie rolled her eyes. "Only you would put that together. You didn't think I'd wash him in the big bathtub, did you?"

He watched Gennie check the water temperature and carefully hold the baby in the bath while she used a soft cloth to gently rub off the blood and grime. All her attention fixed on his care. John's heart fell as he watched Gennie bond with the helpless baby.

He can't stay here. We're too old. He's truly abandoned, but he can't stay here. Besides, he's so sick he may not last the night.

"Gennie, what are we going to do with him?"

"He has to stay with us, of course, while we look for his family."

"A fool's errand. This is the biggest church for many miles. He could have come from anywhere."

"He needs the healer. In the morning I'll take him to Josiah. He might know something."

John sighed softly. "Gennie. He's frail. He may not make it through the night."

"We can start with our own. You and I have lived here all our lives. We know these people and they trust us. I'll ask Sharon to help me, did you know she helps Aleese deliver babies? It's amazing what she knows. Between the two of us we'll find his family. He's so cute…" Her voice trailed off as John watched her coo at the infant.

"And if we aren't successful? If he doesn't live or we can't find his family, what then? We're old now. We can't commit to this child."

"John, how many years did we wish for a child of our own?" She gave the clean boy back to him with a gentle kiss and began to make a compress to help him breathe. "We have always welcomed children here. Old we are, but not so past it we can't help another abandoned child."

"And what if we do find his family? Will you give him back? I can't bear the thought of your heart broken over this. There are too many unanswered questions. Don't attach yourself to this boy. He can't stay here."

Gennie smiled. "I love you. I'll be fine. Let's think about this boy and not ourselves."

Silence filled the room while they pondered their thoughts.

"Tomorrow I'll search for the mother. He'll be back with his family by dinner time."

"Maybe so, maybe not. I'm talking to Josiah and Sharon either way."

The tension rose between them as another silence fell on the room and they listened to the baby struggle to breathe.

* * * * *

Belinda took no notice of the cold as she slowly walked home. Her long, busy shift at the tavern exhausted her, but her mind turned (as it often did) to Antania's plight. Lost in thought, she almost bumped into Aleese at her door. They avoided each other since Belinda's accusations. Now Belinda tried to repair some of the damage.

"Oh! Aleese, I'm so sorry. I didn't mean those awful words I said. I'm just so worried. Can you begin to forgive me?"

"No, you're right. I am complicit and afraid. But now things have changed. Come with me, I need your help."

Belinda finally saw the quiet figure shivering next to Aleese and followed without hesitation. When they entered her cabin, Aleese sat the figure by the fire, gently placed her bag on the floor next to her, and removed the blanket from her head.

Belinda gasped. "Antania" She turned to Aleese. "How…What…Did you…?"

"You're right about everything. I have turned into the very person I used to hate. At least I can do this one thing to try to make amends."

"What happened to her?"

Aleese shared the ghastly tale of Antania's escape and her self-destruction on the road. "I've never seen anyone… I don't know what to do now."

"You have brought her to safety. All we can do is quietly care for her until she comes back to herself. She is strong. I believe she will heal."

Aleese opened her mouth to speak, but Belinda interrupted her thought.

"I will help you care for her. Let's make a schedule. She shouldn't be alone."

"Thank you, Belinda, but I'm busy right now. I need someone who will live here."

A small cry began from inside Aleese's medical bag. Belinda's eyes grew wide and she looked inside.

"You saved her baby. But I thought she carried twins?"

"This one I could rescue. Arbak took the other, a boy."

Now the baby worked up a good cry.

"She wants to eat." Aleese took her to Antania and placed the crying baby in her lap. Antania remained motionless and completely ignored her baby's cries. Belinda held the baby up to Antania's breast and she began to drink.

"This is impossible, Aleese. How are you going to manage?" Suddenly, Belinda made up her mind. She abandoned her queen once. She would not do it again. "I will quit my job and move in. Who else can you trust?" She stared at Aleese and dared her to object. "I'll be the one to live here. Just accept it."

Aleese relented and Belinda went home to retrieve her things. *It is you, my queen. It is you.*

* * * * *

The next day Gennie found a softer, warmer blanket for the baby and they set off to town. The baby breathed easier. She silently thanked her mother for an education in the medicinal value of local plants. Still, she would see the healer today. It would be a walk for her, but she didn't trust her home remedies would be enough.

She liked Beechwood. Modest houses shaded by old growth trees lined lovely lanes in quiet neighborhoods. But the main street bustled with activity. The shops of butchers, dress makers, and craftsmen mingled with the booths and tents of farmers who sold produce and livestock. All the smaller villages came to Beechwood for the market.

The once grand Langley Castle, home of past kings, stood still; a rundown relic, miles out of town. No one knew the man who lived there now. His reclusive habits created nasty rumors about his blood-line. It didn't matter. The Damon never talked to anyone.

She hugged the child close as she wormed her way through the crowd. By the time they reached Sharon's house, he started to complain.

Belinda couldn't believe her fortune. Just a minute more and Gennie would have missed her. Gennie's visit surprised her, but the cries from the bundle she carried surprised her more. Between Antania and this new development, she could barely keep her thoughts straight.

"What in the world are you doing with a baby?"

"He arrived at my door last night. Poor thing almost froze to death."

Belinda began to warm up some goat's milk. She raided a small stash of baby supplies Aleese kept with her and before Gennie finished her story, the baby happily worked on breakfast.

"He can't live on goat's milk, Gennie. There are two new babies in town. I'm sure Marla or Beckie will share their milk with him."

Gennie liked Sharon. Her big heart made her easy to talk to and she knew how to keep a secret. Still, Gennie decided to be careful what she told her. As she told Sharon the story, she picked only the most important facts. Since there wasn't much to tell, she finished quickly. Gennie's decision to raise the child if his family couldn't be found she considered too personal to share.

Belinda did some quick math. *The timing's right. But she carried twins. I need to talk with Aleese. Thank goodness I forgot my brush or I would have missed her.*

"I can't think of anyone I know who could've done this. I'm truly horrified."

Gennie knew she wanted more information, but she refused to say more.

"Would you keep your ear to the ground for us, Sharon? Any news about who he is will be helpful."

"Nothing but an old blanket wrapped around him? Anyone around watching, maybe?"

Gennie shook her head. "If you would talk to Aleese for me? Maybe she has news from other towns. I'm truly desperate for information. This boy needs his mother."

"Yes. And I'll talk to Marla and Beckie. One of them will come to you later today."

"How about I send Father John by to pick them up?"

"Excellent. I'll see what I can do to round up some clothes and diapers, too."

"Thank you, Sharon. What would I do without you?"

She turned away from home when she left Sharon. *I hope Josiah is in today.* Her worries reached a fever pitch when she walked through the gate and saw a sign on his door. "Out on a call, be back soon," but she saw his buggy tied to the fence and she heard noises inside, so she entered the office.

A tall, slender man leaned into a cabinet and read labels on bottles. "Josiah?"

"Miss Gennie, how are you doing?" His smile faded. "Is everything alright?" She raised an eyebrow at his obvious concern, but she pushed her feelings aside and held out the baby.

"Look what dropped on our doorstep last night. He's not breathing easy. I'm hoping you have time to check him."

"Did John walk all this way with you?"

Why is he asking about John?

"No." She walked across the room and opened the blanket. "Could you please look at him?"

Josiah did a quick exam. "It looks like your compress is doing a good job. I've got to get going. There's been an accident on the Wheaton's farm." He picked up his bag. "Your house is on the way. Let me give you a ride home and you can tell me the whole story."

After she finished her tale, they talked about possible remedies for the child. When she arrived home, the healer promised to stop by on his way back to town.

She found John at work in the study.

"Still here? I thought you wanted to find out who the baby belongs to?"

"Just ready to leave. How's Sharon today?"

Gennie stood coyly in the doorway. "She's fine. If you stop by on your way home, you can give Marla or Beckie a ride. One of them will feed him. She also promised to talk around town and find some things for us. When you stop by her place, you can pick up the supplies and see what she's found out."

He looked up sharply from his work. "Gennie. What are you doing? Supplies? We are not keeping him."

"John, we need supplies if only for a few days. You can't expect me to foster a baby with what we have on hand."

He rose from behind the desk and grabbed his coat. "I'll go, but I'm taking over this investigation. See you in a while."

The door closed behind him and she listened to his footsteps fade away. *Now I can get started.* She planned to have the baby so entrenched in their home, he couldn't say no.

She cobbled together a makeshift crib out of a crate and some blankets. The baby slept in it, but now she got serious about his situation.

I've got to get up in the attic. Haven't been up there in years. She thought about all the dust and cobwebs up there. "Here's my first sacrifice for you, little one." she said to the baby as he slept. She screwed up her courage and climbed the stairs.

The door actually creaked as she opened it. *I will not be afraid,* but as she scanned the old furniture, painful memories began to live again.

When she and John first married, they joyfully anticipated their own family. When she became pregnant, they quickly bought everything they could think of for the child. The bright and colorful nursery stood ready to receive when she lost the child. The miscarriage crushed their spirits, but not their hope. They tried again and again. Three pregnancies. Three losses. Gennie couldn't try anymore. Her spirit and soul sank into the murky waters of depression like a wrecked ship.

Eventually, they filled the nursery with abandoned babies, but their efforts to teach parents the value of their baby's life proved successful and no more abandoned babies appeared. They moved the furniture into the attic and shut the door. The nursery remained empty for many years.

Now she gazed on her broken dreams. *It's been so many years, but this is a miracle. He's alive and he needs me. I'll not let him down.*

The crib could be resurrected. The tattered stroller and linens would have to be replaced. She began to make a mental list, but the baby's cry interrupted her. *Diapers are first on the list.* She quickly descended the stairs and went to him.

What have I gotten myself into? Am I really ready for this?" As she picked him up, she thought about what the next 15 years might be. *I'm 52. I'll be 67 when he is just a young man. And John is older than I.* Doubts clouded her mind even as her heart knew she would never abandon this boy to an uncertain fate. He needed her and she fiercely loved him already.

* * * * *

As soon as Gennie left, Belinda hurried through town to find Marla and gather supplies. Then she ran to Aleese's home.

She found Antania and Aleese at the table. Belinda related the story of a baby boy on the church doorstep. They both studied Antania's face for a reaction, but she remained emotionless.

"Gennie wants any information we have. I say tell her nothing for now. What do you think, Aleese?"

"I agree, Sharon. Until Antania is well, the baby is better off with Gennie."

She grimaced slightly at her alias. It wore thin and she missed her real name, but now Sharon became more important than ever. Belinda returned to her rooms to wait for Marla and Father John.

* * * * *

When John finally returned home, he brought Belinda and Marla with him. Gennie proudly showed them the newly cleaned and furnished nursery. The baby fussed in the crib and Marla quickly sat down in the rocker and got to work. Gennie put away baby clothes, blankets, and other necessities in a little dresser. A small fire gently warmed the room.

Father John backed out of the doorway. *This has gone farther than I thought. How am I going to untangle her from all of this?*

"What's that?" Gennie asked as she pointed to a bottle in his hand.

"This? It's goat's milk."

Belinda took over. "It's for night feedings. Keep it outside so the cold will keep it fresh and warm it up a bit before he drinks it."

Gennie took the bottle from him and strode down the hall. "Thanks. I'll take care of it." She saw the shocked look on John's face and wanted none of it. Right now, she made a hasty retreat.

John turned and watched her go. *I will not be swayed. I will not change my mind on this.* His attention focused on the scene behind him. The baby softly coughed and he smiled as Marla cooed at him. *I need to make sure he's healthy while he's here, but he's not staying.*

"I see your concern, Father."

John jumped at Belinda's voice. "I just want what's best for everyone concerned, including the baby."

"I can't think of anyone who can care for him better than Gennie. We will find his family. Until then, he's safe here. Don't you agree?"

"There is so much…" His voice drifted off in thought and Belinda left him to ponder in the hall.

Eventually John wandered into the kitchen for dinner. Belinda hurried off. Gennie stirred stew on the stove.

"How'd it go today? Did you find out anything of interest?"

"No. It's like the mother never existed and the baby popped out of nowhere. I don't get it. How can a mother hide a pregnancy so well?"

All day, Gennie feared his success. Relieved by his failure, now she indulged her curiosity. She sat across from him. "Didn't you hear *anything*?"

"Everyone I talked to seemed just as baffled as you and I. I really thought I could wriggle the story out of someone. What are we going to do?"

As soon as he said it, he regretted it.

"He stays here." Gennie's hand hit the table. "There's no doubt about it. He came here. He stays here."

She shot up and turned her back to him to stir the pot on the stove. John let his head fall into his hands. *I can't do this. I have to find a way out.*

After all their failures at a family and all their foster babies grown now with families of their own, he had resigned himself to a quiet life and the end of the family line. Josiah encouraged him to rest, so he created a routine which sheltered him from extreme emotion. He liked this life. Oh, he loved his wife, but their relationship now became a peaceful and affectionate understanding.

His fragile health he kept from Gennie. A heart thing. "Don't exert yourself," the healer said over and over. A baby in the house would not help his situation. He felt trapped in his deception. Now, he must confess to Gennie. Then she would see the sense in finding another place for the baby.

Marla joined them in the kitchen and they sat down to a hearty stew. They ate in awkward silence broken only by short comments about local news. At the first opportunity, John quickly said, "Well Marla, gather up your coat. It's time to take you home."

As they left, they met the healer at the door.

"Miss Marla, John. Where are you off to?"

"I'm just taking her home. "

The healer spied a hat. "Take this, John. You have to stay warm. A cold is not good for you."

John glanced at Gennie, took the hat, and ushered Marla out the door. As the buggy moved away, Gennie led Josiah down the hall to the nursery.

"Why are you so worried about John catching a cold?"

"It's not good for his heart"

200

What? They reached the nursery and Josiah began his examination. Gennie listened intently to all his "Hmms" and "Ahhs" until he finally straightened up.

"Well, Miss Gennie, he's doing well. Keep the compresses on him until he's breathing easy. The congestion's not too bad. I think he'll be fine in a few days. What's his name?"

"I...I don't know. We've been so concerned about his health and his family we never considered his name. I'll have to think on it."

"Well, when you decide let me know. I have to put it on his records and I don't like 'baby no-name.'"

She laughed. "No. Neither do I." She showed him out the door and returned to the nursery. Her body collapsed into the rocker while her mind reeled. *What a day. I'm exhausted. Oh, you beautiful child. You may be the end of me.*

The child lay quietly in his bed. The soft and warm blanket soothed him. His satisfied belly, and the gentle soothing noises wooed him to sleep. His body relaxed, but as he drifted into slumber his heart cried for the other.

* * * * *

Aleese joined Antania by the warm fire. She bathed her, carefully salved her wounds and clothed her in a warm dress.

"Would you like tea?"

Antania sat lifeless. Her empty eyes stared into the fire.

"I'll fix us some and we can talk." But when Aleese returned with a warm mug, Antania would not lift her hand to take it.

"Come on now. It's good, hot tea. Nothing better than good, hot tea on a cold night." She pressed the woman's fingers around the mug and Antania held the mug, but did not drink. She stared into the fire until the tea grew cold, never aware of it in her hand.

Aleese took the cold mug and Antania's hand dropped limply into her lap. *What has happened to her? What am I to do?* The baby started to cry again and Aleese held her to Antania's breast. *This can't go on. Who knows if she will ever be well?*

She made a hard decision. As long as this child remained in Beechwood, her little life also remained in danger. If Arbak ever found out, they would all die (or worse, end up in his dungeon). If Antania didn't get better, this girl would be oppressed by her mother's illness forever. What child thrives living a secret life? A baby needs her mother's love and Antania couldn't provide it. This poor child faced a dark and dangerous future here. The baby must have a better life than this. Aleese made up her mind to take action.

When the baby girl drank her fill and sported a clean diaper, Aleese wrapped her tightly in a warm blanket, waited for her to sleep, and quietly left the house. She could hide the baby in Gabe and Maya's wagon while they ate. The wagon would be miles away before the girl was discovered. Maya recently gave birth, she could easily care for another and this baby girl would be safely away. Aleese waited in an alley until they went into the tavern for evening meal. She slipped into their wagon and deposited the girl in-between two soft sacks of flour behind the driver's seat. She said a silent prayer and ran back home. She dug a hole in the backyard, put a rock in it and filled it back in. Then she waited.

* * * * *

Two hours later, Gabe and Maya settled in their camp. Small cries came from the wagon.

"What is that?"

"Don't be surprised, girl. *You* wanted a baby."

"Gabe, our Megan is here in my arms."

"Then what…?" They found the baby girl on the flour bags. "Who could have done such a thing?"

"I don't know, but it looks like we are blessed with two daughters." Maya happily cooed and fed the new arrival.

Gabe groaned and stirred the fire. "Just what I wanted," he mumbled to himself.

* * * * *

When Belinda returned, they helped Antania to stand and led her to bed. She laid down and stared into the ceiling. Eventually, she closed her eyes and slept.

202

"Where's the baby, Aleese?"

"Belinda, come over here." They retired to the fire. "The baby's gone."

"What? … What happened?"

"I left to get water and when I returned, the little girl wasn't breathing. I tried everything I know, but she just wasn't strong enough. I rubbed her and massaged her, but she remained stone cold. I buried her by the roses out back."

"I can't believe it. I thought her daughter would be Antania's salvation."

"We mustn't tell her. She has to find a reason to live and this is too much for her to take."

"I agree." Belinda's shoulders sagged as she moved to Antania's bed. She reached out to take her friend's hand and cried by her side all night.

Guilt tormented Aleese. She lied to her friend, put a baby's life at risk, and took a child away from her helpless mother. Her self-loathing turned to anger. *What kind of woman are you now, Aleese?* She lay on her bed and couldn't sleep. In fact, she never really slept again.

✳ ✳ ✳ ✳ ✳

Antania's mind wandered lost in a nightmare. Horrible visions of death whirled around her amidst screams of agony. She wandered through her hell and searched for … something. *So important,* but she didn't remember what she needed to find. So, she wandered and tried to speak to the ghostly visions around her. They answered with horrible screams and moans.

Inside the screams a presence tried to pull her away, but the something she needed to find existed in this hell and she must stay to find it. A soft, silver glow drew her to a thread hanging in the air. She touched it and a tremor of peace invaded her thoughts.

Yes. This is good. The thread felt good in her hand, so she followed it, hand over hand. While she held it the nightmare around her stilled, so she followed it, she knew not where. It didn't matter, as long as the peace stayed around her. Now she felt the presence again and heard a calm voice calling to her.

Is it the man? The voice talked to her about vaguely familiar things, food, fire, warmth, palaces, love. Her awareness of herself outside the nightmare slowly became a reality. But awareness also brought the very real and constant pain in her bones. She vacillated and dropped the thread.

All at once, the pain in her body became unbearable and the screams wailed out of the darkness. She fell under the attack, but the thread gently dropped into the space beside her. She grabbed it in panic. Instantly, peace returned.

"Come back to me, Antania." The thread trembled in sympathy with the voice. Finally, her eyes focused and she saw the cabin around her.

Beside her sat a woman with shimmery blond hair. She reached out to touch it and the woman smiled. She willed herself to stand and walk. The nightmare provided no food. Her nose drew her to the kitchen where someone cooked. She gingerly sat down at the table in the center of the room and watched the someone stir a pot of stew. Belinda followed and quietly sat in the chair next to Antania.

Aleese heard soft steps behind her and slowly turned. She needed to be careful with this fragile chance to connect. She filled a bowl and carefully picked up a spoon. Then she smiled and offered the bowl in silence. Aleese saw the woman's eyes widen, but she did not speak or reach out. She moved closer. The woman hunched down and cast a furtive glance at Aleese, but then refocused on the smell of the bowl. Belinda slowly took the bowl, filled the spoon and raised it to Antania's mouth.

Nothing.

Belinda opened her mouth, put the spoon in and ate the stew. "Hmmm. It's good."

The next spoonful traveled toward Antania and she opened her mouth to receive it. Belinda hand-fed her for two days until Antania began to feed herself.

After four days, Antania began to help Aleese and Belinda with small things. Vulnerable as a child, Belinda's patience and kindness soothed her frightened psyche. *However long it takes, I will save you.*

Aleese found her redemption in Antania. She would nurse her back to health in payment for the crimes Arbak forced her to commit at Langley. Maybe, one day, she would find her daughter and they would be united. Those dreams kept the anger at bay most of the time.

Antania also bore Belinda's hope of redemption. She would bring Antania back to herself; penance for her sin of abandonment.

Day by day Antania slowly improved. Inch by inch Aleese and Belinda guided her to sanity.

CHAPTER 26
DANGER IN SHULE

Every day Ja'el found it more difficult to travel in safety. The price on his head rose the longer he remained free. He came to trust no one outside his little band. And Jacob's trail took them deeper into Umberlan, not north as planned.

He fretted about this one day while he waited for Caleb and Robin to return from a local market. *I know these are Jacob's signs. Why did he turn south? How far ahead is he? Where is Antania?*

He had scryed her many times and always saw black. Only black. It seemed like she didn't exist. *I must be doing something wrong.* He went through the process again and again, but it gave him no answers, just the oppression of worry for his beloved.

Once more he filled the scrying bowl and began to chant. A picture appeared of madness. Images of torture roiled in the bowl. Dead bodies, darkness, confusion, mouths frozen in screams. *What is wrong?!* He felt helpless and frustrated. *We have to hurry, but to where? Where is she?* His heightened sense of danger influenced all his thoughts, and now these images fanned his urgency into panic.

Robin appeared with a bag of vegetables and dried meats. Caleb struggled to balance an armful of books and a small bag of charms. They smiled in greeting and Ja'el fought to hide his distress.

Robin felt proud of himself. "We will eat good tonight." He plunked down on the ground and began to fumble through his bag.

Caleb fought to hold a great stack of books as he walked to the table. "Master, we found a treasure. Crates filled to the brim." Books began to drop from his grasp. "I couldn't decide, so I bought them all."

Ja'el fought his thoughts and emptied the bowl. "You must be careful. An armful of books will arouse suspicion."

"I bought them one-at-a-time and hid them outside the market until we returned. I don't believe anyone noticed."

"Good. Good. I should not have doubted you. Let us see what you have."

Ja'el looked over all Caleb's treasures. Three history books of Umberlan he gave to Caleb to study. The last two held more promise for him.

"Yes. I think these will be good for us. We must find Jacob and begin, Caleb." Ja'el looked at all their accumulated packs. "Unless we buy another horse, we have no more room for these."

"Our funds are almost gone. It's time for us to replenish again and Shule isn't a small farmer's town. I believe we can find work there and stay for a while without discovery."

"Let us sleep on it. I will go with you tomorrow and see this Shule."

Although he felt recovered from the battle at the garden wall, the grey at his temples remained and now peppered through his hair. It gave him the appearance of a much older man. His apparent age and their clothes and grime became a disguise of sorts. Bounty hunters looked for a sage in robes, not a poor farmer with greying hair and two boys. Ja'el put his need to find Antania aside. Caleb spoke the truth. They needed to work for a while.

Shule proved to be a good decision. Caleb and Robin found work at the local blacksmith and plenty of farms surrounded the town. Ja'el worked a few days here and a few there which allowed him to keep a low profile.

The markets in Shule promised treasures. Merchants arrived from Symbia to the west with exotic goods. Market days proved interesting. They settled in nicely and the weeks went by quickly.

Ja'el hired himself out as day labor on farms. He mostly worked in solitude, which gave him the opportunity to practice magic and ponder their next course. His fear for Antania urged him to travel, but they couldn't find Jacob's trail and a wrong turn could add weeks to their trip.

Caleb understood Ja'el's fears, but every day without travel made Caleb uneasy. They usually packed up and left after one week. Now a month passed and Ja'el's ambivalence trapped them in Shule. Robin also wanted to leave, but not for the same reasons.

"How much longer do we have to stay here? I'm tired of working."

"Robin, we are not quite rich enough to leave. Soon. Soon."

"You said 'soon' last time. How long is soon?"

Caleb passed Robin a hunk of buttered bread and turned to Ja'el. "I'm getting uneasy, too. We've been in Shule longer than any other place we've stayed. People are beginning to treat me as a friend. I think they know us too well. We should leave."

"When is the next market day?"

"Next week."

"We will explore the next market and then take our leave."

Caleb sighed and tried to put his worries aside. *At least he's picked a day.*

* * * * *

The new Damon of Solis Castle desired to please the new king. The former Damon, Elios, remained faithful to Salak and had abandoned his region when Varlana fell. Gailen blamed him, even threatened to replace him if Elios wasn't found. Now he held in his hand a report of three new villagers in Shule. He would send soldiers out to question them. Maybe he would torture them to get the information he needed. He rubbed his hands together, convinced this action would bring good results.

The next day his orders dispatched a company of soldiers and the search began.

* * * * *

First thing in the morning, the smithy sent Robin on an errand. He enjoyed errands. It kept him away from the real work. If he took his time, he could use up a good part of the morning.

He stopped to pet a dog, say hello to the baker (who gave him a muffin), and pick some pretty flowers by the side of the road. When he finally arrived at his destination a young woman answered the door. Robin shyly held out the flowers and the young woman smiled down at him.

"Late again, are you?"

"I come with good news. Your order is ready today."

"Thank you, master Robin. Tell your smithy I will come to get it in a few hours. Do you think you'll make it before I do?" She laughed and closed the door.

Robin skipped down the walk and meandered back to the smithy. *Flowers always work. Why do ladies love flowers so much?*

Halfway back he saw two soldiers stop citizens and ask questions. In his experience, soldiers meant danger. He hid behind a barrel and waited for them to pass by. They stopped a man a few feet away.

"Two men and a boy came into town recently. Do you know anything about them? Where are they staying?"

The man shook in fear. Robin watched intently. They hadn't met this man. He would tell them nothing, Robin hoped.

"I…I don't know these people. I'm just shopping today. I live outside of town. I don't know anything."

"If you're lying, we will know and you'll be punished. Your new Damon does not like liars in his region." They let him go and strode past Robin as he crouched as low as he could.

When they turned a corner, Robin hurried to the smithy. Caleb worked at the fire alone.

Robin grabbed his arm. "Caleb, we must go *now*."

"What has happened? Are you alright?"

Robin's body shook with fear as he panted for breath. "Soldiers are searching for us. We must leave now."

Caleb never doubted his young friend. He put down his hammer and tore off his apron. They left the back way and snuck through backyards and alleys to get to their rooms. Hurriedly, Robin packed while Caleb retrieved the horses. Robin left a week's coin on the table to pay for the room and they loaded the horse in the alley. The soldiers walked to the south, so they left town on the north road and circled back to pick up Ja'el on a farm outside of town.

"Master, we must leave. The horses are packed and Robin waits by the road. The Damon has heard of us and sent soldiers into Shule to find us. It is not safe. We must go now to stay ahead of them."

Ja'el dropped his rake. They all knew the risks. Gailen determined to kill anyone loyal to his brother. He suspected any stranger in any town. Caleb spoke truth (again). They should have left before now. He followed Caleb to the horses and they walked beside the road under the cover of the woods. Finally, a mile out of town, they picked up Jacob's trail.

They walked for a week until they crossed the border into Damon Arbak's region. Another week and they neared Nottsville. Market day or not, Shule's close call made them nervous. They gave Nottsville a wide berth and continued south as they followed Jacob's trail.

* * * * *

The man stretched out on the table fought against his bonds. They arrested him and accused him of treason. For weeks he traveled in a cage towards Chimaya Castle. They stopped in every town along the way. He would be left exposed in the town square while his guards drank in the local tavern.

Townspeople would emerge to taunt him, throw rocks and rotten food at him. Helpless, he sat and endured it. Eventually, the soldiers would chase everyone away and lead the wagon to the next town where it would start all over again.

When the soldiers couldn't stand the stench of him, he took a bath in a nearby river or stream. He harbored no delusions. He traveled to his death. He just wanted to last long enough for Noran to reach Oberlan.

Now he struggled, lashed to a table in the basement of Chimaya castle. Gailen entered the room, leaned over the table and slowly smiled a garish grin. He began to speak with a soft, tender lilt, almost affectionate.

"Sometimes, when it's a special person, I like to do this myself. You are a special person, Mortimer. How did you survive the battle at Varlana?" Mortimer stared at him silently.

Gailen picked up an awl and twisted it in his fingers. "It's just my idle curiosity. The real questions are what were you doing in the Aldies and where is Noran? But I think our conversation can answer all of them, don't you?"

Mortimer tensed, but continued to stare at him.

"You won't be quiet for long, Mortimer. I enjoy this too much." Suddenly, the awl pierced Mortimer's side and punctured his kidney. He let out a yell, but continued to stare at Gailen as he fought the pain.

Gailen slowly moved the awl up and down, and tore the kidney to ribbons. "Don't worry. This won't kill you. We still have a lot to talk about." He removed the awl from Mortimer's body.

"Have you anything to say?"

"You are a pig," he gasped.

Gailen smiled again and picked up a hammer. "You won't be needing your fingers anymore. How about we break a few?"

For two days Mortimer suffered Gailen's torture and gave him nothing. When he finally died, Gailen glared at the hunk of meat on the table as he picked up the hammer again. He pounded on Mortimer's body over and over again. "Why – don't – you – talk – to - me?" He finally threw the hammer at Mortimer's head and turned to the guards as he wiped blood from his face. "Hang him outside with the others. Maybe the crows can get something useful from him."

The rocky terrain around Chimaya castle grew no trees, but Gailen created a forest of his own. For miles around the castle the mutilated bodies of men, women, and children hung from posts, fodder for flies and crows. A gruesome reminder of the cost of betrayal.

Chapter 27
The Wagon Returns

One day moved into another and all Father John's attempts to find out the identity of the baby failed. His decision to confess his heart condition to Gennie didn't embolden him. She still didn't know, but they must find another home for the boy

For days he procrastinated. Tonight, he screwed up his courage and decreed today the day. His work done, he moved into the kitchen for evening meal.

"Gennie, I have something to say to you."

"Sit down, John. The meal's almost ready and I have something to talk to you about, too."

After they settled at the table, John's bravado faltered. "You go first."

"Josiah wants to know the baby's name and we can't wait any longer. His family is not going to magically appear. I think we need to formally name him tonight."

His heart sank. *I should've gone first.* All his courage evaporated when he saw the joy in her eyes.

"It looks like you've got a name in mind."

"How about Jed? It's strong. It means 'God's beloved' and the miracles around his life make Jed a good name for him."

Silence.

It's now or never. John decided on never.

"John?"

"Jed it is. We'll baptize him in a few weeks and it will be official. Gennie, are you absolutely sure about this?"

"He's beautiful, John. His congestion is gone and his little personality is beginning to show itself. He really is a sweet thing. I know life won't be perfect, but we can do this! Jed's a beautiful gift from God just for us."

She reached for his hand. "Together, John. We can do this together."

He searched her eyes for any doubt and found only full commitment. He sighed inwardly and let go of his quiet life. She sensed his resistance dissolve and her smile melted his heart.

He cupped her cheek in his hand. "Together," he replied softly.

* * * * *

Aleese answered another summons to Langley Castle. She hated this. *How long must I pay for one mistake? He deserved to die. I did the world a favor. Money didn't make him a good man.*

Now her past sins forced her to leave Antania alone for hours. She tucked her into bed, promised to return soon, and left her in Belinda's care. She stoked the fire and the room warmed up comfortably, but she still worried. Thoughts of danger and catastrophe filled her mind as she walked the lonesome road and finally looked up at Langley's cursed towers. Her memories came alive as Kanane, the man who forced her life into this torment, filled her thoughts.

She used to come to Langley to attend Damon Kanane's wife. One day when she arrived, he led her into a small room and pushed her against the wall. He leaned his body against hers and began to bite her neck and tell her vile things. She struggled and he slapped her.

"I am Damon. You must yield to me." and he lunged at her again.

She pushed him away with all her strength. He stumbled backward, tripped over a table, and smashed his head against the stone fireplace. She stood in shock as his bastard son, Arbak entered the room. As he surveyed the scene his face cracked into a smile.

"He go for ya?"

"Yes."

"Grab his legs. Let's get 'im out a' here."

Aleese grabbed at Arbak's lifeline. They moved the body outside and made it appear he fell from the roof. The proper authorities arrived and performed a quick investigation. Damon Kanane died because of a tragic accident. The true cause remained a secret and Aleese thought the nightmare over.

But the son who inherited Langley proved worse than the father. *A bastard son of a bastardly man.*

She remembered her next encounter with Arbak many months later. He called her to Langley and she screwed up her courage to face the castle again. He showed her the dungeons and explained his new business and her role in it. She yelled her protest and refused to help him. As she stormed out of the room, he violently grabbed her arm and swung her back inside. He reminded her of her indebtedness to him and threatened to turn her in. If the law discovered everything she would be killed.

Trapped by her fear, she agreed. Now, if she went to the castle when he called, she faced the horror of Arbak's cruelty. If she refused, death.

Tonight, she swallowed her dread, entered a worn oak door and descended the stairs to the cold, damp dungeon. *These women might as well be the prisoners of old.* Malnourished women sat chained to the wall in every cell. The smell of waste and decay clung to the dark walls. Once again, her heart broke and she wept. *How can I be a part of this? Is my life worth more than theirs?*

"Over here, woman."

His voice grated over her nerves. She stood before yet another woman in labor distress. All her anger and self-hatred exploded. "How much longer are you going to kill these women? How can you believe this is a good business? Selling babies and killing mothers is horrific and I won't do this anymore. I can't."

His fist hit her jaw. She flew across the cell and landed on the stone floor with a grunt. His boot found her stomach and she felt the vomit fill her mouth.

"You shut yer mouth and git on with it."

She crawled through the straw strewn across the floor and tried, once again, to do the impossible. Arbak didn't care about fitness. If the female could get pregnant, he made a baby with her.

Aleese cried when she saw this "woman." A child much too young to birth a baby. Aleese could do nothing. Arbak summoned her too late. The baby died in the birth canal. The girl almost immediately after,

Her soul screamed within her. She swallowed her tears, afraid of more violence, and leaned against the wall. Her hand brushed a cold something under the hay on the floor. Quietly she searched and discovered an old hammer. She stood and backed away, afraid of her thoughts.

"You done in there?"

"She's dead. They're both dead."

"Why do I keep callin' you if you keep lettin' my bitches die? You worthless whore!" He slammed and locked the door. "Stay in there with your mess and maybe you'll do me a better job next time."

"No! You can't do this! People will miss me. They'll look for me. You can't leave me in here." Panic rose for the woman asleep in her home, but she couldn't divulge her secret. She tried in vain to plead her cause. "There are women in the village under my care. You'll bring suspicion on yourself if you keep me here. I'll be missed, I tell you."

He spat through the door slat. "This is my house and I say you stay." The slat slammed shut and she wiped her face as she stood in the blackness. The smell of blood and death overpowered her. She cried through the night and the next day. Her stomach began to scream for food and still he didn't come. She went wild with worry for the woman at her home. The stench of decomposition filled her nose and mouth.

The stench drew rats. She heard them rustle and guarded the woman's body against them, but then they turned to her. Too many to fight off, she finally let them eat the woman's remains to save herself. After three days in the dark with the dead and the rats, she gave into her darkest thoughts and plotted to kill him.

The old hammer became her friend. She and it would get revenge for these women and their children. The hammer's presence spoke to her of heavenly intervention and gave her permission to kill such an evil man. She refined her plan constantly and by the time the man came back, she knew every step by heart.

"Are ya ready to work?"

"Yes" came the weak reply.

The key turned in the lock and the door swung open. Like a banshee she screamed, threw herself at him, and knocked him to the floor. He rolled away from the first hammer blow and cursed as he scrambled to his feet. She snarled and ran at him again. She swung the hammer in a wide arc and caught his shoulder. Bone snapped and he lurched away from her. He kicked her and she stumbled, but caught herself and turned to him again. He swung at her and broke her nose, but the pain just seemed to energize her. Nothing stopped her rage. The white of her eyes gleamed through the blood on her face. He trembled at her ferocity and fumbled for his knife.

"You will die before you leave this place!" she screamed as she hurled herself at him again. He stabbed her in her side as the hammer connected with his skull and he dropped to the floor. The pain and blood fueled her fury. She sat on his back and hit him again and again until the hammer finally broke. Brain matter sprayed the walls. Blood and bone matted in her hair.

She hurled the useless handle away and fell over to lay beside the battered body. She gasped and wheezed to fill her lungs, slow down her heart, and fight the pain that throbbed in her side. She forced herself to move. *There's more to do, girl.* She rolled his body over and searched his pockets until she found the keys and staggered toward the cell doors.

＊ ＊ ＊ ＊ ＊

The next morning Gennie heard the wagon again. *Those horrible squeaky wheels. Don't they have any grease?* It stopped at the front door and Gennie grabbed the arm of her chair, filled with dread. *Have they come to take Jed back?* Fearful, she rose on shaky legs and opened the door.

Young women dressed in rags filled the back of a wagon. They shivered in the cold. Aleese drove the rig, covered in blood and falling out of her seat. Gennie ran to help her down.

"These… all I could save… must go home… So sorry…" She collapsed in Gennie's arms, barely breathing.

"JOHN! JOHN!" She looked to the dazed and confused girls in the wagon for help, but they needed help themselves.

Father John appeared. "Holy Mother of God!"

Gennie helped the girls out of the back while John carried Aleese into the house.

"Go get the healer. I'll stoke the fires and do what I can here."

John threw on his coat and grabbed his hat. He bridled the horse and rode him bareback to the healer's house. Out of breath, he pounded on the door.

Josiah opened it in seconds. "John, what are you doing to yourself? Come in. Sit down by the fire."

"No. You must come… to my house. A wagonful… of sick women… Aleese…covered in blood…" He fought for breath.

"I will go. You stay here and recover. Don't leave until I get back. You've strained your heart enough for one night." He gave him some sedatives and set off for the parsonage.

* * * * *

Gennie grabbed some clean towels and bandaged the wound in Aleese's side. Her hair matted around meaty balls of … something? Her filthy clothes stank. Her torn fingers drew back claw-like against her chest. *She hardly looks human.* One of the girls put pressure on the wound while Gennie fixed a bath.

They're going to have to take more than one. It'll be days before the grime is off these girls. She helped them in and out of the tub as she evaluated their general health. The girls cooperated as if in a trance. They didn't seem to know how to behave in a home.

But, when Jed woke up, they seemed to come alive. They cooed and fussed over him, so Gennie left him to their care on one side of the room while she frantically cared for Aleese. *Where is the healer?*

Just as she thought it, the healer arrived. "I saw the wagon outside. Where are all these women…" His voice trailed off as he took in the sight. There by the fire four young women stood, some wet, some dirty. Another soaked in a tub by the fire. Gennie pressed bloody rags against the stomach of a disheveled unconscious woman on the couch.

"What in the world?"

"Josiah. Help me."

Gennie's voice snapped him out of his stupor and he quickly moved across the room. "Leave me with her. You tend to the others. Don't worry about John. He's recovering at my house."

Recovering from what? But she lost the train of thought as she turned her attention to the girls.

A few hours later all the girls finished their first bath and they helped remove the tub from the parlor. The girls now slept on beds and sofas all over the house while Josiah inspected his stitches in Aleese's side.

"She's lost a lot of blood. She may not make it through the night. If she does, her chances improve. The next few days are critical. Is everyone else asleep?"

"Yes. Josiah, every one of them is pregnant."

"Where did they come from?"

"The same squeaky wagon brought them with Aleese in the driver's seat. Maybe she has the answers."

"Then you and I need to give Aleese a bath. She'll never survive if she gets an infection. We can't submerge her, so you take the right side and I'll take the left. Get some clean rags and water. This will take some time."

They spent hours slowly cleaning her. The healer found bite marks on her legs. "Looks like rats. Not infected though." he cleaned them and applied salve and they moved on. He set her nose and checked a nasty bruise on her leg. "She might have been in a fight. The rats came first, though. Aleese, where have you been?"

They shaved her head and burned her hair. Josiah recognized the bone and brain matter and began to make mental notes. *This looks like more than just a fight. Murder?* He looked around at his sleeping charges. *No one will know anything until these women recover enough to talk.*

The sun broke through the windows when they finally sat down. Aleese rested fitfully, but still lived. The others still slept. Gennie put Jed back in his crate by the fire to stay warm. He drifted to sleep as soon as he felt the blanket over him.

Josiah and Gennie listened to soft snores for a while until Gennie broke the silence. "Where did they come from? And why did they come here?"

"Well, Miss Gennie, you and John do have a reputation for cherishing babies and their mothers."

"So many questions. And now what are we supposed to do?"

"They should stay here until they recover. There's really nowhere else for them to go. I think you need to ask Sharon to stay with you for a few days. They all seem calm enough, but until we know more you shouldn't be alone with them."

"I'll have John with me."

"He arrived at my house in pretty bad shape. He needs quiet for a few days. Let him stay with me for a while."

"Josiah, why do you keep saying that? What's wrong with John?"

"His heart, Miss Gennie. You can't tell me you don't know. It's been fragile for more than a year."

"What?"

"Think about his low energy and shortness of breath. Remember his reluctance to take on a baby. Pay attention, Miss Gennie. Your husband needs you to watch out for him, not gallop around the countryside on a freezing cold night. When he returns you two need to have a serious, honest talk about his health." He turned briskly and strode out the door.

Gennie sat frozen in her chair, stunned by the healer's revelation. Amid the peaceful sounds around her, she sat alone in her confusion.

* * * * *

Panic filled Belinda's mind. *Aleese, where are you?* Her stomach growled as she looked in the empty pantry. Wood needed to be replenished. *I can't leave. She has suffered too much. I will not leave her again.*

She could think of no one to help without awkward or dangerous explanations. Antania's existence must remain secret for more reasons than Aleese knew. She would wait.

Antania slept. Belinda laid down to rest.

Suddenly, Antania screamed and tore at her clothes. Belinda ran to her and tightly held her until she calmed. When Antania lay back down Belinda began to weep. *What have they done to you, my queen?*

CHAPTER 28
ANOTHER LONG-AWAITED MEETING

Aleese drifted into delirium. She tossed and turned while she spoke in broken phrases about death, babies, rats, a mad woman, and countless things Gennie didn't understand. Her knife wound became infected and soon the infection riddled her body. Gennie did all she knew to stem the sickness, but in just a few days Aleese died and left more unanswered questions.

The wagon was recognized and a posse gathered to investigate Langley as the possible source of these recent mysteries. They found a nightmare. The whole of Beechwood watched in agony as the body count increased. They seemed to litter the castle and its property. Father John officiated a service over a mass grave of nameless lives found too late.

* * * * *

Father John recuperated nicely and soon moved back home. Gennie hovered over him too much, but he appreciated the new openness between them. They began their life anew.

The girls eventually returned to health. Marietta and Jeanette married local farm boys. Joslyn miscarried her child and left at the first opportunity. She vowed never to return. Meg found her happiness at the dressmaker's shop and hired on as a nanny and seamstress. She moved into a room above the shop with the family.

But Evelyn stayed reluctant to leave. Gennie grew to depend on her care and attention to Jed and also didn't want her to go. No one spoke their feelings until the tension of secrets filled the house. Finally, Gennie sat her down for a talk.

"Evelyn, you know how much I appreciate everything you're doing here."

"Yes, mam."

"And I like you very much"

"Yes mam."

"But don't you have a family somewhere missing you?"

Evelyn drew back. "No mam. I got nobody nowheres. Are you makin' me go? I got nowheres to go." Her eyes filled with tears.

"No, Evelyn. I didn't mean…" She took the scared girl's hands in hers. "I would love for you to stay here forever, but I don't want to hold you back from someone else. Where are you from?"

"A ways away. It took days to get here. My folks are dirt poor. There's so many childs runnin' around. I guess I didn't pull my weight, 'cuz that awful man came and they sold me to him."

"They sold you?"

"I guess I's worth more than the others. The man promised good work, but you know what happened. I can't go back. They don't want me. Oh, mam. I want to stay. I love my room. I love little Jed. An' when my little baby comes, Jed and him can be family. Please let me stay, mam. I got nowheres else to go."

Gennie reached out to hug her. "You can stay as long as you want. John and I don't want you to go. How about we be a family together?"

Now the tears flowed freely. "Oh, mam. I'm so happy I could bust! I was so afeared, but now I'm flyin' like a bird."

Evelyn eventually added a baby girl to the household. "I'm gonna call her Mavis." And Mavis and Evelyn became an essential part of the parsonage family.

* * * * *

Complete emptiness. Belinda stretched all the supplies to the limit and now she learned Aleese died, caught up in the tragedy at Langley Castle. She must leave to get food and wood. She made a sleeping draught and, when Antania dozed off, she slipped out of the cabin and ran to town. *I will only be gone a little while. Please, don't wake up.*

Antania awoke when she heard the door softly close. For days she heard the other someone say words like "castle" and "bodies" while she talked with people who walked by. Her stomach growled and she rose to find the other someone gone.

Her search for food turned up empty and hunger drove her to leave the house. As yet another group of men walked by, she ventured out to follow at a distance. Like a timid squirrel she hid behind trees and scampered low to avoid detection.

The group of men turned off the road and she followed them to a big building. As the men disappeared into the building, she moved into the trees. The building repulsed her, but the woods around it offered plenty of places to hide. She felt safe among the trees and plants; a little chilly, but for the first time she felt peace.

* * * * *

Belinda returned to find her worst nightmare come true. Antania left the house on her own. *I wasn't gone long. She can't have gone far.*

She ran out of the house and saw another small group of townspeople on their way to the castle. It seemed the whole of Beechwood wanted to gawk at the horror. She remembered how Antania followed them around the cabin and wondered if she simply followed someone to Langley.

She joined the procession. Halfway to the castle she saw a small piece of cloth on a sticker bush by the side of the road. Twenty more steps and she found a footprint in the mud. Small clues led her to enter the castle gates. Then they disappeared.

She moved off the road to the cover of trees. She stood still and scanned the area. *There!* A figure deep in the trees. Anyone else would have missed her. The figure turned and disappeared into a willow tree.

So, you've found a garden. She smiled and returned to pack a bag. When Antania ventured out again to the edge of the trees, she found blankets, food, and clothes.

Over time, she discovered she instinctively knew what plants tasted good and which to avoid. She quietly watched the people dig a very big hole and shake their heads. They filled their hole with strange things of all sizes. Then a tall man spoke to them all and they covered it all up. They left and never came back. This land belonged to her now. Sheltered in these woods, the nightmares seemed distant and peace reigned the day.

Huge locks and chains kept the gates and doors shut and the town turned its collective back on Langley Castle. The guilt and shame of such horror happening so close to home with no one's knowledge drove them to never mention the incident again. Langley stood abandoned. She felt safe.

* * * * *

Every day Belinda stole into the castle grounds and sat still for an hour or two. She would leave packages behind when she left. Although she never saw Antania approach, the packages disappeared. Days passed and still Belinda persisted. *Come to me. I am your friend.*

One afternoon Belinda finally felt a soft presence beside her; the odor of humanity wandered into her nose. She froze and Antania sat down, but eventually Belinda moved and Antania jumped up and ran away. Patiently Belinda persisted and over the days Antania relaxed. Their silent visits were a joy. To connect with Antania in this fragile way filled Belinda with hope.

One day, she felt Antania's fingers touch her hand. Belinda turned her palm up and, when Antania moved her hand over Belinda's, she gently closed her fingers and smiled. Antania stiffened, but then her shoulders dropped. They remained hand-in-hand for another hour.

* * * * *

Ja'el and Caleb talked in low tones as Robin slept by the small fire.

"I don't like this, Caleb. Why did Jacob travel so far south?"

For many weeks he didn't scry, afraid the bright glow of the bowl might attract soldiers on patrol. But questions needed to be answered and they decided to risk it. They filled the bowl.

An image emerged.

Caleb leaned closer. "Jacob."

They watched as Jacob handed papers to a guard at one of the northern checkpoints. The guard examined his papers closely, but gave them back and Jacob moved through. The image disappeared.

"Do you think they made it?"

"He is not driving his own wagon. I am not sure what this means. We must trust he keeps his vow."

They returned to the bowl.

"Where is the queen?"

"Let us try Belinda. I try Antania night after night and see only blackness." Belinda packed a bag. She rose and left the room.

"Well, it doesn't look like she and Jacob are together."

"True, but she remains alive and free. Now, where is Antania?"

Before they scryed again, Robin began to stir. They quickly emptied the bowl and returned it to the pack.

* * * * *

Slowly, Antania came to believe Belinda offered friendship. Eventually, they began to walk the land together. Childlike in everything, Antania silently shared her world and Belinda began to talk to her. Then the day came when Antania spoke.

"You are good to me."

"I want to be. I want to take care of you."

"Why?"

"Because you are special to me, to a lot of people. You are loved."

"You love me. Who else loves me? This is not a place for love."

"Yes, this is a bad place. I don't know what happened to you, but whatever it was, it isn't truth. You can have your wonderful life back again if you want."

"Tell me about myself before this."

And Belinda began to tell her all she knew about love and joy and gardens and palaces. Suddenly, Antania stopped her and stared into her eyes. She touched her golden hair.

"Belinda"

"Yes, my queen." Tears streamed down her face. "Yes, I am your Belinda."

"And I ... Ja'el ..." She cried out as her hand went to her belly and she collapsed in tears. They cried together for a long time. Eventually, they sat in silence while they tried to measure the magnitude of what lay before them.

* * * * *

Ja'el stood in the road perplexed. Outside of Nottsville Jacob's trail suddenly stopped.

"We have come too far without a sign. We must have missed a turn. Let us go back and look more carefully."

They scanned both sides of the road for 300 paces over and over until the sun began to set.

Robin stopped and whined. "What do we do now? I'm hungry."

They sat down on a log to eat and ponder this new development.

"We can go back to Nottsville or on to Beechwood."

"Master, if we go back, we'll learn nothing new. I say forward."

"Robin, what say you?"

"Mmgrnsft."

"Swallow and try again."

Robin's gulp echoed off the trees in every direction. "I tasted everything in Nottsville. What kind of food do they have in Beechwood?"

Ja'el stood. "Beechwood it is."

As they walked a great wall appeared along the road.

"Do you think Langley Castle's behind this wall?"

Robin began to jump up to see over the top. "You mean the place where they found all the bodies? People don't like to talk about it, but I heard some things."

"What did you hear and who did you hear it from?"

"Well, yesterday Peter wanted to play Adonna, the warrior queen."

"What!" Caleb's fingers went to the medallion in his pocket. "She lived here?"

"She built Langley Castle. Now be quiet, Caleb, and let Robin finish. Who is Peter?"

"Just someone I met. He told me about a man who kept women in there and sold their babies. Adonna rose up out of the grave to kill him and set those women free. They found his body in the dungeon and buried it somewhere in there."

At this point they came to a gate in the wall. A big chain covered it, locked with a huge lock, but Robin jumped up and scrambled over easily.

"We could stay in this castle. Nobody lives here. Nobody even comes here. I've always wanted to live in a castle."

"Robin, get back over here right now."

"Wait, Caleb. Robin may be right. Look at the chains and locks. We could live in secret. I could study without fear. Its story may be gruesome, but it will work in our favor."

Caleb's jaw dropped as Ja'el climbed over the gate. "Wait, what about the horses? And all our supplies?"

Ja'el found a rock and began to bang at the hinges. "People lock the middle and forget about the sides." Soon one side of hinges opened and they pulled back the gate. "Welcome to your new home." Ja'el said as Caleb led the horses through. "Now help me put this gate back in place."

* * * * *

Antania's thoughts continually focused on Ja'el. He consumed her. *Do you breathe, my love?* So much time gone. So much wasted time. Her son. Ja'el. Jacob. Her thoughts whirled around her mind and made her dizzy.

Belinda encouraged her to wait in the castle. She realized how vulnerable living in the open made her and agreed. *How did I survive? A mad woman in the woods.* She laughed at herself. *From queen to animal.* It humbled her to know how low she fell.

As she wandered the halls, she studied the portraits on the walls. *I dressed as a fine lady once.* She remembered her luxurious dresses and the maids assigned to meet her every need. She didn't care about any of it. *Belinda's faithfulness is worth more than a hundred maids and a thousand dresses.* The beautiful dresses on these beautiful women meant nothing to her now.

The last portrait hung next to a mirror. Antania wondered why such an ugly, unkempt creature would adorn these walls. Her hair stuck out in a tangled mess. Thick globs grew next to bald patches. Eyes shone out of a black grimy face, her clothes torn and tattered. She stood on bare feet. Scratches striped her arms and she stood a little twisted.

Antania's hand went to her face. *I wonder how dirty I must be. This poor woman is a wild thing.* The arm in the picture moved. She jumped back in alarm and then slowly approached the wall again. She held up her hand and wiggled her fingers. The portrait did the same.

A wretched cry screamed through the hall as Antania realized her mistake and stared at herself in the mirror. This disgusting, ugly, wild woman used to be queen of Umberlan.

Screams filled the halls as she ran away from the grotesque image. She stumbled into a big room, a library, and hid under a big desk. No one should see her. How could Belinda smile at this hideous creature?

Her self-loathing drove her to climb out and look for water. Even shivering in a cold bath seemed better than this dirt and grime. Belinda said they would bathe tomorrow, but she couldn't wait.

She searched every room downstairs and then climbed up. Halfway through those rooms she heard a loud bang and then another outside by the gate. Two men and a boy walked with two horses down the drive. *I will hide and Belinda will drive them off tomorrow.* But she couldn't move from the window. The tall one seemed vaguely familiar. The way he walked and the way…

"Ja'el!" *How could he be here?* Her heart raced and she fought the urge to run and hide. She followed them as they walked up the drive. She knew his walk even without his robe. She looked at her tattered clothes and ran her hand over her tangled hair. *He will think me a mad thing and throw me out! Why today, Ja'el? Tomorrow you will know me, but now?*

She hoped they would camp in the trees, but no, they found an open door. She heard them explore the rooms. She ran behind dusty drapes to hide. No. Under the desk in the Library would be better. She tip-toed quickly down the stairs and slipped into the big room.

The soft click of the door made Ja'el turn. Before him stood a wild woman, dirty and unkept. Her out-of-control hair framed a grimy face. Scrapes and scars pitted her arms and feet. Her eyes opened wide with fear.

And yet the turn of her nose filled his dreams. Her full lips spoke tender words he remembered every day. For almost a year, he loved and searched for her. And right now, she looked more beautiful than any other in all his life. Tears spilled out of his eyes as he said her name.

"Antania."

The love in his voice drained all the strength out of her legs and she slid to the floor. "Ja'el. How can you know me? I look a fright."

He shot across the room and gathered her into his arms. "You are beautiful, my love. You are the most beautiful, wonderous woman in the world and I have found you at last."

She laughed. All the pain of the past vanished and she laughed in the joy of it. Ja'el caught her joy and they laughed until their stomachs began to hurt. Then they laughed some more.

All the commotion brought Caleb and Robin in at a run. They stopped dead and stared in disbelief. Their Master sat on the floor and cradled a crazy woman while they laughed together.

Ja'el finally took a breath and said through his tears, "Everything is alright. Go. Explore. Everything is alright."

* * * * *

Noran crossed the Aldies into Oberlan, a bittersweet moment. He tarried at the mountain pass as long as he dared and Mortimer never came. The only reason he would have missed the meeting Noran dared not think about. When he approached King Ardenna he silently vowed revenge for his companion's sacrifice.

"My king. Thank you for sanctuary."

"Damon Noran, you are welcome in my house. Come. Let me take you to your comrades."

He led Noran through his castle to a map room. Several serious men stood around a big table and studied a map of Umberlan.

"Elios. Notok. You live!"

"Noran. It's good to see you here. Come. We have a war to plan."

Noran strode quickly to the table. *Mortimer will not die for nothing. It's time to join the fight.*

* * * * *

Jacob pulled up his wagon at the outpost. Once again, he showed his papers and paid the guards the acceptable bribe. Two miles before the northernmost guard station, Jacob pulled off the road and down a small trail.

He stopped and began to unload his wagon. A woman and a child emerged.

"You must walk the rest of the way. Take this trail until it turns away from the mountains. There you will find a smaller path headed north. It will take you to Oberlan. You should arrive tomorrow. Stay quiet and light no fire."

"Thank you, thank you, thank…"

"Be on your way. We have already stopped here too long."

The woman and child hustled off down the trail. Jacob waited until they walked out of sight. He returned his wagon to the road and walked back down the trail to gently wipe away any trace of their stop. Satisfied, he returned to his wagon and continued north. He carried supplies for the next outpost. After this delivery he would turn back.

He had made many of these trips since Gailen seized the throne. The Damons paid well for their families to arrive safely. The wealthy merchants loyal to Salak also made him good money. Slowly, strategic refugees found him. He hid them under his wagon and transported them to safety. The resistance grew and so did his money.

This time, Jacob's "cargo" related stories of Arbak's death and ghosts of the murdered at Langley Castle. The ghastly ghosts he ignored, but the downfall of Arbak opened the roads around Beechwood. His spirit lifted. Now he could return and continue his search for the queen.

*****

When Captain Dugan crossed into Oberlan, his soldiers filled the taverns and markets with tales of his heroic leadership. King Ardenna heard of his valor and called him to the castle to greet the Damons as they arrived. He called Dugan Umberlan's unsung hero.

The Damons intimidated Dugan, especially inside the map room. But they relied on his hard-won experience. He had fought Gailen's patrols and found little used trails to lead his people to safety. The Damons took his advice seriously and honored his leadership among his men.

His network sent news of Gailen and he kept the Damons informed. They made him their General and he realized he just might be the leader Ja'el told him he would be. He hoped so. Soon there would be war.

END OF BOOK ONE

READ ON FOR A SAMPLE OF *THE RISE OF ECHLYS*
BOOK 2 OF THE RULE OF WISDOM

Excerpt from *The Rise of Echlys*

Robin had witnessed the argument in silence. He knew better than to comment during one of Antania's rants. The meal over, he took the opportunity to explore a little on his own.

He pushed familiar places in the wall and entered the secret passages. He'd made a mental map. Now he would test its accuracy. He set his mind on the knife room and began. Twenty steps forward then a turn to the right. Ten more steps and a turn to the left, but only for a few steps and then right again. After two wrong turns he doubled back and reached along the wall for a loose stone.

No stone. Well, I'm good and totally lost. So much for map making.

He rooted around and found a mysterious length of wood that jutted up from the floor. Robin folded his hand around it and pulled toward himself. Nothing. He pushed. Nothing. What is this? He tried to rock it side to side. Still nothing. About to give up, he spied a hole about knee high in the wall. On a whim, he pulled up on the wood and it came out of the floor. The wood piece fit nicely in the hole.

"I'll have all your secrets, Langley." The castle creaked in response.

Now what? He pushed and pulled and twisted and then did it all again. Nothing. He kicked at the wood. If it broke, who cares, it seemed useless anyway. He kicked it a little harder. The wood rose up and the wall moved away.

A shaft of red light broke through the gloom in the hall. What's this? His plans didn't include mysterious red rooms, but his curiosity overcame all his apprehensions. He walked through the door.

Stained-glass windows lined the wall and cast a rainbow of colors over a dark stone altar. Scenes of fantastic flying creatures played out on every side. As Robin walked around, his hand traced the images. They seemed to move under his touch and pointed him to a center circle on the back. When he touched it, it opened and a drawer slid out.

A faded velvet cushion cradled an old black book. The leather cover cracked and curled, but the creature pictured on the cover pulsed with life. A dragon, wings unfurled, stood radiant and beautiful, outlined in a green thread that sparkled with light. The air rippled around it. Robin stood transfixed.

Whispers filled the room and compelled him to reach out. In a trance, he picked up the book and began to read. He'd never seen anything like these strange words, but he knew them somehow. Magic curled around his arms and began to wrap him in tendrils of desire. Power. Power is everything. Power will give me everything I want.

A beam of light cut through the room and shocked his hands. He dropped the book and looked up to see intense blue eyes and a frown. A woman in white stood before him, her hair as white as her gown. She seemed to float just off the floor.

"COME AWAY FROM HERE. THERE IS DANGER IN THIS ROOM."

"No. There is truth. I understand now. Power is what I need."

"WHAT WILL POWER GIVE YOU?"

He became confused and struggled to remember the revelations of the book. "Everything I want."

"AND WHAT DO YOU WANT?"

Her soft voice cut through the clouds in his mind. "I don't know. I mean, I don't remember."

"COME WITH ME AND WE WILL DISCOVER WHAT YOU WANT."

Appendix:
Characters and Places

Aldies (All-deez)	A mountain range separating northern Umberlan from southern Oberlan
Aleese (Ah-lese)	Midwife in Beechwood, bribed into service for Arbak
Adonna (Ah-don-nah)	Ancient queen of Langley known for being a fierce warrior from Symbia
Antania (Ahn-tah-nee-ah)	Chosen by Ja'el to be Salak's queen
Arbak (Ar – bahk)	Damon of Langley castle, ally of Gailen
Ardenna (Ar- dehn-nah)	King of Oberlan
Beechwood	Town south of Langley Castle
Belinda	Attendant to Queen Antania
Bitterlands	A region near Varlana made desert to provide water to the capital
Caleb	A boy roaming the gardens at Evan castle who becomes Ja'el's apprentice
Chimaya (Chim-ay-ah)	Gailen's castle
Damon (Day-mon)	A governor of a region of Umberlan, passed down through bloodlines or appointed by the king
Devonshire	Town near Evan Castle
Dugan (Doo-gan)	Captain in the army, Janell's assistant, engaged to his daughter, Marguerite
Echlys (Ehk-liss)	Black dragon imprisoned inside books of magic
Evelyn	Mother of Mavis (child of rape by Arbak), lives with Gennie and Father John
Father John	Local minister, adopted father of Jed

Gabe	Once business partner to Jacob, now loyal to Gailen
Gaffian Sea (Gaff-ee-an)	Body of water that forms the western border of both Oberlan and Symbia
Gailen (Gay-len)	Salak's brother, set on betraying his brother and taking the throne
Gennie	Wife of Father John, adopted mother of Jed
Ingrid	Gailen's wife who died young. All his women since he called Ingrid.
Jacob	Smuggler, friend of Morcon and Ja'el
Ja'el (Jah-ehl)	Son of Marcon, Damon of Varlana
Jakfa (Jahk-fah)	Gailen's son, loyal to his father
Janell (jah-nell)	General of Salak's army
Janella (Jah-nell-ah)	Ja'el and Antania's daughter, Jed's twin sister, raised by the Ingrids of Chimaya Castle
Jed	Ja'el and Antania's son, Janella's twin brother, raised by Gennie and Father John
Josiah (Joh-sigh-ya)	Healer in Beechwood and surrounding area
Mara (Mah-rah)	Gabe's wife
Marguerite	Daughter of Janell, engaged to Captain Dugan
Mavis (May-vis)	Daughter of Evelyn, adopted sister to Jed
Morcon (More-con)	Damon of Varlana, father of Ja'el
Mortimer	Hired to care for Noran
Noran (Noh-ran)	Damon of Evan castle, father of Antania
Nottsville	Town northeast of Langley castle
Oberlan (Oh-ber-lun)	A country north of Umberlan, ruled by King Ardenna
Omilian (Oh-mee-lee-an)	White dragon, Echlys' sister
Robin	Boy saved by Caleb in market, becomes a member of Ja'el's household
Salak (Sal-lack)	King of Umberlan
Sharon	Belinda's alias in Beechwood
Symbia (Sim-bee-ah)	Country of warring tribes to the west of Umberlan

Tenebray (Ten-eh-bray)   Town north of Chimaya Castle

Terrell (Teh-rell)   Trusted attendant to King Salak

Tobin (Toh-bin)   Captain of the king's guard, secretly loyal to Gailen

Umberlan (Um-ber-lun)   A country south of Oberlan, ruled by King Salak

Varlana (Var-lah-nah)   Capital of Umberlan

CPSIA information can be obtained
at www.ICGtesting.com
Printed in the USA
LVHW050431040222
710074LV00015BA/2080